KITES
of Good
FORTUNE

To Alf
With best wishes

Therese

"For Jim"

KITES
of Good
FORTUNE

Therese Benadé

KAART VAN DE
CAAP DER GOEDE HOOP
waar in aangetoond werden de Voornaamste
Plaatzen met de Naamen van der zelver Bezitters.

Duytsche Mylen 15 in een Graad

NIEUWE KAART
VAN
CAAP DER GOEDE HOOP
in hare rechte jegenwoordige staat
vertoond door
FRANÇOIS VALENTYN.
J. van Braam et G. onder de Linden exc Cum Privil

Duytsche Mylen 15 in een Graad

First published in 2004 in southern Africa by
David Philip Publishers, an imprint of New Africa Books (Pty) Ltd
99 Garfield Road, Claremont 7700, South Africa
www.newafricabooks.co.za

© in text: Therese Benadé
© in published work: New Africa Books (Pty) Ltd

ISBN 0 86486 600 3

Cover and text design: Fresh Identity
Editor: Karen van Eden
Proofreader: Angela Briggs
Typeset in 10pt (Administer) by Fresh Identity
Printed and bound by MSP Print

Map on previous page taken from *Description of the
Cape of Good Hope with the matters concerning it*,
François Valentyn, Amsterdam, 1726
(Van Riebeeck Society, Cape Town, 1971. Part 1, Second series No 2.)

TABLE *of* CONTENTS

CHAPTER ONE

Homecoming

What a glorious day! It is exactly how I imagined the day of my homecoming should be. A few clouds over the Table Mountain, golden in the first rays of the sun. To the left, the Devil Mountain, its peak clear and true like a loyal companion, and to the right, the Lion Mountain, flying the flag of the Company. Further down to the right, another flag flying from Signal Hill. It is from here that the Captain will receive the signal to proceed into the Bay, drop anchor and begin to unload his passengers and cargo. Many of the passengers are already gathered on deck, as I am, eager to put the long voyage behind them and feel solid earth under their feet.

Europe seems a very long way away now but, in my mind's eye, it is still very real. Since my childhood, fragments of Europe had come to me at the Cape, washed ashore by the tide, spilling out of ships. European people bringing bits and pieces of their language, their art, their fashions, their manners, their science, their ideas, which I had adopted eagerly in an effort to be European myself. I was encouraged to be a Europhile by my mother, my husband.

'Look at Annie,' people would say in amazement, 'born and bred in the Cape and yet so European!' But all the while I knew that I would only be a look-alike, that my understanding would be incomplete until I had seen for myself, touched and smelled the original on which my African copy was based. And now that has been accomplished: I, Annie de Koning, have a complete picture of Europe in my mind rather than a disjointed creation of fantasy.

I have seen for myself the great cities of Patria, I have heard fine music in grand halls, I have watched great painters at work. I have conversed with aristocrats at their own elegant tables and walked in stately parks and gardens and, above all, I have experienced snow. The rough-cut puzzle piece that once was Europe has taken on the precise shape to fit the larger jigsaw of my life. This is why I had to make the journey.

It took a long while to fulfill my ambition to see Europe; it was only after my dear Olof was in his grave that I was free to go. And go I did, against the advice of many who doubted that a woman of sixty-four could survive the voyage there and back, could adapt to the climate and the rigours of travelling. Only Simon understood my ambition, my stubborn insistence. Since he was eager to leave his disappointment at the Cape and search for new possibilities, he accompanied me, leaving his brothers to mind the farms and businesses and his sisters to keep the home fires burning. At one point I thought he would stay behind to make a new life in Sweden but, in the end, his obsession with Sophie brought him back.

We understand each other, Simon and I. It is an understanding founded in intuition, a single-mindedness that drives us to pursue our passion for people and art. Of all my children, he is the only one who never expressed wonder about my devotion to Olof until his death at eighty-one, the only one who never made fun of my artistic endeavours.

There is the gunshot now, the smoke clearly visible from the top of Signal Hill. The anchor is weighed and a gentle breeze slowly moves us toward the Bay. The early morning sun is strong and warm. As we get closer I can begin to distinguish the Castle and the Company and private warehouses in the foreground and, to the right, the Church, the Gardens and the houses of the town. As we draw closer, I see the smoke rising steadily from my beloved house on the Heerengracht. Johanna knows we will soon be home! Where is that Simon? He is no doubt tarrying in the cabin, gathering courage to face our arrival.

Here he comes, with that tight look on his face. I know if I babble enough he will soon relax.

'Look Simon! Think of those who came before us and saw the Cape for the first time. When your grandfather, David Koning, came here in 1652, there was nothing, not a single building – a complete wilderness. When your grandmother Angela came, three years later, there was a wooden fort where now you see the Castle. By the time your father arrived here as a Sergeant in the service of the Company, the Fort and warehouses were prominent, the Gardens and Church clearly recognisable and the houses of Table Valley well established along the river.'

'It still must have looked pretty primitive to all of them,' replies Simon. 'It looks pretty primitive to me, now, after Amsterdam and Gothenburg.'

'You're not regretting your return already? Too late now, my son. You'll feel better when you see your brothers and sisters. Look at the dock! I think I see Martinus! Yes, it is unmistakably your younger brother: he looks exactly like your father did when I first met him. Who can mistake the blond head and broad shoulders? Is that Olof de Wet with him? It looks as if they have brought a chair for me. I will be carried through the streets in style, and everyone will know that Annie de Koning, widow of the late Honorable Captain Olof Bergh, is home!'

'Happy Annie and nervous Simon,' he says ironically.

The lighter approaches the ship and soon we will be transported across the last little stretch of water to the shore. My

3

heart pounds in eager anticipation. When we reach the dock, Martinus reaches out to help me up and enfolds me in his strong arms. He is just as tall as his father and hugs me with the same energetic affection. For a moment I am filled with the physical memory of Olof, with the sad realisation that he will never hold me like this again.

'Mother, how well you look. But how pale after the weak European sun!'

'Nonsense, child, it's just an old woman's way of protecting her shrivelling skin. Now you, you are your usual golden self.'

Olof de Wet comes to hug me. He is my daughter Christina's son from her infamous first marriage to Jakobus de Wet. He is only two years younger than his uncle, Martinus, and seems more like a son than a grandson.

'Grandmother,' he says, 'welcome back. Everyone is gathering today for the big feast to celebrate your return.'

Before we go any further, let me quickly introduce you to my large family. Yes, I have had a productive life, conceiving and bearing children easily. Of my eleven children, seven survive today. Christina arrived first, in 1679, exactly nine and a half months after Olof and I were married. Today she is the wife of Matthias Bergstedt, a Swede like Olof. Three years later came Maria, who is married to her second husband, Johannes Visser. Her son Albertus Koopman is nineteen years old and from her first marriage. Apollonia is my third daughter and married much later than the first two. She has two children by her husband, Jan Alders. Johanna, my fourth, is still unmarried and has been keeping my house in my absence.

Then there is Simon about whom you already know. He is artistic and nervous, and the reason for this anxiety will become apparent in due course. One year younger than Simon is Martinus, Assistant Merchant, formerly Magistrate at Stellenbosch and father of two children by Cati Ley. My youngest surviving child is Albertus, the farmer and father of one small Olof whom I have not yet seen.

Of all my children who are gone, I will miss Engela the most today. Sweet Engela who lost her life soon after she gave birth to Johan Rhenius's second son. Of all my daughters, Engela was the most like me in looks and character though, sadly, not in stamina. I'm hoping her young boys, Tobias and Jan, will be at the feast today. The three children who did not grow into adulthood were Petrus, Carolus and Dorothea, poor little struggling plants who never bloomed or bore fruit and are still so dearly present in a mother's heart.

People find it difficult to understand how I could have had so many children and have loved them all equally. I have always thought of my children as colours, each with his or her own variety of tones. They have come to me bright or subdued, inviting me to place them in the painting of my life, apply them in the expression of my love. With every new colour, the possibilities of my heart expanded, until I stand back now and am amazed at the rich and complex patterns their lives have imprinted on mine.

The chair in which I am being carried moves away from the dock between the Castle and the Company Warehouse along the river, towards the town. Soon it gathers a following of people who have heard of my arrival. Soldiers and slaves, old and recent acquaintances, all come to welcome me.

It is strange to be important again; there were weeks in Holland when I could be completely anonymous and unrecognised. Who bothers with a dowdy, provincial woman between middle and old age? Who cares about her thoughts and impressions, whether she behaves with dignity? Who knows that somewhere at the southern tip of the dark continent she is a known quantity, her influence and opinions heeded? Here my history and status are part of the order of things, my deeds, and those of my late husband, affecting the lives of many people in this small community, providing work and leadership, interest and gossip.

I know that those who come to greet me feel reassured that I have survived my trip; those who wish me gone are probably skulking in doorways in sour disappointment. I

5

am not pretending to be loved by all. Power and position have their pitfalls. Sometimes one is forced to choose one person above another, or to reprimand and dismiss the unsatisfactory, which leaves an inevitable trail of disgruntled individuals. It took my late husband many years to get me to accept this fact of life philosophically. I did not have his soldier's disposition, his administrative second skin, his unswerving belief in being strict but fair. I am more inclined to giving second chances, the benefit of the doubt. A weak humanitarian trait, I know.

Simon comes to the window of the chair. 'Would you like us to go past the Church, Mother?' he asks.

He knows I would like to assure myself that Olof and Mai Angela are still safe in their resting places in the church-yard. And indeed there they are. Olof in a prominent place under the opulent gravestone with our family crest and well-executed Latin inscription. Mai Angela rests beside my stepfather, Arnoldus Basson, in a more modest part of the consecrated ground.

I still feel a little guilty about her burial here, although it was unclear what she really wanted towards the end. I have had nightmares about her spirit escaping that grave beside Arnoldus and making its way towards Maccassar.

But now the bright sunshine dispels that possibility and I turn my attention to my home on the other side of the Heerengracht. I think of the same street in Amsterdam, with its grand houses, impressive staircases and heavy doors, the large windows and decorative gables and, yes, my house is small by comparison, a farmhouse, in fact, but it is my very own. It contains my life's store of worldly goods, all my accumulated memories.

I stop the chair and cross the *gracht* on foot. Johanna is waiting for me at the door under the pergola, now ochre with autumn. I am consumed by the embraces of big and little arms. I am mother and grandmother, I am mother-in-law, I am mistress, I am friend. I am loved and I am welcome.

I am Annie de Koning and I am home!

CHAPTER TWO

Angela and David

MY MOTHER, ANGELA, IS most fondly remembered for her stories. Throughout my life I heard her recount her own life, episode after episode. She had a canny way of suiting her narrative to her audience as an illustrator chooses her medium: crude woodblock prints with obvious morality for the common reader, fine engravings with subtle allegorical reference for the learned, soft water colours for the sensitive and, for the connoisseur, rich oil paintings with detailed foreground and background.

Her listeners were invariably astounded that an illiterate woman who could not write her name could so enchant them with her rich language, so charm them with her dramatic monologue, so involve them in her life's true history. I do not claim to have inherited her talent but will attempt to recount that episode from her life pertaining to my origin.

Angela already knew who David Koning was when his ship drew into Table Bay in 1661. She had seen him eight years previously as a guest at the house of Captain Pieter Kemp in Enkhuizen. Although nominally a slave, Angela was living in the Kemp household as an ordinary domestic servant. Contemporary social thinking in Europe obliged those who kept slaves in the New World to pretend that the practice did not exist once they returned to the Old.

Angela played the game and pretended that she was a nursemaid like any Dutch nursemaid, but bondage hung over her like a permanent cloud. She and Captain Kemp both knew that she could, at a moment's notice, be transported from Holland and sold as a slave. She liked her work, however, and much preferred her present master to the Portuguese sea captain from whom Captain Kemp had taken her as part of his privateer's loot.

Angela loved the Kemp children: Joos, Jacob and little Marieke, who treated her as an exotic playmate and patiently taught her all the Dutch she knew. She felt a special loyalty to Marijke Kemp, who both clothed her generously and provided cast-off clothing from her own children's wardrobe for Angela's three-year-old daughter and the son of Domingo, also part of Captain Kemp's booty. She was aware that she and Domingo could be expected to work for the Kemps without the children being accommodated, clothed and fed. Instead, they were given the run of the attic and generous accommodation on the scale of things.

In other circumstances, as Angela reminded herself, she and Domingo would be able to earn money on the open market and better themselves. This they knew they were not free to do, but because of the kindness shown to them by the Kemps they accepted their role. They did not have to look far to see servants, ostensibly free, treated far worse than they ever were.

It was in April of 1653 that the Kemp boys had announced in a flurry of excitement that their uncle, David Koning, was to visit. They showed Angela the splendid silk kite he had brought them from Japan and told her that he was an expert at flying kites. They were surprised and delighted to know that Angela also knew about kites. Her brothers had flown them in her village. and probably still did. She helped the children prepare special gifts for their uncle and shared in the anticipation of his arrival.

When David arrived, Angela was not disappointed. He was a tall man with a granite-grey gaze that seemed to find the walls of the parlour too close. His deep, infectious laugh filled the room and embraced the company. His tanned skin looked incongruous against the fine white lace of his collar and cuffs. He was a man of the outdoors, made uneasy by walls.

Angela, present but in the background, had ample opportunity to observe and marvel at this man who seemed to her the most handsome she had ever seen. She studied him in detail, the way he tossed his head and shrugged his broad shoulders, the way he eagerly ate the little cakes, the enthusiasm with which he quaffed his wine. She understood enough Dutch by now to understand his jokes and quietly hid her laughter while those in the company doubled over with mirth.

After the refreshments and an exchange of gifts, the children had little difficulty in persuading David to fly the kite. He seemed relieved to have an excuse to escape the indoors. The original plan excluded little Marieke who, at three, would be capable of doing no more than watching the kite. But she was old enough to know that she would be missing a whole lot of fun and clever enough to find the answer to her dilemma.

'Angela, take me with you!' she cried.

And thus Angela was brought from the shadows to be first noticed by David Koning.

'Does Angela know about kites?' he asked doubtfully.

'She does! She flew them with her brothers all the time!' cried the boys enthusiastically.

'Angela may go along to mind Marieke. Don't forget your duty in your enthusiasm, my girl,' admonished Mrs Kemp, knowing the playful nature of this girl-mother. 'Keep an eye on her, David. She gets carried away.' Her fondness for the girl did not escape David.

It was a fair walk to the eastern town gate. The boys carried the kite and chatted to their uncle while Angela followed a short distance behind them, carrying Marieke. After a while, David turned around and took the child, falling in beside Angela.

'From Bengal?' he asked.

She confirmed this with a sideways nod of the head.

'You must know from going to slave auctions? Or perhaps you have studied those catalogues so popular with slave

9

traders? You know, those books with pictures of indigenous peoples from Africa and the East?'

Her Dutch was halting and childlike, but the implied reproof did not escape him. He knew what she was talking about, having only recently been shown a catalogue of Brazilian Indians, splendidly beplumed. The sea captain who showed it to him had been especially excited by the prospect of such attractive merchandise.

'It is an inevitable part of one's duty in the service of the Company,' he said, justifying himself. 'I try to avoid discussing it with the actual victims of the trade.'

He could see she did not understand the last remark. There was questioning in her bright, dark eyes, a small frown on her brow, and her mouth produced a puzzled pout.

'*Fala Português?*' he asked.

'*Falo*,' she replied, relieved. At least in Portuguese she would appear less of a fool.

And thus they continued the conversation, much to the aggravation of the boys. Between the town hall and the town gate she gave him a brief account of how she came to be in Holland. She was pleased that she did not have time to dwell on the painful parts of her story. To recount events without emotional details always made her feel more in control.

These were the facts of her young life:

At thirteen she was reluctantly sold into slavery by her village during a famine. Anjali became Angela, the personal property of Pedro da Silva, the Portuguese sea captain who bought her. Like all Muslim slaves, she was forced to convert to Catholicism and joined da Silva's other concubines in his household in the Portuguese territory of Goa. Here she gave birth to her daughter, Manuela.

Soon after, she had found herself and her baby on board Captain da Silva's ship, the *Centaur*. With them came, amongst others, Domingo, Da Silva's household slave from Angola, with his small son whose mother had died in mysterious circumstances. Somewhere between Goa and Batavia, the *Centaur* was attacked by the *Amersfoort*, and

Angela and Domingo and the two children became part of the booty of Captain Kemp, who brought them with him to Holland. It was here that Domingo fathered my half-sister Maria.

'How old are you now?' asked David Koning, amazed at the apparently objective way in which she told the facts, each one carrying such personal trauma.

'Sixteen,' she said, with a tremor in her voice that showed him she was more vulnerable than her factual narrative would have him believe. Her head was held high on her long neck, her shoulders proudly pulled back.

'You are very brave.'

'I'm a survivor. It is easy during the day when I am with the children. What I do when it's dark and I am alone, is something else,' she said, setting the limits of her privacy.

They passed through the gate near the church and soon reached the hill above the wooden breakwater. This was a popular place to fly kites since there were no trees and a skillful kite flyer would know to fly the kite out to sea and not into the windmills beyond the hill. The activity soon took over and any discussion of Angela's life became impossible.

Angela took the child from David and began giving instructions on how to get the kite off the ground. The breeze blew out to sea and was just strong enough to keep the kite at a manageable height. Soon the red, black and white dragon adorned the leaden lowland sky. Her throat tightened with the memory of the blue sky of her native Bengal. As though he could read her thoughts, David said:

'That kite would look a lot better against a sun-filled sky with a few palm trees around! You boys don't know what is in store for you! You should sail with your father as soon as he will let you. The East is a wonderful place.'

This recognition of her place of origin cheered Angela and she gave him a wide smile. Just then Joos let his concentration slip and the kite came crashing down on the large stones of the breakwater.

'You idiot!' cried Jacob, reaching the kite first. 'Look, the

11

bamboo is broken! It will never fly again!'

They all ran to inspect the damage. The mainstay of the kite was cracked, though not completely broken.

'It can easily be splinted but we need some sticks and a tape of some sort,' said David.

While the boys were away looking for sticks, Angela asked David for a knife. He duly produced one and she turned her back to him, fumbling inside her cloak. Soon she had cut a petticoat tie and handed it over shyly. For a moment lust flared between them.

'What a sacrifice,' he teased. 'I hope you won't be dropping intimate garments on the way home?'

'I don't know what you're talking about,' she countered innocently, but her smile told him that she knew exactly what was on his mind.

'You know I desire you, don't you?'

'Yes. But I am not yours to have. I am like that kite, apparently flying free in the wind, but in fact securely held by the strong silk twine in the hand of the master.'

'If I did not have to leave tomorrow, I could be that wind, taking you to the heights of passion,' he said, his voice tight with regret.

She shrugged her shoulders and the tense little smile made her look much older than sixteen. 'You are a married man, Sir. You'd best spend your passion saying goodbye to your wife.' The reprimand was unmistakable.

'I stand corrected,' he said. 'I see you are a woman with Christian morals.'

'Christian morals, Muslim morals, they're all designed to protect a poor defenceless girl like me. It is a pity that desire and lust cause so many men to forget about morals. I have already been the victim of one such man. I would not choose to be the victim of another.'

'And what about love? What if I were to love you?'

She gave him a long, steady, searching stare and said, as though repeating a sentence, 'Love is a luxury of the free, but to those in bondage it remains a dream.'

She was relieved when the boys returned with the sticks and put an end to the conversation.

The kite was mended and provided another hour of fun. On the way back Angela tried to speak as little as possible, but before they reached the house of Captain Kemp, David Koning made a little farewell speech that stayed imprinted on her memory.

'I have a strange feeling that we will meet again,' he said, 'and when we do, circumstances will be different. Don't forget me. I will most certainly remember you.' He took her hand in a formal goodbye.

'Goodbye, Captain. I shall never forget this afternoon.'

A year later Marijke Kemp died giving birth to her fourth child. All Pieter Kemp could think of doing was to place his children with relatives and take to the sea as quickly as possible. Angela and Domingo had no choice; they would have to go back to the East on the *Amersfoort*.

'I have heard that Commander van Riebeeck at the Cabo de Boa Esperança has been given permission to own slaves. We will see if has need of the two of you.'

The idea pleased Domingo. He would do anything to get his feet on African soil again. Once there, all one needed to do was to keep going north to get home.

For Angela, thoughts of home were not an option. Captain Kemp had obviously thought he was showing them kindness by selling them as a family, it being not uncommon for to separate parents from each other and from their children. Angela was hoping they would be rejected by the Commander at Cabo and taken to Ceylon or Batavia where, at least, one would occasionally see a mosque and hear the calls to prayer.

However, this was not to be.

Maria de la Queillerie, wife of Commander van Riebeeck, was only too happy to have a nursemaid who knew the ways of the fatherland and a house slave who had been trained to the high standards of Dutch hygiene and cleanliness. That Domingo and Angela were not married did not seem to bother the Commander or his wife and they accepted the three children as part of the deal. They were healthy and well cared for and would, in due course, make useful slaves themselves.

The Van Riebeeck household included two little Arab girls who had been given to Maria de la Queillerie by a sea captain. They were used as house and kitchen maids and needed much reminding of the routines of a Dutch household. There was also Eva, a Cochoqua girl who had been given to the Van Riebeecks by her uncle, Autshumato, whom everyone called Harry. He was the leader of a Hottentot group, the Strandlopers, who had lost their cattle and lived by scavenging on the beaches.

After only three years in the household of Jan van Riebeeck, Eva was already fluent in Dutch. She was often used as an interpreter in the Commander's dealings with cattle traders from the interior, and had, more than once, shown her natural skill at diplomacy in delicate negotiations between Dutch and Hottentot.

Eva was more like a daughter than a servant in the Van Riebeeck household. She was free to come and go and, on occasion, did so without informing anyone, causing the Commander much concern. She returned each time to find herself more valued as an interpreter and protégée. She was to stay on at the Fort until 1664, when she married the junior surgeon Pieter van Meerhoff.

Eva fascinated Angela. She had seen people from many different races in her young life, but Eva was different from all of those. When she smiled her eyes closed completely and her mouth pushed her high cheekbones even higher. She had a great sense of humour and showed her kindness by offering to look after Angela's children when Angela herself was required to sleep near those of her master. Eva shared much information about the ways of her people, and told amusing animal stories.

When she heard Angela and Domingo speak Portuguese to the children, she immediately expressed a desire to learn this language. She picked it up with ease and could soon offer herself as a Portuguese interpreter as well. She was curious about Angela's conversion to Christianity and found it difficult to grasp the difference between Catholicism and Protestantism. Angela explained that it was much like the differences between clans of the same tribe. It was a matter of politics and power but, in essence, the same.

Eva herself was under pressure to adopt the Christian religion to be completely accepted by her Dutch patrons. Although Catholic slaves like Angela and Domingo were not told in so many words to become Protestant, it was always implied that their souls would otherwise be in danger. Angela liked the ritual of going to church, the social gathering, the singing and the prayers. It was a weekly occasion that relieved the tedium of the work routine. She soon professed a desire to be baptised in the Reformed faith saying privately that it was like a change of clothing. It had nothing to do with what really happened to the soul.

Domingo, however, clung to his Catholicism. He saw no reason to be forced yet again onto the same God in a different way when everyone knew that it was really the Orixas that ordered and influenced events. Eva saw similarities between the Orixas and Heitsi Eibib who was worshipped by her own people. She agreed with Domingo that the gods of Nature were far less confusing than Angela's abstract God.

So it was at the Cape of Good Hope that Angela and David met again, on the bright morning of 18 June 1661. The arrival of *'t Wapen van Holland* at the Cape had been eagerly awaited, since it would bring Commander van Riebeeck's replacement, but when it dropped anchor in Table Bay, together with the yacht *Overveen*, it brought disappointing news.

The new Commander had died on the way to the Cape. The news was softened by the fact that its bearer was such an old and dear friend of the Van Riebeecks. It had been David Koning who had brought them to the Cape in the *Drommedaris* nine years before.

From the kitchen Angela heard David's unforgettable laugh and rushed to the parlour door. In this low-ceilinged house he looked even larger than in Holland. She stood there for a good few minutes before he felt her stare and turned. Happy recognition flashed across his face and his broad smile took her in; yet he did not greet her. Puzzled and disappointed, she returned to the kitchen.

Soon, however, she was given instructions by the mistress to get linen and provisions ready for the house at Bosheuvel.

'You know, when Captain Koning was last here, there was not a single building in this place. The Commander is going to show him the Gardens, the farms along the Liesbeeck, the redoubts and the almond hedge, and leave him at Bosheuvel for a few days to enjoy some hunting and fishing.'

She added, 'It is his wish that you go as housekeeper. He says you must still be able to cook some of Juffrouw Kemp's special dishes. I was surprised that he still remembered you. Did you see him often at the Kemps?'

'Only once. I am also surprised,' said Angela, hoping to hide her excitement. 'Will Domingo come to Bosheuvel also?' she asked.

'No, he has to stay here and help with the rest of the guests. We'll send Klaas, the Hottentot, with you to make the fire and see to the Captain's horse.'

Early the next morning, Klaas and Angela set off for Bosheuvel along the wagon road that followed the Liesbeeck. They took the track to 't Rondebosje and from there found a newly made path to the Commander's own farm, Bosheuvel. The farm hugged the back of the Devil Mountain. Angela had been there once before and thought of it as paradise. The two-roomed house was basic but sturdy and the kitchen was outside. She was hoping the good weather would hold.

In the late afternoon, Commander van Riebeeck and his guest arrived. The house was swept, the rugs laid, the beds made and a fire was blazing in the hearth. David Koning did not miss the flowers in the jug and the fine table linen.

'Such simple elegance in the wilderness,' he said. He still had not addressed her by name, and was not to do so until the next day after the Commander had left.

Then it was as though a sluice had been opened.

He found Angela kneading bread on the table outside. He watched for a while, her fists and face seemingly consumed by concentration. She felt his stare and looked up with a smile.

'We're alone now,' he said in Portuguese.

'My Dutch is much improved. And Klaas will be bringing wood soon.'

'I told you we would meet again. How lovely you have become. You're a grown woman now.'

'You seem to continue where you left off eight years ago, but you forget how that meeting ended. I reminded you that you were a married man and I a woman in bondage.'

'Yes, like that kite, you said. What would you say if I told you that I could cut you free? Because I am free now, a widower.'

'There is still the question of love.'

'We have three days. We could learn to love each other in that time, seeing that we already want each other.'

'We are not alone. Klaas is here.'

'Klaas can be paid to disappear. But you have to tell me to pay him. You have to choose; it will be your first act as a free woman.'

She looked at his twinkling eyes, the colour of the mountains, his broad shoulders under his shirt, his large hands.

'Yes, pay him.'

I never knew my mother to include the erotic details of her life in any narrative. These were her secrets. But, oh, the joy and fulfillment she implied when she said that for three days they shared so much, body and soul, that they were ready to pledge themselves to each other forever. He would settle his affairs in Batavia and come back for her on his journey back to the fatherland, early in the following year. He would buy her freedom and marry her.

'And what if I am with child? What if something should happen to you?' She spoke as one familiar with misfortune.

'I will make arrangements with the Commander. You will be looked after.'

This he did and he must have been very persuasive not to incur the wrath of his friend Jan van Riebeeck, who presented himself to the public at large as a man of strict morals who did not tolerate fornication. In this case he seemed to make an exception, and Angela even found herself treated with a certain amount of deference. A trestle bed replaced her mattress in the children's room where she slept with Maria, her youngest child. Whereas she had been accustomed before to sit on the ground in the yard, she was now encouraged to use a chair in the kitchen.

Angela and David had said their sad farewells in private the morning he left. She stood on the quay for a long time watching 't Wapen van Holland sail away in a small fleet with three other ships, slowly leave the bay and disappear over the horizon. She was unable to control her tears and people wondered amongst themselves for whom she could be weeping.

The gossip started in earnest when it became obvious that she was with child and Domingo made it known that he had not lain with her for many years. How could he when she was sleeping inside the Commander's house and he in the slave lodge? No, it was not his child, but it could be the child of someone important. Had nobody noticed the attitude of superiority Angela had adopted, the unspoken hope in her eyes? Had no one heard the hints about her future, how she would leave this place when she was free, as though she had some real prospect of freedom?

Surely they must have noticed how she mysteriously clammed up about the patrimony of the child?

It was in January of 1662 that Angela was called to the Commander's office. The formality frightened her: slaves were always instructed in the yard. She was even more alarmed when she saw the Commander's wife already seated in the office with a sombre face. Both women were six months pregnant. The Commander's face looked pained rather than angry.

'Sit down, Angela,' he invited in an unusually kind tone of voice. His dark eyes were filled with tears.

Angela's heart began to pound. Bad news, it must be bad news.

'We received news this morning from St. Helena of the loss of *'t Wapen van Holland* and two other ships sailing with her. All who sailed in them were lost in a storm south of Ceylon. There were survivors from the *Arnhem* who managed to make their way to St Helena and send word of the disaster.'

Stunned, Angela stared at him and as his words sank in. In one fell swoop all her hopes were extinguished. The room became a blur. She swooned and fainted.

For a week, she hardly knew where she was. Delirious with grief, she screamed his name over and over again, leaving the whole community in no doubt as to who my father was. The Danish doctor, Van Meerhoff, prescribed tranquilising brews and Eva sat with her day and night, now praying, now whispering animist incantations. My mother was finally persuaded that she would lose me if she did not pull herself together.

When she was on her feet again, the Commander called her to his office once more. This time Cretser, the former clerk from *'t Wapen van Holland*, was present.

'Look, Angela,' said Commander van Riebeeck, 'this is the undertaking Captain Koning made before he sailed. Mr Cretser and I signed here as witnesses. It is a provision for you and the child in case something should happen to him.'

It was as though a faint light shone at the very end of her dark tunnel.

'Read it to me,' she said. And as she heard the words, she memorised them and could still recite them in her old age.

'I, the undersigned, David Koning, in front of these witnesses, Jan van Riebeeck, Honorable Commander of the Cabo de Boa Esperança, and my trusted friend, Jacob Cretser, in solemn earnest and love, wish to make provision for the future welfare of the slave Angela of Bengal.

I charge the undersigned witnesses to attend to the following instructions, should I fail to be able to attend to them myself. First, that the aforenamed Angela of Bengal be manumitted at a fair market price, and be allowed the freedom of the Cabo de Boa Esperança or be transported as a free person to her native Bengal under the protection of a trustworthy sea captain. That the cost of this be charged to my estate. Second, that the child she may be carrying be baptised in the Reformed faith and be known by the name: De Koning. Third, that an annuity be made available from my estate to provide mother and child with a suitable income.

I moreover charge my friend, Commander Jan van Riebeeck, to protect and advise Angela of Bengal in my place.'
Signed this 25th day of June, 1661

David Koning
Co-signed as witnesses: Jan van Riebeeck
Jacob Cretser

Angela held the paper as though it was made of precious silk and asked which letters made my father's name.

'And this will happen?' she asked. 'Because of this paper I will be set free and my child will have her father's name?'

'Yes, I will now present a copy of this document to the authorities in Patria and petition for this request to be included in the settlement of Captain Koning's estate. But you'll have to be patient, Angela. It may take years. After I leave, Jacob here will see that you get your due.'

And so it was that I had a Dutch Reformed christening on the same day as my friend-to-be, Grisella Mostert, and was welcomed into the Protestant community as Anna de Koning.

My mother's manumission took longer. When Commander van Riebeeck left that April, he sold her to the Fiscal, Abraham Gabbema, with an understanding that she should be set free as soon as the funds to buy her freedom arrived at the Cape. Four years later word came that the money was on its way and Gabbema told the world that he was releasing us because of 'pure affection'. Thomas Mulder paid him a fair price for my mother and released her when the money finally arrived six months later.

My mother explained that by now, being so accustomed to European ways, fluent in Dutch and a practising Christian, she had abandoned the idea of returning to Bengal. Above all, she thought that I should grow up in the place where I was born. A new life in a new land!

In February 1667 she was given a piece of land, 57 by 50 Rhineland feet. With our annuity she built a simple little house, bought a cow and a few sheep and set about doing what most Free Burghers of the settlement did in those days: grow fresh produce for the many ships on their way to the East.

CHAPTER THREE

Learning things

MAI ANGELA WAS ILLITERATE. She never learnt to sign her name except with a nervous, self-conscious cross. This did not mean she was stupid; she spoke her native Bengali, Dutch and Portuguese fluently and could recite long passages from the Bible in Dutch, prayers of supplication in Latin and, as we later discovered, devotions in Arabic. Her memory was phenomenal and nobody tried to cheat her with money because she could do complicated calculations in her head.

My mother impressed upon her children that her own freedom from slavery had given us the opportunity and time to learn the things of which her enslavement had deprived her. Study was never an option for her. Her life was spent working, first for her owners and then to give us a better life. It was not that she made herself into a martyr because of this; it just always seemed to be understood that we would avail ourselves of the opportunity to acquire the learning that could move us into a life beyond that of manual labour.

There were enough slave children around to serve as an example of our good fortune. They were taught to read and recite hymns and Bible verses in order to praise the Lord, but few of them were ever taught to write. Maria, Pieter and I went to school with Grisella Mostert from next door. Grisella and I were exactly the same age. Her father, Wouter Mostert, owned a mill and a brewery and was a great support to Mai Angela in the early days when she first got her land between the Company Gardens and the Lion Mountain.

Wouter Mostert had received his own education in Utrecht and prided himself on finding the best tutors for his children among the ever-transient array of lay preachers. Apart from academic credentials, he insisted that a tutor should possess a sense of humour. Learning was a sweet thing, he said, and, on these grounds more than one sour- or sad-faced potential teacher was turned away. This meant that we sometimes went without lessons for months, but the next fleet would always bring new possibilities and, once a jolly tutor was found, our lessons would continue.

Though the Bible and Catechism was the primary source of reading material fancied by our tutors, given their profession and persuasion, Wouter Mostert insisted that we use books from his own collection as readers. He owned a copy of the *Neder-lantsche gedenck-clanck* by a poet from Zeeland named Adriaen Valerius, from which we learnt of the enslavement and the oppression of the Dutch people. Because they were God's own chosen people, they were finally liberated from Spanish oppression.

From this book we memorised songs of praise and hymns in which God was thanked for restoring the Promised Land to the Seven Provinces of Patria. We stared for hours at the allegorical engraving in which the Seven Provinces, represented by seven women, thanked God, alongside the Stadholders. Hester Mostert, who had actually seen some of the Dutch princes, said that the artist had produced an accurate image.

From the engravings in *Neder-lantsche gedenck-clanck* we became familiar with the Leo Belgicus, that symbol of Patria featured in books and maps everywhere. This book inspired in me a strong feeling of Dutch patriotism that made me feel connected to my own father in a curious way. It seemed that I could somehow channel my love for him by knowing his history and cultivating a passion for his country. At least half of me had a right to belong to a great nation. Even though I knew I would probably never set foot on Dutch soil, it made me a devoted student.

My favourite history book was the edition of Wouter van Goudhoeven's *Oude Cronijcke van Holland* commonly known as the *Divisiekroniek*. From this book we learnt about the ancient Prince Bato, who settled on the Rhine with his Batavians, and his brother Salandus, who settled in Zeeland and named Middelburg after his father Mitellus. These stories involved us in European geography. Soon the lands and rivers of Europe were better known to us than our own wild and unexplored colony, where only the mountains and streams in our immediate vicinity were known to have names.

The *Divisiekroniek* was beautifully illustrated with woodcut pictures of many noble lords and ladies. I was always puzzled by how the artists knew what people looked like. I was also fascinated to see how the costumes changed through the centuries. I loved the story of Til Uijlenspiegel and, while we were encouraged to model our behaviour on that of Griselda the Meek (the real 'Griselda'), I soon decided that we were far too interesting to be meek all the time. My favourite nobleman was Count Floris the Fat in his fur cloak and hat, pointed spurred shoes and curious sash with folly bells.

Our moral manuals were the *Complete Works* of Jacob Cats and Roemer Visscher's *Sinnepoppen*. Cats' moralistic verse guided us from childhood to adulthood. According to these catchy rhymes, girls were meant to stay close to home and hearth while boys prepared to defend king and country.

We were well guided in our interpretation of the illustrations in Cats' volume on children's games. Recognising the symbolism of these games was, for a while, a favourite pastime: bubble blowing and hoop rolling represented futility, bladder balls the inflated emptiness of worldly affairs. The stiltwalker showed conceit, and blind man's bluff the folly of those who grope in the dark.

I discussed much of this with my mother, but Cats' interpretation of the folly of the kite flyer I shared only with Grisella, who knew all my secrets. It seemed to me to truly represent the relationship between my mother and father. Together they had flown a kite, believing they had escaped the constraints of all earthly objections to their union, and then the cord snapped, the kite crashed to the ground and their dreams turned out to be 'just so much paper'.

Hester Mostert was very fond of the poetry of Vondel and encouraged us to memorise his two famous poems on the death and funeral of his child, though when the time came for public recitation she always took the stage. Her well-proportioned blonde presence instantly demanded attention and, when she fixed the audience with her clear blue gaze, people knew they were in for a stirring performance.

At the end of *Kinder-lyck* she would usually give those in tears a pause in which to compose themselves and prepare to follow her to the funeral in *Uitvaert van mijn Dochterken*. Everyone knew she could recite these poems with such depth of feeling because of the death of her own little Cornelia in the year Grisella and I were born. In a community where child mortality was commonplace, just about everyone at our small gatherings had cause to remember a lost child.

Of all my mother's friends, Hester Weyers (as Hester Mostert was known before she married) was the most practical and down to earth person I knew. She had a great sense of humour and a bright laugh and could not abide gossip. This quality gave my mother a sense of security; she knew that anything she confided in Hester Weyers would not reach the ears of our small community. People were always eager for scandal, especially scandal involving those like us who seemed to be prospering beyond our particular station in life.

Thinking back on it, I realise that I owe much more to Hester Weyers and Aaltje Elberts, our local expert on bobbin lace, than the sewing skills I learnt from them. My exposure to them during my formative years taught me social graces and the niceties of feminine behaviour that my mother could never teach me. Mai Angela was aware that she was not as refined in proper Dutch manners and encouraged me to learn from them. This came about quite naturally, since Grisella was being taught at the same time, but they did not need to include me. They showed me a kindness I will never forget.

Grisella stuck with the lace making, but increasingly I turned my hand to embroidery until the opportunity for pursuing my other passion arrived. An interest in plants came to me almost naturally since it was by gardening that my mother earned a living. Our plot was not far from the Company Gardens and from early on my mother was on good terms with the Company gardeners.

In the early days my mother helped the gardeners Boom, Jacobz, Van Roosendael and Gresnich establish a medicinal garden and found for them specimens of indigenous flowers to show the collectors who called. These collectors were especially interested in bulbs and seeds as these were dry and could be easily transported.

My mother's advice was also sought when specimens were brought from the East to be cultivated at the Cape in an acclimatisation stage before being transferred to the gardens of Europe. Some of these she recognised from her childhood and could remember whether they grew in wet or dry places, were hardy or frail. She always remembered the colour and shape of the blooms and whether or not they were fragrant.

Thus, 'plant talk' happened around me as long as I could remember and, as I grew up, I came to know where all the different narcissii, ericas and *carduus* grew. My mother came to trust my ability to identify a plant when not in bloom and, by the time I was nine, I was allowed to go with the gardeners on local plant hunts.

In 1672, when I was ten years old, an interesting German botanist called at the Cape on his way to Ceylon. He was

Doctor Paul Hermann, a dapper young man of twenty-six, full of enthusiasm for our plants. He spoke quickly, laughed easily and had a nervous habit of examining the lace of his cuffs when thinking. He had seen some of our lilies growing in Holland, England and even Padua in Italy where he had studied, and was anxious to see the ericas and *carduus* of which he had heard so much.

My mother was persuaded to abandon her garden for once and climb the Table Mountain with Doctor Hermann, in search of plants. After some discussion as to whether a ten-year-old would make it up the mountain, I was allowed to go along. I regarded it as a test of my stamina and knowledge. We took with us three slaves and a German soldier to explain some of the Doctor's language, though his Dutch was quite good since he had studied in Leiden. He was delighted when he heard I was only ten.

'Such was my age when collecting plants I had my first adventure,' he said, stringing his words together in his peculiar German way. 'Then was it that I almost drowned in the river a very special reed to pick. You do well to start so young.' He let me carry one of his special collector's knapsacks.

No serious misadventure befell us that day. The weather remained excellent, and we did not come across any dangerous animals. The good doctor saw more ericas and thistle flowers than he had ever hoped to see.

He himself knew of no one who had managed to cultivate *carduus* flowers outside Africa. He had only seen illustrations of the large variety and had not known it was such a lovely pink with such a handsome black beard. The variety of lesser *carduus* also filled him with wonder. He made us feel that, by showing him these plants, we were giving him a precious gift.

My big achievement was that my legs held up and the party never had to stop for me, though I suspected that they sometimes lingered a little longer over some particular plant in order that I might recover my strength. I was

27

rewarded by a promise to be part of another expedition to the kloofs of the Devil Mountain to find some special lilies. I was excited; I was now old enough to have deduced that this was the place where I was conceived and this would be the first time I would see it with my very own eyes.

But first the Doctor wanted to press and classify his collection from Table Mountain and he chose me to be his assistant. He personally supervised the making of the presses and gave the carpenter special instructions on the exact measurements and fit of the wooden screws. Before pressing the plants, he made accurate sketches of the entire plant, flower, leaves and roots, naming each plant according to the system used in Leiden and Copenhagen.

It was my job to prepare his drawing cards for him by making an outline of accurate margins. For this we used *stylos* of soft graphite. Soon he let me finish the roots and, later, the leaves, after he had positioned them on the stem and outlined them in proper proportion. I was not yet trusted with the delicate task of finishing the flowers. He said colouring the sketches with paint would come later and he made careful notes as to the true colours of each plant.

Doctor Hermann was a bubbling fountain of information and seemed to like talking to me, perhaps because I was young, with few opinions of my own but many questions and a mind like a sponge, hungry for information about the world out there, the Europe to which, ridiculously, I felt I belonged. He patiently answered my questions and sometimes even complimented me on their perceptive nature. He told me about his friends in Italy and England, Denmark and Holland, their lives and interests.

The Doctor had promised some plants and seeds to his friend Professor Bartolinus in Copenhagen who wanted to include information on the rare plants of the Cape in a new book he was writing. Doctor Stolle, a ship's surgeon, had already agreed to take these to Europe for him.

After the drawing came the pressing. I was taught how to lay out the leaves and flowers, cover them with paper and place them on the press, taking care not to disturb the arrangement. This I did, layer upon layer, and the good Doctor praised my delicate handling of the plants. Every layer was meticulously labelled in Latin before the next was added.

And so I built up my first botanical vocabulary and started calling plants by their proper names. Doctor Hermann told me that if I were a flower, I would be called *Anna Regis Capitis Bonae Spei*. Griselda disapproved of this Latin affectation and told me not to be ridiculous, making up Latin names for myself, but that was just because she was jealous.

Our trip to Bosheuvel was made more exciting by the necessity of camping overnight in order to climb the kloof early in the morning. Our small party called at the Gardens at Rustenburg and 't Rondebosje on the way. We made a big campfire that night and instructed our slave Scipio to keep it burning all night to keep the lion and leopard at bay. Even so, I heard their calling intermittently through the night and was glad my mother was close by to snuggle against. She seemed particularly happy to be in that spot and when we woke at dawn to break our fast before setting off, she gave me a tender hug and said:

'It's around here that you were made, Annie.'

I was enormously flattered because I knew then that she thought of me as old enough to understand the facts of life. I had menstruated for the first time the previous month and was entering into womanhood. I loved her for being candid with me in that particular place, at that particular time. But when I think about it now, I realise that she probably had a need to share her happy memories with someone and who better than me, the product of that happiness?

We found the spotted red lilies that my mother had promised Doctor Hermann, and many other exotic mosses and ferns besides. We watched the river otters at play and caught some fresh trout for our lunch and talked of many things.

'Your daughter a good scientist will make, *gnädige Frau*,' Doctor Hermann told my mother. 'She has excellent powers of observation and the *enthusiasmus* neccessary as a collector.'

'My daughter is going to have to find herself a husband to keep her, Doctor, and I don't think too many men will seriously consider marrying a scientist.'

'Don't worry, Mai. If I plan to do anything in a botanical line, it will be the drying and the drawing. That is the part I enjoy most and that is more artistic than scientific.'

'Also more feminine,' said my mother, relieved.

I was sorry to see Doctor Hermann go. He was the first truly educated person with whom I had spent time, and I must honestly say that the thrill of intellectual stimulation far overshadowed the thrill of impending womanhood. I was careful, however, to keep this feeling to myself.

When Doctor ten Rhyne arrived on the *Ternaten* the next October, I was the obvious choice for his assistant. He approved of me immediately on the grounds that I had the same name as his mother. He was about the same age as Doctor Hermann, but more of a scholar, curious but less energetic. He took meticulous care of his thick flowing black hair and his moustache was neatly trimmed.

Doctor ten Rhyne's well-manicured hands were almost too soft for a naturalist known to spend much time digging in the earth. His speech was slow and considered and his smile a rare but warm occurrence. He was known to be most proficient in written and spoken Latin, and showed me the Cape flowers in books he had brought with him to make sure I knew where these were to be found.

It was by looking at these books that I first discovered the difference between Germanic and Italian style; the former formal and serious, the latter more flowing and fanciful. I particularly liked the illustrations in a book by the Italian Ferrari, in which the plant names appeared on ribbons draped around the stems, filling the page with flowing elegance.

Dr ten Rhyne promised to teach me how to draw and shade these ribbons, which he called scrolls. In the same book there were intriguing illustrations depicting seven days in the life of Flora. I looked at them for hours trying to figure out the symbolism, admiring the figures and the architecture, transporting myself into a world of generous dimensions and large proportions.

To our delight, we found about eighty plants for his collection, but since he stayed for only a month on his way to Java, he mainly pressed the flowers and processed the bulbs for drying. He did few illustrations himself, but allowed me to do some drawings and helped me with the Italian-style scroll work. He was a very good teacher and seemed to enjoy instructing me and expanding my knowledge of botanical terms. He was surprised that I already knew some Latin and encouraged my attempts to figure out the text in his books.

The Doctor was very knowledgeable about the indigenous peoples of the East as well as Brazil. He was intrigued by the local clans, and when Mai Angela heard that Eva van Meerhof was back in town from Robben Island she introduced her to the Doctor. Few knew more about the many tribes and clans of the Cape than Eva, herself a Cochoqua.

Eva's life had taken a sad turn. Pieter van Meerhof had been murdered in Madagascar some years previously and, without a husband to protect her. or Jan van Riebeeck to employ her, she was lost. She found no sympathy at the Fort. The new administration distrusted her and had no use for her as an interpreter. It was said that her own people rejected her because she had become too Dutch. As her security and confidence decreased, so did her control over her behaviour. She drank too much and, when inebriated, lost control over the European code of conduct she so scrupulously observed when sober.

My mother felt very sorry for Eva. She knew about a broken heart, she knew about shattered dreams and lost hope. She knew about the kite string snapping. Eva's wayward behaviour was tolerated to a certain extent, and her friends

tried to protect her. My stepfather often brought her home
from the tavern, having rescued her from some imminent
promiscuous entanglement.

We would put her to bed and send word to the old
Pottery where she lived with her three children. Her loyal
slave, Jan Vos, would then know not to expect her home
and to mind the children until the next morning.
Eventually, the wife of Jan Reynierz took pity on Eva's children and was given permission to take care of them. Jan Vos
was put under the protection of the Church Council.

Time and again, Eva was sent back to Robben Island to
cool off. She did not seem to mind this, since it was there
that she had spent her happiest years with Pieter van
Meerhof when he was Superintendent of the prison. She
said she could still feel his presence there and it calmed her
for a while until the loneliness grabbed at her heart again
and she had to see her children, the living proof of her love
for the Dane. It was on such a visit that my mother caught
her before she had begun the downward spiral of a binge.

Eva was much cheered by the thought that she could be
useful to a scholar and a doctor to boot. They sat under the
mulberry tree in our garden and spoke together for hours
on end, Eva talking and the Doctor furiously taking notes
in Latin. He said he was happy to hear the history from the
perspective of a native female, which differed much from
the information given by local burgers and what he called
'domesticated' male Hottentot.

Eva told him her version of the conflicts in the early days
of the settlement, of the rivalry between the Kaapmans and
Strandlopers and the tribes further to the north-west of the
district that bore the name Hottentots Holland. They discussed the power and wealth of the Cochoqua and their
chief, Oedasoa, her brother-in law, and his deputy, Gonnema.
Eva explained the methods of warfare used to subject
neighbouring tribes, the Chariguriqua and Chainouqua.

The Doctor listened, and carefully noted Eva's anecdotes
about plot and counterplot, deceit and intrigue that formed

the intricate political story of the relations between the Dutch and the first peoples of the country. Mai Angela had cautioned him that Eva's accounts might be coloured by her own disappointment with European ways, but he insisted Eva was an invaluable original source of information.

The Doctor was eager to meet Eva's relatives, including Oedasoa and his brother Hanibal, but Eva was against an overland expedition. The commander and soldiers at the outpost of Saldanha had recently been murdered, and the conflict between the Dutch and the Cochoquas was escalating, with the possibility of a full-scale war. She suggested that one of the Saldanha traders might be persuaded to take them to Saldanha Bay by sea, from where a message might be sent to Oedasoa to send a safe escort for the Doctor. Then, she said, he would meet Koina, proud and free, in their natural state, unspoilt by too much smoking and drinking and the decadent ways of the Dutch.

It was the beginning of the seal trane season and Bartholomeus Borns was set to sail up the West Coast to deliver equipment for the trane burning on Dassen Island just south of Saldanha. Everyone in the settlement of Cabo de Boa Esperança knew Barth Borns. We all depended on him and the other Saldanha traders for the seal trane that kept our lamps burning, and for penguin eggs and salted fish and penguin meat to feed the slaves.

Barth Borns was quite a character with his eye patch, grisly unkempt hair, weatherbeaten face, and his large pipe, rarely out of his mouth. It was said that there was really nothing wrong with his eye, but that he wore the patch to match that of his terrier dog, Klepje, a fierce rat catcher. This dog was almost better known than his master. Of all the rat catchers in Cabo, he was the most intrepid, often seen with a dead rat almost as big as himself.

Barth was reluctant to take a party such as ours. He made it clear that we would have to camp and could expect no luxuries, since the outpost was closed. He pointed out the dangers from wild animals and said he took no responsibility for our protection. Eva, however, was determined to go. She borrowed our slave, Scipio, for the journey and her former slave, Jan Vos, both known to be loyal and fearless.

Before we set off, my mother gave me a list of things to be collected: gannet down, plover eggs and cormorant guano, which also interested Doctor ten Rhyne. He made sure we took the proper bags to collect enough of this fertiliser for him to take some to Java.

Barth Borns grumbled when he saw that Eva was also bringing Pieternella and Salomon van Meerhof. When Eva explained that this would be the children's first chance to see their aunt and uncle, he grunted and waved them onto the boat. Klepje, whom children were always warned not to touch, immediately and miraculously took to Salomon, softening Barth's heart towards Eva's children.

We sailed off in the *Bruijt* on a clear morning in late October. The freshness of spring was still in the air and everyone on board was in a holiday mood. As we passed the prison island, Eva pointed out to Pieternella and Salomon that this was where they lived when their father was alive and that she now lived there with the baby when things became too much for her.

On the way out, we called at Dassen Island, where Barth dropped the trane kettles and checked on the sheep that had been left behind when the outpost was closed earlier in the year. He knew this island well. He told the Doctor that the Company had allowed the Saldanha traders to keep sheep on the island some years before, but because the sheep got so fat the Company withdrew the privilege and placed their own sheep there.

I remembered from when I was tiny how Theuntje Borns, Barth's wife, was exiled to the island for six weeks after she spread the rumour that Hester Weyers had borne two illegitimate children in Holland and that she had murdered one of them. What a sensation that caused! Eva recounted this scandal to Doctor ten Rhyne with glee but, of course, not within hearing of the Saldahna trader. She also told how

Barth Borns had helped the French to occupy Saldanha Bay, the cause of Commander van Quaelberg's dismissal.

Two days later, we reached the entry to the Bay and made for Schaapen Island. Barth Borns thought it best to make our camp here rather than on the peninsula at the abandoned outpost at de Craal. We would be safer from preying wild animals and attacks from hostile tribesmen. Eva sniffed contemptuously at this last remark and said that the Koina and Cochoqua were peaceful people who were driven to hostility by indiscriminate acts of the Free Burghers.

We all knew, however, that the island gave us better protection, and pitched our camp near a fountain of fresh water. Smoke signals had to be sent to the kraal of Eva's brother-in-law, inviting him and her sister to visit us. I was thrilled to be allowed to accompany Eva and Jan Vos to the lookout point on the mainland from where the signal was sent. After a steep climb, we were met with an amazing sight. On the one side there was the lagoon with its turquoise water. On the other, the undulating interior stretched endlessly toward the far horizon.

Jan Vos set a fire. We did not have to wait long. Soon smoke was clearly visible on a distant hilltop. Eva sent signals and answers were received. She smiled with satisfaction.

'They'll be here in two days, Oedasoa and my sister,' she said happily.

While we waited for Eva's relatives, Doctor ten Rhyne and I continued our botanical collections of dune flowers on the coast. We rowed up the lagoon to the marshland to inspect the reeds and waterplants. The weather was unbelievably kind and we managed to go to Malgas Island to collect the cormorant guano for my mother's garden.

The Doctor told me that using bird excrement as fertiliser was a custom brought to Europe from Brazil. This opened a whole new area of discussion between us and while collecting guano and gannet down, I had a lesson on South America. I was filled with wonder at the vastness of the earth, the endless variety of its people, plants and animals and I felt intensely my own insignificance before the Creator of so many wonders.

On our return from Malgas Island, we found a very excited Eva. Word had come that her sister would arrive with a party from her kraal the following day. We were to meet them on the beach across from Schaapen Island.

Eva was up early the next morning, inviting Pieternellie, Salomon and me to come and watch her dress for the meeting. She had brought a bag of tribal clothes with her and proceeded to unpack it carefully, explaining the garments to us as she did so. There was a *karos*, which was a blanket lined with sheepskin, which she said was made of skin only in the days before the Dutch, as was the skirt that she would wear around her waist. The skirt had a wide belt, to which was attached four triangular pieces of soft, furry skin – one to cover her buttocks, one to cover her genitals and two longer panels for the sides.

Tied at the end of each of the side panels of the skirt was a bunch of seeds that made a pleasant rattling sound. Eva said that the rattles scared away snakes when one walked and made a good sound when one danced. When I asked about a bodice, she laughed and said that Khoi women were proud to show their breasts since that was where they kept the food for their children.

Eva unpacked many strings of coloured bone beads that she said would go around her neck and torso and a quantity of large and small bangles for her legs and her upper and lower arms. Some of these bangles were made of smoothly carved ivory, showing the lovely grain of the bone; others were made of copper. Her pride and joy were a new set of red and yellow copper bangles, recently made for her by a Javanese exile on Robben Island. She had had these made specially for her sister. Her own outfit was completed by a small peaked grass hat and earrings consisting of large double copper hoops with ivory beads.

Now she was ready to dress, to transform herself from Eva van Meerhof into Krotoa de Cochoqua. We watched wide-eyed as she draped herself in beads and carefully placed the bangles and skirt. She asked Pieternellie to hold the mirror while she greased her hair with great dexterity and divided it into segments to which she attached small glass and copper ornaments. Finally, she rubbed some charcoal on her cheeks and declared herself ready to meet her relatives.

Doctor ten Rhyne was astounded by the metamorphosis. Barth Borns said he had seen her 'in skins' before, but never as handsome. What he meant was that this morning she was sober and happy. Eva smiled her best eye-closing smile and began to do a little dance.

'This is the real me, this is Krotoa, not Eva.'

A look of bitter irony replaced the smile as she began to sing aloud: 'Cochoqua, Guriqua, Chainouqua, Hessequa, Attaqua, Houteniqua ...'

She was obviously enjoying the effect of the assorted clicks she was producing. Doctor ten Rhyne interrupted. 'What on earth does all that mean?' he asked.

'Those are the names of some of the tribes of my people, the people the Dutch call "Hottentot".'

'It is more complex than I thought,' observed the doctor.

I noticed that Bart Borns was showing a lot of kindness to the children, and gave Salomon special little jobs to do. Now he sent him off with Jan Vos to go and meet his relatives. They arrived at noon, and as soon as we saw them appear over the sand dunes we jumped into the boat and rowed across, taking with us the food we had prepared.

The visiting party consisted of Eva's sister and two women she had known as a child. They were accompanied by a number of young men. Because of the war, not many men could be spared and Oedasoa was suspicious that this might be a trap to take him hostage.

Nevertheless, it turned out to be a happy gathering. Pieternellie and Salomon were much admired, amidst clicking and smiling and touching. I became the object of special attention when it was explained that my mother came from the other side of Europe and had been a slave of the Dutch. That I was *mestiza*, the same as Pieternellie and Salomon, but of a different ethnic mix, seemed to fascinate everyone present.

Encouraged by Doctor ten Rhyne's motto that 'that which won't kill you, will fatten you', we were all very polite, eating each other's food and drinking sour milk from calabashes. The visit lasted until well after sunset, when the Cochoquas insisted on leaving. It was obvious that Eva, now very much Krotoa, was very sad to say goodbye to her sister. Maybe she felt intuitively that she would not see her again.

The next morning we set sail for the Cape. Eva gave Pieternellie and me an ivory bangle each. I treasure mine to this day. She was very quiet during the trip home, dressed again in European clothes, staying close to Pieternella and Salomon, almost as though they were the adults and she the child.

They never saw her alive again.

The night after we landed at the Cape, Eva got drunk and was banished to Robben Island, where she died the following year. Not long after her funeral in the Fort, where we were all present, Barth and Theuntje Borns were given permission to take Pieternella and Salomon with them when they went to live on the Island of Mauritius.

Doctor ten Rhyne left in November, taking with him folios of dried plants, a huge bag of guano and many notes on the Hottentot. These he included in a book he later wrote about our country.

CHAPTER FOUR

Olof and Annie

WHEN SERGEANT OLOF BERGH arrived at the Cape in 1676, I was fourteen years old. Too young to think seriously of marriage, but old enough to understand why several young women at the Cape fell instantly and madly in love with him. Many a romantic imagination was set ablaze by tales of his bravery in Ceylon, his noble origins and the fact that he was unattached. For these it was convenient to ignore the rumour that he had a family in Ceylon.

Since I told myself that I was too young to be affected by this madness, I took the opportunity to observe the cause of their affliction objectively. I did this from behind my lace cushion when the handsome Sergeant visited the home of my teacher and mentor, Aletta Elberts, wife of his senior officer Hieronimus Cruse.

Thanks to Aaltje, I was a good lace-maker. She taught my friend Grisella and me everything she knew about needlework, especially embroidery. She believed in perseverance and kept us on task until we finished whatever project we started. When I was nine, I completed my first sampler of cross-stitch patterns of Dutch motifs: ships and windmills, birds and flowerpots, complete with Adam and Eve and the Tree of Life.

After cross-stitch came the more delicate drawn thread and cutwork techniques that we were encouraged to apply to our bodices and petticoats. After we had passed this apprenticeship on underwear, we were allowed to make ker-chiefs and cravats. In my youth, clothes were not nearly as elaborate as they are today and we used our embroidery skills mainly in household articles such as bed sheets, tablecloths and shelf cloths. Lace was in much greater demand to trim collars and cuffs.

It was from Aaltje that we first learnt to make a simple border lace, graduating first to wider inlays and finally to larger rectangles and ovals, to decorate tables and chests and add the true Dutch touch to the windows of our simple homes. She had her contacts in Holland, from whom she ordered her supplies of fine thread, and she supervised the local manufacture of bobbins and cushions, teaching us how to upholster the cushions to exactly the right thickness.

Grisella was a little suspicious of my renewed interest in lace-making, but I could legitimately plead a trousseau that I was commissioned to do, and managed to convince her and myself that I was not smitten. I do not think Aaltje was fooled. She gave me one of her teasing looks, her brown eyes twinkling, her fine eyebrows raised, but she discreetly said nothing. What I did not know then was that Aaltje had secretly sent to Ceylon to establish whether the gossip about the existence of a Bergh wife and children there was true. This took more than a year, because of the snail's pace at which our news travelled.

During this time I had plenty of time to observe the Swede. He was tall and fair, with golden curly hair down to his shoulders and eyes that matched the Cape sky on a fine day. His skin was biscuit brown and his broad shoulders bulged beneath his jacket. To see him fencing was a joy: he was so quick and nimble on his feet. He was soon known to be one of the top swordsmen in the Garrison and not a man to cross. Yet his manner was mild and friendly and people rarely saw him angry.

At the Cruse home he joked and laughed and teased the ladies in Aaltje's parlour. Sometimes he brought his lute and sang ballads in Swedish and Portuguese. My favourite was the medieval ballad about the unicorn, which he sang in old German. He had a rich baritone voice which the community heard every Sunday in church singing our Dutch hymns with an amusing Swedish accent.

I also saw him play his part in the social life at the Castle. Under the pretext of delivering or collecting clothes, it was quite possible for a person of my position to linger on the periphery of a tea party and watch life in the Commander's parlour, the most elegant I had ever seen.

My mother was wont to scoff at the modesty of the Commander's parlour, comparing it to the parlours of Amsterdam. Be that as it may, it was here that officers from the Garrison were sometimes invited to take tea with the ladies. Although he was not a high-ranking officer, Sergeant Bergh's birth and social ease caused him to be included in the entertainment of important visitors.

Fluent in Portuguese and the Scandanavian languages other than his native Swedish, and with a good working knowledge of German, French, Spanish and English, a man like Olof Bergh was an asset in a port like ours. His Dutch had a soft Swedish inflection that made it sound more like singing than speaking. His physical presence was charged with energy and a mannered charm that he extended to bold and shy alike, and he moved with the precision of a swordsman, clicking his heels and bowing most elegantly. This courtly behaviour made every lady feel respected and esteemed. I noticed that he listened to women with his eyes and this is perhaps what gave the smitten hope.

If in the parlour he was a ladies' man, in the library he pursued masculine interests. He could read and write Latin, and had a good knowledge of the geography of Europe, Batavia and Ceylon. His wide general knowledge was known to all, and I frequently saw him called away from the ladies' company to verify one fact or another in dispute amongst the men.

Sergeant Bergh's cultured company reassured us that the Cape was not such a savage place after all. I found his learned side much more attractive than his social grace. It made him a substantive man in my eyes. I hoped that if I ever conversed with him it would be on some historical or geographical topic.

A year passed and Olof Bergh's presence was as that of the sun: warming everyone and shining on no one in particular. As I became fifteen and then sixteen, I began to harbour a secret wish that I could be like a glass and pull his rays in on me alone. I knew I would be playing with fire; the concentrated heat could consume me. I was excited, but shy. Would I have the power to capture his attention? He knew who I was, but we had exchanged words only in passing.

Whenever the opportunity for a real conversation arose, the watchful Aaltje would intervene and find something else for me to do. It was obvious that she was keeping me away from him. This puzzled me, but I was too timid to ask her for her reason. Perhaps she thought me too young for a man of thirty, although many older men married young girls. Grisella herself was engaged to Tobias Vlasvath, the Fiscal, and he was twelve years older than she.

Deep down I wondered whether this was where Aaltje was drawing the line of the social divide, whether she considered Annie de Koning good enough to be a pupil and protégée but, because of her illegitimacy and mixed blood, not good enough to marry a man such as Olof Bergh.

Aaltje's attitude changed suddenly after the return fleet brought her a letter from a friend in Ceylon. I was surprised when she insisted on reading a large part of it to me.

'Listen, Annie, Katryn writes all this about Sergeant Bergh: "... *as to his marital status, the eligible young ladies of the Cape can go ahead with their flirtations: the man is unattached. He did have a long friendship here with a woman named Catharina de Wit, but it never resulted in marriage and she is now married to an Under Merchant though people still say she pines for the handsome Swede".*

'What do you think of that, Annie? Your chances are as good as anyone else's now.'

'What do you mean "my chances", Aaltje? We both know that you are the one who has been keeping the Sergeant away from me this past year. I suspect you think I'm not good enough for him.'

'Nonsense, Annie, I just didn't want to encourage something that would lead to heartbreak. I had to make sure the man was not keeping a secret family in Ceylon. Now the coast is clear and we can work on matching him to you.'

I gave an incredulous snort. 'And what about Sweden? Maybe there's a wife and children in Gothenberg? Had you thought of that?'

'Funny you should say that. I just got that part of the story from Jeroen last night. There is a friend of Olof's in town, a naturalist on his way back to Sweden, and he told my husband that Olof ran away from Sweden partly to escape a marriage his family was forcing upon him. Apparently she was beautiful and rich, but stupid.'

'But speak of the devil!' she added, as Ensign Cruse and Olof Bergh came walking up the steps, accompanied by a very blond, fine-featured Norseman. There was no escape.

We were introduced to Doctor Christiansen, who had come from Java and Ceylon and was on his way back to Stockholm. For the first time Aaltje invited me to join in taking tea.

'What, Miss Annie de Koning is not at her bobbin lace today? Is the trousseau finished?' asked Olof Bergh teasingly. I did not know that he had been aware of what I was doing behind my lace cushion these past months.

'It is,' I said, trying not to blush.

'Well, that's good, because we really came here to ask for your help. My good friend Christiansen would like to take with him a small collection of plants. In our discussion last night it turned out that our common friend Doctor Paul Hermann spoke highly of your knowledge of the location of the botanical treasures of the Table Valley.'

I relaxed. I would not have to play the parlour games of tease and counter-tease. I could talk about that which was near to my heart.

'How kind of Doctor Hermann to remember me. I was his apprentice when he was here about six years ago. I would be delighted to show you where to find not only the common flowers of the Valley, but perhaps also some of the rare ones that grow on the other side in the kloofs of the farm Bosheuvel.'

We arranged to go on our first expedition the following day and I rushed home to prepare the picnic food I had boldly offered to bring. I was not sure that Sergeant Bergh would be part of the party and told my hopeful heart to prepare itself for a disappointment. After the inconclusive but encouraging talk I had had with Aaltje, I was ready to fly the kite of my ambition.

When I told my mother about the excursion, I saw a new light in her eyes, not exactly scheming but rather considering the opportunity.

'And Sergeant Bergh will be there? I do hope so. It's time he noticed my pretty Annie.'

'Mai,' I protested, 'let's not raise our hopes. The Sergeant has resisted many a beautiful girl and I'm not even sure I want to think about marriage yet.'

'So you say, Annie, but I have seen you look at him in church and when he passes on horseback in the street. He would be a very suitable husband for you.'

'He plans to go back to Sweden, Mai, I've heard him say so himself. You would not want me to marry a husband who would take me away from you?'

'You could persuade him to stay, Annie'

'Wait a minute Mai, I only spoke to him properly for the first time today. Let's not fetch the baboon from the other side of the mountain.'

We were still having breakfast the next morning when the party arrived on horseback. I was surprised to see Aaltje Elberts amongst them and realised that she had appointed herself as my chaperone. Olof Bergh was the first to dismount and come to the door. He greeted my family very cordially and thanked my stepfather for allowing me to be their guide.

'Do you ride, Miss Annie?' he asked

'Not very well, Sir. I don't have a horse so I have no opportunity to practice.'

'We did bring a mild-mannered horse with a lady's saddle, just in case. The riding today won't be too taxing and if we do decide to go further up the mountain than you can manage, you could ride with one of us.'

He was reassuring without being patronising. This was not the time to confess the fear of horses I have had ever since my little brother was fatally kicked by one but a few years before. I took the bull by the horns and pretended I had always loved horses.

We rode up the Valley to the foot of the Table Mountain to collect the first specimens. That I would find the plants did not surprise my companions, but that I knew them by their Latin names drew their admiration.

'How unusual to find a young woman so informed in this remote place,' said Doctor Christiansen.

'It is the only place I know, Doctor, and fortunately I had the opportunity to learn from some knowledgeable philosophers like yourself.'

'It says something about your character that you used those opportunities to your advantage,' said the Doctor.

'Also about her intelligence that she has retained all these names and information,' said the Sergeant.

'Thank you, gentlemen, that is enough flattery for one day,' I said, trying to hide my pleasure. 'Doctor Hermann and Doctor ten Rhyne gave substance to my natural passion for plants and made me part of a greater world by teaching me how to name them.'

Doctor Christiansen was lucky to be there in the flowering season of the *carduus*. The Europeans who had read the descriptions of our flora by Doctor Clusius knew about this plant. They were all keen to see it.

'Clusius calls it "an elegant thistle",' Doctor Christiansen commented.

We found some superb examples of the large king-sized

bearded flowers and also an abundance of delicate blushing brides and pincushions. The gentlemen found the common names for these flowers charming.

We left our collection of plants with the horses at the entrance to the gorge and began to make our way on foot up the mountain. Aaltje kept close to me, but I noticed she called on the Doctor for help to cross the stream or scale the rocks and left Olof Bergh to assist me. This he did most attentively, pulling away bushes and finding the least troublesome route.

All the while our conversation covered just about everywhere he had ever been, from Sweden to Ceylon. He had a sense of detail and a way of comparing people and places that fascinated me. He did not flirt and he did not brag that day, though I knew he was capable of both. It was as though we could be ourselves completely in each other's company, without having to prove anything.

For the first time I heard Swedish spoken at length, since the two men naturally lapsed into conversation in their mother tongue. I loved the soft, round, musical shapes of the language and was surprised that by the end of the day I could figure out some simple meanings. At one point Olof saw me smile at an interchange between them and realised I could understand.

'Christiansen,' he said, 'better be careful. Miss Annie here is picking up our language. Pretty soon we won't be able to gossip anymore!'

'Yes, watch out,' I joked, 'before you know it the Honorable Company will dress me like a boy and send me to spy on one of your Scandinavian ships!'

'A spy I can believe, Miss Annie. A boy, never!' he laughed, and that was as close as he got to complimenting me all day.

Early the next morning Olof Bergh came to our house with disappointing news. He was needed on a cattle trading expedition to the interior. He had permission to take Doctor Christiansen with him and would be able to show him the aloes in the arid country to the north. The excursion to Bosheuvel would have to be cancelled. Mai Angela was almost more disappointed than I was; it seemed she had been looking forward to visiting Bosheuvel more than any of us suspected.

'There'll be another time, Mistress Basson,' the Sergeant promised. 'In fact, I would like to ask your permission to teach your daughter to ride a little better when I come back. That is, if you would like it, Miss Annie? You could use the same horse you used yesterday, until we can get you a good horse of your own.'

This last announcement astounded me and completely dried my mouth. He was organising a future for us in such a practical and natural way.

'How kind of you, Sergeant,' accepted my mother before I could get a word out. 'Will you have breakfast with us?'

'I was hoping you would ask,' he said. 'After the excellent fare with which your daughter sustained us yesterday, I feel I have discovered one of the better kitchens in town. It was such a well-balanced feast of Eastern and Western flavours, much like the young lady herself.'

'Such flattery, so early in the morning, Sergeant,' I cautioned, struggling to overcome my excitement.

'You haven't told me whether you will go riding with me when I come back, Miss Annie?'

I had to warn him. 'You may be taking on more than you're bargaining for, Sergeant Bergh. You must have noticed my timidity yesterday. I have no great fondness for horses; I have avoided them since the death of my brother. I realise there is much freedom in being able to ride and that I should make the effort, but I may be too feeble a pupil. As for my own horse, even if we could afford a horse, we have nowhere to stable it.'

To my relief he made light of my anxieties. 'It is quite natural to be cautious after an experience such as yours. I promise you I will be a patient teacher. We'll worry about a stable once we have the horse.'

I resisted asking whom he meant by 'we' and followed my mother to the kitchen where breakfast was ready.

The Sergeant was very interested in the early history of the settlement and encouraged my mother to tell him exactly where the old buildings were and when the new ones were built. She could tell him who the first Free Burghers were and where they lived. She knew the first farms along the Liesbeeck and could recount the details of the many conflicts with the Hottentot. They spoke mostly in Dutch but sometimes switched to Portuguese. After two hours he reluctantly took his leave.

My mother said goodbye to him at the door. 'Annie, see the Sergeant off,' she said rather obviously leaving us alone together. All of a sudden I felt clumsy and shy, but he was quick to put me at my ease.

'I'm sorry to take Christiansen away from you. When I come back we'll go riding?'

'The interior is a dangerous place even for a brave man like you. I'll pray for your safe return.'

He clicked his heels formally and kissed my hand. My cheeks were burning and when my eyes met his I knew something between us had changed. He mounted and rode off without another word.

Not long after his departure Grisella appeared at the door.

'Was that who I thought it was? Yesterday and today? What's going on, Annie?'

She was excited, but I was cautious. My friendship with Olof Bergh was in its infancy, but already seemed too precious to include even my best friend.

'Business, Grisella,' I said to put her off. 'It all has to do with this Christiansen and his plants.'

During Sergeant Bergh's absence a marauding lion terrorized our settlement. Night after night it came down from its lair in a gully on the Lion Mountain and helped itself to whatever animals it found unprotected. People reinforced their fences and set slaves to keep fires burning through the night, but the sly creature still found his nightly prey among the animals on the outlying properties.

When, finally, it became so bold as to steal a sheep from our neighbour, Wouter Mostert, a hunting party was gathered to track down the miscreant. But the beast must have had advance notice. When the hunters got to his lair, he was nowhere to be found and for a few nights he seemed to have disappeared completely.

This was the story on everyone's lips when Sergeant Bergh returned from the interior. Having just confronted lion, rhinoceros and elephant during his mission into the interior, the Sergeant was eager to prove that he could rid the community of this scourge. Another hunting party was mounted.

It set out long before dawn, calling at our house to collect our slave, Scipio, who claimed to know exactly where the lion's den was. There were several soldiers and slaves in the party. My stepfather and Wouter Mostert were the only burghers allowed.

The party moved towards the gully by moonlight, carrying no torches. Sergeant Bergh said that it must have been the torches carried on the earlier occasion that alerted the lion and caused him to flee. Everyone was instructed to move as quietly as they could, since it was quite possible that the lion was on his way to find another meal. And this was exactly how it turned out.

In a thicket half-way up the gully, the hunters were surprised by angry growling from the underbrush. As the lion leapt out at Scipio, Sergeant Bergh rapidly pulled out his sword and attacked the animal. The lion fought back fiercely, gouging a part of the Sergeant's shoulder, but this did not deter the intrepid swordsman. After several more blows from the sword, the lion lay still.

By the time the victorious hunters arrived at our house, carrying the lion, the Sergeant had lost a lot of blood. My mother suggested he be put to bed right there and the doctor sent for. We took him to the room I shared with Maria and bade him lie on my cot. I then set about cleaning the wound and applying a poultice of yarrow and sage to stop the bleeding. He was pale and exhausted but obviously excited by the success of his quest.

'It's good to see you again, pretty Annie, your face kept appearing in front of my eyes every day I was in the wilderness,' he said excitedly.

Suspecting the onset of delirium, I gave him an infusion of mint, rue and valerian to calm him until the doctor came. I drank a little myself to calm my nerves. Seeing him there on my bed prostrate and wounded had a strange effect on me and I was aware of something more than a sisterly concern, but I was not going to let his wild talk upset my equilibrium.

'You should rest,' was all I could say without giving myself away.

When the doctor came he approved of everything I had done and, after some discussion with the patient, decided not to move him immediately.

'He is delirious,' I protested.

'All the more reason that he should be kept as quiet as possible. Consider this. It is an honour for you that such a hero should choose you for his nurse.'

First his sister, now his nurse, I thought. What role would I have to play next? But whatever was required, I could do it.

I took care of Sergeant Bergh through the next few days, dosing him regularly with sorrel cordial to contain his fever and barley water to soothe his stomach. I carefully instructed our slave, Fransien, on how to wash him and change his clothes. There would be no talk of how I took advantage of a sick man!

With his robust constitution, Olof Bergh was soon able to graduate from gruel to a hearty soup, from lying on the cot to sitting in a chair. The wound was healing well, but a week after he should have been back at the Castle, he was still in our garden teaching me to read the Latin text of his *Bestiary*.

'You should be back on duty,' I said in the presence of the Doctor and my mother one morning, hoping they would back me up.

'A man has a right to recuperate,' said the Doctor.

'Don't make the Sergeant feel unwelcome, Annie,' scolded my mother.

When we were alone that afternoon Olof asked: 'Don't you know why I am reluctant to leave, pretty Annie?'

'Yes,' I said. 'It's because you're getting fed and waited upon and forgetting your duty to the Company.'

He took my hand and I began to tremble. I looked away, hoping he might not notice my excitement.

'You try hard to sound like the strict nurse, my dear. You must know I'm staying because I cannot tear myself away from you. Don't you remember what I told you about thinking of you constantly on this last trip to the interior?'

'Yes, but I thought you were ranting. You can't be serious. This situation has gone to your head. What about your plan to go back to Sweden? You must know that I would not contemplate anything of a temporary nature. I may be the illegitimate daughter of an ex-slave woman, but my honour means a great deal to me.'

'I am proposing to marry you, not dishonour you, dear Annie. You are the lady who has tamed this wild unicorn. I am destined to stay with you for the rest of my life.'

His loving eyes, the colour of forget-me-nots, engaged my hazel stare and would not release me until I changed my look of protest to a look of love. Slowly I felt myself surrendering. He held me close and kissed me, sweeping me up in his passion.

He waited until Mai Angela and Arnoldus Basson were both home and asked their permission to marry me.

'You haven't gotten our Annie pregnant, have you?' asked Arnoldus immediately.

'You should have more faith in the moral character of your step-daughter. Her purity is unblemished. Of course, we will marry as soon as possible. I have reason to believe a Lutheran minister will be on one of the incoming ships and Annie has agreed to be married in my faith.'

'And are you planning to take her away to Europe?' asked Mai Angela in an accusatory tone.

'My dear Angela, the more I see of this country, the more attached I become to it. And now I have a serious commitment to its most precious native. I doubt I will ever be able to leave it.'

While we waited for the right minister to arrive, my riding lessons began. Olof found me a handsome white horse with blue eyes. All this horse needed to make it into a unicorn was a horn, so I called it Licorne, the Portuguese for unicorn, after its donor. When I showed reluctance in accepting such a generous gift, he said I had earned it by nursing him back to health. Wouter Mostert was kind enough to allow me to stable Licorne next door. I made good progress and soon I was able to gallop on Licorne for long distances.

Since we were engaged to be married, it was easier for us to ride together unescorted, but we mostly went riding in company. Although the townspeople were generally pleased by our intended marriage, we knew that gossip in such a small community lurked around every corner. There were those who would have been only too happy to see the illegitimate daughter of Angela of Bengal disgrace herself. Olof was also very aware of protecting my good reputation and we chose our private moments together carefully.

We waited no more than two months before a Lutheran minister arrived to marry us. The whole town celebrated our marriage with song and festivity. And if your imagination is as vivid as my memory, you could fancy for yourself the delicious passion and consummate love of our first union.

It was the auspicious beginning of a marriage that was to last forty-five years during which eleven children were born. It was a marriage that joined our energies and confirmed our enduring friendship.

CHAPTER FIVE

Friends

OLOF ALWAYS SAID THAT the Cape would remain nothing but a victualling station without vigorous and visionary leadership. Before 1679, this had not been the case. After the pioneering work of Commander van Riebeeck, a succession of well-meaning but uncommitted individuals had run the Company's business, their sights set on the greater opportunities for material advancement in the East.

We had to listen to their constant unfavourable comparisons between the opulent and elegant life in Batavia and Ceylon and the drudgery and struggle of life at the Cape. I was happy that Olof dissociated himself from this annoying grumbling and attached his affections to those better disposed to our way of life. And occasionally such a person arrived to amuse us for a time and we knew to enjoy the company while it lasted.

We had hopes that Commander Bax would stay and 'make something of the place', to use Olof's expression. He certainly tried to get the Castle in good shape, though Olof did not think the construction sound and said that, compared to the Fort at Galle, it looked like a doll's house. But the Commander tried to make us all believe that the Castle was essential to our security and the ultimate answer to the French threat.

I will never forget how every man, woman and child was made to carry baskets full of dirt out of the moat, following the good example of the whole Bax family. When Commander Bax died, soon after our first child, Christina, was born, the whole community was downcast. The uncompleted church at the bottom of the Company's Garden stood like a symbol of poor Johan Bax's unfinished business at the Cape. When the bells tolled on that dismal winter's day of his funeral, our hearts echoed every mournful measure.

But as sure as spring follows winter, so did the arrival of Commander Simon van der Stel bring new hope and, to Olof, a friend who shared his dreams about the Cape of Good Hope.

The new Commander and his family were met by a guard of honour formed by soldiers in their full splendour and a salute was fired from Signal Hill. Not a soul was absent from the crowd gathered at the dock. We watched as the dark, dapper little man stepped off the lighter, followed by his wife's sister, Cornelia Six, and his children. As is so often the case with small men, Simon van der Stel's smile and energy exuded a friendliness that more than compensated for his stature. His dark eyes fixed every new acquaintance with an intensity that assured them that they would be remembered. This proved no illusion. He had an excellent memory and soon called everyone by name.

Simon van der Stel was the perfect picture of groomed elegance, with his dark periwig curled to the shoulders, an immaculately trimmed moustache and beard, and his cravat tied into a bow above the long coat buttoned to the waist. His coat sleeves were edged with a finely pleated cuff over lace-trimmed shirtsleeves. His full breeches were tied at the knee with satin ribbons that matched those on his heeled shoes and his long walking stick. On his head was a flat wide-brimmed hat with feathers and more ribbons.

The apparel of Miss Cornelia and the children echoed this high fashion. She wore a long mantle that revealed a pleated satin skirt with a fine pleated edge. She had a single row of large pearls at her neck. A small cap trimmed with ribbons and lace sat on the immaculate curls that clung close to her head. Her face was serious in repose, but when she smiled, an unexpected radiance lit up her whole face. One could see why she was adored by her niece and nephews. Kindliness clung to her like an invisible garment.

We escorted the Van der Stels to the Commander's house just outside the Castle and set about celebrating their arrival. The Commander, in his quick manner, gave orders to open vats of *momm* in the taverns at his expense so that the ordinary folk could drink his health. This was our first taste of his generous and sometimes extravagant hospitality.

It was obvious from his initial remarks and speech at the celebration at the Castle that night that the Commander was a Dutch nationalist who seemed to disapprove of anything *mof*, as German customs were called. He was surprised that there were so many Lutherans around and frowned when he was told that we observed our sacraments with the Dutch only when no Lutheran minister could be found.

The Commander jokingly rebuked me for having adopted my husband's Lutheran faith, but seemed satisfied when I quoted him the example of Rachel. Olof must have impressed him with his tales of the interior and his experience at bartering cattle because, as the evening drew on and conversation turned into merriment and, in turn, carousing, Commander van der Stel made the surprising announcement that 'the Swede' would be on the team that was to inspect the settlement.

Miss Cornelia and young Catelina made a big fuss of my Christina. Who could blame them? She was adorable, with her father's round face but my big brown eyes, her chestnut brown ringlets escaping from her cap. I was happy to share her with them as long as it afforded me the privilege of being present whilst their stylish clothes were being unpacked.

The lavishness of the new fashions thrilled me; they seemed almost whimsical compared to the serious lines and colours that were used before. The bow trims on the sleeves, the scooped necklines, and the looped overskirts all were delightful improvements on the pious plainness of my youth.

'It's the French and Italian influence, Miss Annie. You see it everywhere in Amsterdam these days: in the clothes, in the gables on the houses, on the decorated ceilings, in the music. Curly ornamentation is what everyone pays for these days.'

While the men were away inspecting the farms along the Liesbeeck and then went all the way over to Hottentots Holland, Aaltje Elberts and I made it our business to show Miss Cornelia and the children the amenities of our small town. We stopped at the Warehouse shop to show off our supplies of domestic merchandise.

I could see from the look on Miss Cornelia's face that she did not think highly of the goods, although she tried to keep her comments neutral. When she felt the quality of the bolts of fabric on display, her fingers betrayed her disapproval.

'Don't worry, Ladies,' she said, 'we will soon improve on this situation. I have sources in Batavia who can get me the finest fabrics from India, China and Japan. All the women of the Cape need in order to improve their appearance is a knowledgeable person like myself directing the purchase of textiles and haberdashery.'

Aaltje and I smiled; we did not mind being patronised by someone with contacts, so fashionable and obviously so interested in improving our drab style of dress. Access to the right sources was always a problem for us, living at the far ends of the civilised world. Elegant people came and went without affording us the means of imitation. We knew that if only we could lay our hands on the right stuff we too could look the way we felt we ought to.

We walked up the Sweet River to the Company Gardens, pointing out where the different craftsmen had their workshops, describing the special skill of each as we went. Word of our presence soon spread and people came out to meet us, some just to wave and smile, some bold enough to come forward to extend a personal welcome. When I saw Johanna Victor with little Josina on her hip, I tried unsuccessfully to divert our course. Of all people I did not want her to have the privilege of speaking even one word to Miss Cornelia.

Johanna Victor was the most vicious gossip in town and had already put about a scandalous rumour about Miss Cornelia.

Why was it, went the story, that the Commander's wife had stayed behind in Holland? Everyone in Amsterdam knew about the wife-beating case brought against him by his mother-in-law. Sure, nothing was proven, but why was it that Miss Cornelia had spent nine months in England, ostensibly to study music, while her sister retired to Utrecht and was hardly seen by anybody? Why was it that Miss Cornelia was back in Patria for the christening of young Ludovic whose name is really Cornelis? Was it perhaps because she was the mother of one that she had now taken her sister's place as mother of all? What else might her duties include?

Johanna was very good at asking questions that implied scurrilous answers and set the evil minds of her listeners to construct the turpitude of their choice. She was after Olof before she became pregnant with Josina and married the father, Johannes Pretorius. For a while, I was her special target because, of course, Olof chose me, and she suspected he must have told me about her various attempts to get his attention.

Josina had tried to spread rumours about my immorality, but was proved a liar when Christina arrived a full eleven months after Olof and I married. And here she was with her flat peasant face smiling, her shallow blue eyes scrutinising every detail and storing it away to ornament the substance of future inventions.

But Miss Cornelia, so secure in her patrician superiority, was not even aware that she was in the presence of a cobra. She responded to Johanna, as she did to us all, in that friendly, though distant, manner, always maintaining her own private space. She took Josina's pudgy little hand and with the other held my Christina's long fingers.

'I suppose these two will make good little playmates soon?'

Not on your life, I thought, rather upset that she thought the snake my equal. But that comment was rather ironical in view of what happened much later.

'Hester Mostert is expecting us for tea,' I said, trying to end the conversation. 'And look, the children are ahead of us. They don't know where to go.'

I was anxious that Miss Cornelia should meet those dearest to me: my mother and the beautiful Grisella, now engaged to be married to the Fiscal, Tobias Vlasvath. I knew my mother would be ready and waiting with her special *kolwadjib* and a bouquet of roses.

Miss Cornelia responded exactly as I wished, taking tea and then accepting supper, talking and talking as though the day had no end. Willem, my half brother, was the same age as Henrico van der Stel and took the three older boys, Willem Adriaen, Adriaen and Frans, for a picnic up the tail of the Lion Mountain.

Young Catelina was perfectly content to spend the time in the company of women, but little Ludovic was disappointed when the gang of big boys refused to take him along on this expedition. My mother, always good with children, went over to her house and brought back a branch on which sat her pet chameleon, Suleiman.

This creature, with its rotating eyes and ability to change colour, entranced the little boy. He spent the whole day coaxing it to climb onto stones, bark, soil and various plants. All we heard from him were periodic peals of delight as the curious creature blended with a new background. Suleiman showed his liking for small boys by catching a few flies and demonstrating the flashing speed of his peculiar tongue.

Asked about the name, my mother replied that he was a good Muslim chameleon, serious and always alert to the great gifts of Allah. It always made me smile to see how my mother, now a good Calvinist wife, made use of the beliefs of her youth in such amusing ways.

Aaltje and I were invited to join in the unpacking of Miss Cornelia's harpsichord the next day. This I had to see! There had not been a harpsichord in the colony since Maria de la Queillerie took hers with her to Batavia and that was before I was born. My mother told me much about it and said that sometimes Olof's lute sounded exactly like a harpsichord. The concept of a keyboard eluded me, and the fact that I would see one for myself kept me awake for hours.

The harpsichord came in a strong wooden case and had to be carefully lifted out. The instrument sat on a carved six-legged gold painted pedestal. The inside of the lid was elaborately decorated with floral designs, framed in gold. On the sides were woodland scenes of nymphs and satyrs playing various musical instruments. The detail of these paintings took my breath away. French and Italian style exemplified!

Miss Cornelia was gratified to find all of the ivory and ebony keys on the double keyboard undamaged. The plectra also seemed intact. The strings had been disconnected for the journey and were attached before the tuning could begin. Alhough Miss Cornelia had acquired the necessary practical skills when she studied music in England, she was happy to know that Olof had experience in tuning his sister's spinet and could be of assistance. It seemed that the last thing she wanted to do was to ask her brother-in-law for help in such a precise and methodical task. He was not always a patient man.

By evening the instrument was at last fit to be played on, and her nimble fingers could finally produce a coherent piece of music. I was transfixed by these ricecares and fantasias, old-fashioned tunes standard in the music-making of Amsterdam.

There followed a modern suite of dances by Henry Purcell and soon the older children were summoned to add the sound of their recorders to that of the harpsichord. They played so sweetly, in such perfect harmony, that I felt moved to tears.

That evening, Willem Adriaen, who was but a few years younger than me, made me an offer that would change my life.

'I have brought an extra set of recorders with me just in case the climate or the voyage did not agree with the wood, but everything seems to be in perfect working order. It is obvious that you have a great affinity for our music. Would you like this set on permanent loan? One of us could easily give you lessons. There are only two sets of fingering you need to learn. And, heaven knows, we could always do with an extra pipe. Once we add Papa's viol, we will have a proper consort.'

A wooden box with four pearwood recorders was presented to me. They were disassembled, each piece resting in its own space on a velvet lining. Willem Adriaen explained:

'The smallest is the sopranino, and then comes the descant, then the treble and the biggest is the tenor. We also have a bass and a contra-bass that we use between us. Now if you learn the fingering for the descant, you have it for the tenor. Similarly, if you learn it for the treble, you have it for the sopranino. Look at your lovely hands; I can tell you are musical.'

Charming Willem Adriaen. Thus was he always, full of enthusiasm and flattery.

My throat was dry, my heart pounding. I could feel myself transported to a higher plane. Never did I dream I would be able to play music, to belong to such an echelon of society! And here they were offering me instruments, lessons and a place in their musical club.

'I would love to try,' I said, caressing the recorder pieces in their bed of velvet.

By the time Olof arrived back from Hottentots Holland, Catelina had already taught me the airs of *La Folia*, Go From my Window and Amaryllis. On these airs I would later learn to improvise divisions. I watched in fascination as she danced, explaining the steps and character of pavanes and galliards, corrantos and allmaines.

Olof's enthusiasm over his trip took precedence, however, over my musical news. He proceeded to praise the new Commander in such extravagant terms that I wished I could have recorded them for reference during those years to come when circumstances soured his opinion of Simon van der Stel.

'This man is a true Joshua, Annie; he is the one who will lead us from this small settlement into the promised land of the interior. He has already named the island in the Eerste Rivier Stellenbosch, and means to offer land to farmers as soon as he can.

'He is as charmed by this country as I am and sees its great potential. He says the climate reminds him of his early childhood in Mauritius. Of course, we were lucky to have such an unusual stretch of windless days. That always helps to create a good impression. Though the country in the lee of the mountains at Hottentots Holland is very sheltered, as one can see by the way the trees grow straight up, unbattered by the wind. It is really very beautiful there. When there are a few families there, I will take you to see it.'

According to Olof, the new Commander had great sympathy for soldiers like himself who worked for a pittance with no means to improve their material situation. He had even said that soldiers would be allowed to buy property outside the Castle.

'Think of it, Annie, we can have a home of our own and you won't have to spend the rest of your life quartered in the Castle. I'm telling you, this is a new beginning. What is more, the man likes me, trusts my opinion on security and construction and was very impressed when we came across a small band of Hottentot with whom I had bartered before. They greeted me with the kind of friendliness that must have made it plain to the Commander that I had treated them well in our previous dealings.

'And I must tell you, he is no coward. The night we camped in the forest at Constantia, a hyena slipped past the Sufis who were there to keep the fire going, and entered the Commander's tent. Without hesitation he attacked that beast and drove him off into the night. This is the kind of man I can work with, my dear. This is going to make all the difference to my life. Before, I was prepared to stay here for your sake, but now I feel I could stay for my own sake as well.'

It was heartening to see my energetic husband so inspired with new purpose. I had privately wondered to myself how long it would be before he decided that the pull from his birthplace was stronger than my own. Now it seemed that with the prospect of property and promotion there was a hope that he might put down permanent roots here.

Our friendship with the first family grew as we made music together and the Commander and I discovered our mutual interest in botany. He had brought with him a number of recent books on the subject. Of particular interest to me was a book by the Danish professor, Bartholinus, to whom Doctor Hermann had given four plates and descriptions of numerous plants as well as a report on the two plants he had managed to grow from the seeds we collected on his visit.

My excitement at seeing the engravings of the very ericas and the leonotis we collected when I was only ten convinced the Commander of my indisputable passion for flowers. When he saw me reading the Latin text he expressed his open admiration.

'Mistress Bergh,' he said respectfully, 'you certainly are a surprising young woman! Who would have thought ...' He stopped himself, realising that he was patronising me. But I finished his sentence for him.

'Yes, Sir, who would have thought that the daughter of a Bengali slave woman would read Latin and play music? I agree, I have come a long way from reading only the Heidelberg cathechism and sewing for a living. But it was the annuity from my father that allowed me to be better educated than other slave children and dress respectably in order to be acceptable in middle class homes. That, together with my mother's unfailing love, has allowed me to fly much higher than one would expect from my very humble beginnings.'

I was surprised at my own boldness, but the Commander was not offended.

'Well said, Mistress Annie. Come, let me show you this brand new book by Johann Schreyer. It's in German. See, the author himself signed it. Did you ever meet him? Just before we came here I visited him in Leyden specifically to see the Cape plants in his botanical garden there. He has managed to grow one single aloe, which he keeps in a special place in a greenhouse, fussing over it as though it were a baby. In the same greenhouse he has some lilies, but the pelargonias and ericas are thriving outside.'

I remembered Doctor Schreyer well. He was detained at the Cape with scurvy when I was barely seven. I remember how he advised my mother on her medicinal garden and grafted our first orange tree onto a sturdy grapefruit sapling. Mai Angela would be glad to have news of Doctor Schreyer and I asked to borrow the book to show her.

'I thought she was illiterate,' said the Commander.

'That is precisely why books have a magical meaning for her. She loves to hold them and to be told what is in them and, of course, the pictures anyone can understand as long as their allegorical meaning is biblical. I must confess I need Olof to explain the classical figures to me. But that, after all, is how I learn.'

'Your curiosity is the most attractive part of you,' said the Commander. There was velvet in the tone of his voice and his black eyes flashed above his prim moustache. For a moment I could swear he was flirting with me. Polite but immediate discouragement was called for. His friendship to Olof was too valuable to be soured by a diversion with me.

'That is the opinion of my husband also, Sir,' I replied, reminding him where my loyalty lay. He took my point and proceeded to show me more books without ever paying me another personal compliment.

The seeds of civic pride sown by Commander Bax now grew under the well-planned, energetic direction of Simon van der Stel. Loads of stones and shells arrived from Robben Island for the construction of new homes and the repair of old ones and the paving of streets. It was at this time that we bought our first town house, to the south of the Company Gardens near the market square. It was not large but it was our own.

Above the large room downstairs, we had a big bedroom for ourselves and a smaller room for Christina and Maria, who was then on the way. We had a big kitchen with an ample hearth and enough garden to grow our own vegetables and herbs, with the stables opening on the alley at the back.

We even made a small pond for the ducks and set up a henhouse. Olof built a dovecote to a Swedish design he remembered from his youth and introduced the ritual of feeding the birds at Christmas time. This seemed a little eccentric since the birds had plenty to eat in the middle of summer!

The Commander built himself a splendid house inside the Castle. A drawing room, just off the grand dining room upstairs, served as the music room and became the venue for our club. I applied myself to the satisfaction of my instructors and soon became a versatile recorder player, taking up whichever instrument was required for a specific part.

I became so much at ease with the music and the instruments that occasionally I was brave enough, to stray from the tablature and contribute my own improvisations. This secured my an undeniable place as a member of the consort.

A blight was put on our music-making when Miss Cornelia came down with a fever barely eighteen months after the Van der Stels arrived. She died twelve days later and was buried on the Sunday of Pentecost.

The Commander and the bigger boys put on a brave face, but Catelina, Frans and Ludovic were inconsolable. I channelled my sorrow into being with them as much as I could, trying to divert them with special outings: picnics on the mountainside collecting plants, or on the beach flying kites, collecting shells and making *trombas* out of sea bamboo.

And then a kindred spirit arrived and came to live next door to me. It happened while the newly-promoted Ensign Olof was on a bartering trip to the Hessequa that I was advised by Pierre Couchetez, one of the Company's assistant gardeners, of the imminent arrival of Doctor Heinrich Claudius and his wife. Ever since Pierre had received notice that the couple were on their way to the Cape, he had spared no effort in finding them suitable accommodation. When our neighbours left to take a farm in Stellenbosch, their house was the obvious place for the botanist and his wife.

I helped Couchetez to clean the place and provided basic linen and kitchen equipment. On the morning of their arrival, he went down to the quay to meet them while I decked the house with flowers and set a bredie to stew on the hearth. Then I kept a vigilant eye on the street.

They were unconventional from the outset. Through my window, I saw them arrive on foot, both carrying large valises, their uncovered blond curls giving them a somewhat vagabondish appearance. I allowed them time to put down their luggage before I went over with bread and beer.

'I'm Anna de Koning, your neighbour, wife of Ensign Bergh.'

Both smiled together, revealing perfect rows of pearly teeth, simultaneously extending their hands in a modern way of greeting. They could have been brother and sister though they were nothing of the sort.

'Heinrich Claudius and my wife, Marie L'Estrange or, as you Dutch would have it, Maria Vreemd,' said the Doctor, firmly grasping my hand. There was nothing but reassurance in that handshake and I felt a current of happy approval pass through my body.

Her hand was softer, but no less sure and filled me with goodwill.

'I believe you are responsible for this nourishing and decorative welcome, Mistress Bergh? We thank you so much.' Her face, framed by ashen curls, was curiously animated and in repose at the same time. Her voice was melodious yet strong, and there was an inflection in her accent that I could not place.

'Won't you take lunch with us?'

During lunch they proved most forthcoming. The first thing they explained was the hand-carried valises. These were their most precious possessions, irreplaceable and guarded with their lives. The bags contained their paints and sketching and engraving equipment and the precision optical equipment used by Doctor Claudius in his study of plants and medicine.

I had already guessed that one case contained some sort of viol. But even this was special. It was a lyra viol made by Barak Norman of London, better than any that could be found anywhere in the world, according to Marie.

'You see, Mistress Anna, we are very particular about tools and instruments. How can one produce work of quality with sub-standard equipment?'

'You will like my husband. Those are his sentiments exactly. And please call me Annie. "Mistress Anna" makes me feel so old.'

Heinrich Claudius told me about his birthplace in Silesia and his voyages and work in China and Batavia. He was sent to the Cape to do work for Doctor Andreas Cleyer, a senior physician in Batavia. He had met Doctor ten Rhyne and was very interested to hear of my connection with him.

I went next door, put Maria in her cradle and brought my poor copies of Doctor ten Rhyne's illustrations. He nodded approvingly and his smile extended an invitation.

'Good lines and scale, Annie, and a certain delicacy in the petals of your flowers, though to be scientifically accurate one would need more detail. Marie, I think we have found an assistant.'

'Excellent, the sooner she begins the better. You know, Annie, we have many commissions to fulfill. There is a great demand in Europe for herbaria of exotic plants. You should see the rooms at the back of Mr James Petiver's apothecary in London! That is actually where Heinrich and I met, at the sign of the White Cross in Aldersgate Street.

'My father is a musician with a passion for plants and one day, when he took me along to go and inspect Mr Petiver's new consignment of specimens from Virginia, who should we meet but this handsome specimen from Silesia? It was love at first sight, I can tell you. Among the chaos of piles of engravings, dried plants, bulbs and seeds, this man stood like a beacon of sanity!'

'She has since discovered that was an illusion,' said Heinrich playfully.

'But one that suits my own temperament,' countered his wife.

This was a recurring theme. They seemed to enjoy cultivating the idea of their mutual eccentricity. I found it amusing, especially as experience proved that they were the best-organised, most practical people I had ever met.

Heinrich and Marie were happy to find a room in the house with windows both to the north and east and decided immediately to make this their studio, even though it was meant for a bedroom.

'Sleeping is done with closed eyes, it doesn't really matter where you do it,' said Marie. 'But painting and drawing require all the light one's eyes can get.'

The next day I organised some extra help to move the furniture around and find them some tables to work on while proper drawing desks were being made. Then we unpacked the equipment: pestles and mortars, pigments and gums, fine plumbago *stylos* encased in resinous wood, fine sable pincels of various shapes and sizes, quills and plates, inks and presses. They laughed when they saw my own improvised brushes made from the hair of my mother's dog, but they approved of the quality of quill produced by my own geese.

Heinrich dressed up and presented himself with his letter of introduction from Doctor Cleyer to the Commander, who immediately commissioned him to inspect the Gardens and make his own recommendations as to improvements and expansion. He invited him on an inspection of the forests and promised to take him to the southern tip of the Peninsula.

I could tell from all this attention that the Commander was impressed. Lucky Heinrich; everyone in the Colony knew by now that Simon van der Stel had only friends or enemies, nothing in between.

Heinrich was quick to conclude this for himself.

'I am fortunate that he wants so much from me. It will

not be difficult to stay on the right side of him. I have a feeling that being on his wrong side could be disastrous.'

In the dismal years to come, I often thought how prophetic those words were. But for the time being, the sun shone on good relations everywhere.

Olof and Heinrich instantly formed a firm friendship based on their common curiosity about the world around them and beyond. They disagreed on security and the severity of punishments, on the material advancement of one race at the cost of subjecting another. But even though the one was radical and the other conservative, they were both reasonable men who enjoyed arguing.

Will I ever forget those debates that went on late into the night? Olof, the soldier for whom violence was an integral part of the job, and non-violent Heinrich whose job was to preserve life. And me in the middle, seeing both points of view, but careful not to take the radical side.

Fortunately, the debates were often interrupted by intense music-making. Marie's spinet was plainer than Miss Cornelia's harpsichord, but to my mind it had a sweeter tone. Marie was an accomplished player with a wide-ranging, rich voice and a varied repertoire of English and Italian songs, some elevated, some profane. She also played the recorder while Heinrich played the viol. They had brought with them the most recent music from England. Divisions were the latest thing and the lyra viol the most fashionable instrument.

That this instrument was both plucked and bowed delighted Olof. It seemed as if he and Heinrich transferred their political debates into a debate of music as they vied with each other on improvisations of plucking and bowing on lute and viol. Marie and I added our own harmonious extemporisations on descant and treble recorders.

The members of the Castle music club, that is to say all but the Honorable Commander, sometimes joined us in these adventures, but whenever we went to the Castle to play we curbed our wild spirits and played only prescribed music. We knew better than to court disfavour by radical behaviour. The Commander never heard Marie's repertoire of mad songs and street cries. As far as Simon van der Stel knew, she only sang songs about nymphs and shepherds.

The arrival of Marie and Heinrich Claudius not only brought a new life of recreation; it also changed my working life. I began to reduce my activities as seamstress and threw myself into becoming a botanical artist. First I copied and coloured engravings, but soon I was able to draw from live specimens.

I spent hours in that studio with Marie working in quiet concentration, recording the details of petals and leaves, stems and stamens, learning to shade and speckle in the right places to create dimension. The paints became my friends. Reds and greens, browns and yellow used in a variety of shades to represent the infinite variety of the inventions of the Creator.

The silence was sometimes broken by a burst of conversation, now and again about personal history but mostly about thoughts. I had never had a friend like this; we seemed to know each other's minds, often needing only half a sentence to explain something.

It turned out that she was also born out of wedlock. Her mother, a painter from Amsterdam, was married when she fell in love with Roger L'Estrange, an exiled Royalist from England. When Marie's mother died, soon after she was born, her husband insisted L'Estrange acknowledge the baby girl as his own, which he did.

Marie was raised by a Dutch nanny and, when Cromwell pardoned her father, she returned to England with him and was placed in the household of her father's sister who lived at Greenwich on the banks of the river Thames. Her father was quite elderly by then but, before his death, saw her as often as he could. His will specified an amount of money for lessons in music and painting.

'How lucky you were to have known your father, to have had him guide your life like that. All I had was a basic education and my fantasies of what he could have been like.'

'Sometimes I wonder if fantasies are not preferable to reality. I have dreams about my mother and what life with her in Holland might have been. I imagine a bohemian life of great creativity. My father's will imposed a direction on my life that my aunt implemented austerely. I had no choice in it. The first free choice I made in my life was to run away with Heinrich.'

This was news to me.

'What do you mean, you ran away? Are you not married?'

'Oh, yes, some priest quickly blessed the two of us somewhere between London and Amsterdam, but it was not what my aunt would have chosen for me,' she laughed. 'Oh, Annie, you look so funny when you're shocked!'

'I'm not shocked, Marie. It's the thought of your boldness that fills me with awe. The insecurity of it all.'

'Boldness my foot. My mother was much bolder than I, and Heinrich is the only security I need. We are but specks in the universe, bits of dust, buffeted by the winds of destiny.'

When she spoke like that, I loved her. She so eloquently expressed my very own thoughts. This was the first person with whom I could talk about the riddles of philosophy and the wonder of creation without having to refer directly to the Bible. I liked the idea of being buffeted by the winds of destiny much better than submitting to the will of God.

Such opinions, however, would be considered blasphemy by some in our conservative community and I kept them to myself. It was in my own interest to appear to everyone, including my husband, to be an unquestioning, God-fearing Protestant. But with Marie I could speculate freely on the mysteries of the universe and the complexities of human nature.

While we both despised arrogance and hypocrisy, Marie had a boldness of criticism and a disrespect for authority that I admired and longed to emulate. My childhood friend, Grisella Mostert, was a case in point. She had become the greatest beauty in the Colony, or thought she had, because a previous Fiscal, Pieter van Neyn, had written a poem about her that was published in Holland.

Now that she was engaged to be married to the Fiscal, Tobias Vlasvath, Grisella had adopted his air of superiority. No longer did she come to fetch me for a stroll in the Gardens or spend some time gossiping over tea and embroidery. She was too busy seeking confirmation of her own importance in the drawing rooms of the Castle. She had been given a new place for her chair in church and barely acknowledged me anymore on a Sunday morning.

Grisella did ask me to make her wedding dress, but by then I was so hurt by her arrogance that I pleaded my painting as an excuse.

'Why, Annie, I would have thought you could do with some real income. We all know what Olof earns. And Claudius can't be paying very much for those little drawings.'

'No, Grisella, I do it free for my own satisfaction and would have made your wedding gown for the same reason if we were still real friends. But you have become a stranger now that you think yourself so important.'

This rebuke did not touch her at all.

'Make no mistake, I will be really important after my wedding and you would do well to remember it.'

Marie's comment on this conversation was that Grisella had only her beauty and position on which to depend. Stripped of that she would be nothing.

'At least you are skilled and can earn your own living no matter what, Annie.'

These, too, were prophetic words. How good it was to have such a friend now that my childhood friend had abandoned me!

Our friendship flourished. Heinrich went with Olof on both trips he made to Namaqualand and brought back a large number of specimens, including exotic aloes and *asteraceae* hitherto unknown. They also brought an amusing little meerkat whom we named Wotan and several snakes that were too poisonous and ugly to have names.

Heinrich was good at drawing live animals, working quickly and even capturing their motion. The only animal I ever tried to sketch was Suleiman because he, at least, kept still. Heinrich honoured me by using that drawing for an engraving.

On the second trip to Namaqualand, Heinrich made accurate readings and produced the first maps of the northwest of the country. Whereas Heinrich found more than he expected, Olof was disappointed. On both occasions, drought forced them to turn back and dashed their hopes of making any significant discovery. The position of the river Camissa, the supposed location of the city of Vigiti Magna, and the rich land of Monomotapa remained a mystery.

It was Olof's failure to find copper, however, that rankled most with the Commander and led to their first major argument.

'Twice now you have come back with nothing but stories of an arid and inhospitable terrain. Excuses, excuses. I'm tired of excuses, I want results, I want copper. How can we persuade the Lords XVII that this is a viable Colony if we can produce nothing more than wine?'

'Forgive me, Your Honour, I am a soldier and a man of courage and perseverance and, as such, I explored the terrain to which you sent me. Read my journals. I did not make up stories about the lack of water or the inability or unwillingness of the Hottentot to show us the Copper Mountain or the big river and fabulous Vigiti Magna or Monomotapa. I did the best I could, but I am not a rainmaker or a magician.'

His sarcasm did not please the Commander.

'No, nor are you a competent explorer. I will remember in future to use you only for the things you are good at – cattle trading and construction.'

'Not to mention salvaging shipwrecks and secretly bringing back species. Hast thou forgotten how greatly the Company profited from my efforts at the wreck of the *Joanna*? I have not forgotten my meagre reward.'

Friends

His use of the polite form of address emphasised the growing distance between them. The Commander softened somewhat.

'Misplaced self pity, Bergh. You have been made Ensign, you have acquired property. You are doing well for yourself. But the next expedition to Namaqualand will be led by me personally.'

'I hope Your Honour has more success. Perhaps you should wait until we have reports of good rain in the region. That will solve the water problem. And perhaps you should take some mining engineers instead of depending on the favour of the Hottentot to give or withhold information about their source of copper.'

'You should have followed your own advice.'

Olof did not hesitate to point out that this was not for want of asking. The penny-pinching attitude that governed the entire realm of the VOC had prevented him from taking the equipment and expertise he needed. The Commander, on the other hand, would have access to the best of what was available when he himself ventured into that desert to find copper.

This was in 1683. So much was still to happen before Simon van der Stel made the journey into the interior and claimed to have discovered mountains of solid copper. Neither the Company nor anyone else became rich from the discovery. As far as I know, no one had the courage to establish a mine in that inhospitable region.

CHAPTER SIX

Fortune smiles

FOR THE FIRST SEVEN YEARS of our marriage, Olof and I seemed propelled by our progress. Olof had risen in rank and was a member of the Marriage Council. He was well regarded by his superiors, especially Hieronimus Cruse, the Captain of the Garrison and an old friend of my family.

We had our own house on the Heeren Street close to the entrance of the Company's Gardens and in the same block as the Cruses, though their property was much grander than ours. We had three lovely children, all conceived in loving passion and born without any of the many possible mishaps.

Olof was particularly thrilled that the third child, Petrus, his first son, looked so much like him. He was a blond, blue-eyed little fellow, so different from his darker sisters. My cupboards and chests were stuffed with good clothes and linen, my dressers and mantelpiece laden with fine china, my kitchen well equipped with every latest gadget. We had five slaves to work in the house, garden and stables.

Every day either the admiration or envy in people's eyes assured us that we were a lucky couple. We felt such a bright confidence that any small loss or insecurity could easily be dismissed.

This was our situation when a splendid party arrived on the *Bantam* in 1685. To me it was as though a missing piece in the puzzle of Olof's past had appeared that morning in April. How often had I heard reference to Hendrik Adriaan van Rheede tot Drakenstein, the Lord Mydrecht, with whom Olof had gone on his first expedition to Jaffna and Mannar in 1665 as a twenty-year-old soldier.

When Van Rheede returned to Ceylon as First Captain and Sergeant-Major of Ceylon, he and Olof had fought together in the siege of Tuticorin. It was Van Rheede who awarded Olof the coat of arms that he so proudly used to adorn his shield and swords.

In many ways Olof used the Baron as a model. Here was a man who began his adult life as an ordinary soldier and had risen through the ranks through bravery and perseverance. He was also a well-bred, educated, thinking man and a shrewd politician. Now, at the height of his career, he had been sent by the Lords XVII as Commissioner General to inspect the Company's colonies in the East. He was given almost unlimited power to change and implement policies on the spot without reference to Holland.

We knew that the Baron would be accompanied by another acquaintance from the past, Isaac St Martin. He, the Baron and the late Commander Bax, had formed a threesome at the beginning of their careers. What we did not know was that Baron van Rheede would also bring with him such a jolly crowd of young people: his adopted daughter Francina, her companion Sandrina Beets, and two young men, Maurits de la Baye and Jan Huydecoper, son of the director of the botanical gardens of Amsterdam.

The Baron recognised Olof immediately, even in his place in the guard of honour, and requested specifically that he be part of the official inspection tour. The whole party did a walking tour of the town in the late afternoon, stopping on their way back for refreshments at Captain Cruse's house. Marie and Heinrich went with us to meet them and we were soon immersed in botanical talk.

It seemed everyone knew everyone. News about the Doctors Hermann, Ten Rhyne and Cleyer bounced back and forth. The conversation then moved to collections, and plans were made for us to see the Baron's pride and joy, his great opus, the *Hortus Malabaricus*. In return, Heinrich would show the Baron his collection of illustrations for the planned but unpublished *Hortus Africus*.

75

A week before, a shipment of fresh betel leaves had arrived from the small Indian Ocean island, Joanna. I was sent to fetch the *tempat sirih*, the box in which the paraphernalia for the betel ceremony was kept. The Baron watched in eager anticipation as I sliced the areca nuts with the *kacip*, the special single blade iron cutter in the shape of a winged horse.

'This is a real treat,' said the Baron. 'I thought I would have to wait until Batavia before I chewed *sirih* again. And I'm glad to see that you have tobacco as well as spices to add to the concoction, my dear Mistress Bergh. The *pan* they chew in the East just does not seem right to me without a little tangy tobacco.' The company seemed to agree with this expert opinion.

I smiled as I ground the sliced betel nut into a paste with lime, spread it on a the heart-shaped *sirih* leaf and added some cardamom, caraway, anise and sweet little coloured pastilles. Last of all came a generous chunk of chewing tobacco before the leaf was rolled neatly into a small parcel. I handed the chew to the Baron.

'Mistress Bergh, your husband will never be without an occupation. If he fails as a soldier, he can always set up shop as a *penjual sirih!*' joked the Honorable St Martin, happy to show his familiarity with the Javanese terminology.

'A *penjual sirih* will not be able to keep me in the manner to which I have become accustomed, Sir!' I countered. 'No, I think he should stick to his profession and think of *sirih* very much as recreation!'

Maurits de la Baye and Jan Huydecoper were introduced to *sirih*, but the ladies were not offered any. Sandrina was about to ask for a chew when Francina explained to her what we all knew: in Cabo ladies were never offered *sirih* before dinner. It was a very relaxed Baron who left the Cruse house some time later amid much back slapping and hand kissing.

The Baron's recognition of Olof bode nothing but good for us. For a while now Commander van der Stel had been overruled by Commissioner Rijklof van Goens, an invalid who was making unreasonable demands and criticisms from his bed in his country house at Newlands, turning a blind eye to corruption and inefficiency. This frustrating situation was now changed, since Baron van Rheede outranked Van Goens and had no high opinion of his abilities.

The animosity between the Baron and the Commander and the Van Goens, father and son, went back a long time. Everyone in Ceylon knew about their disagreements. Olof said that the Baron agreed with him that both father and son were self-seeking cowards.

'You'll see, Annie, how many wrongs will have been righted when the Baron leaves. I have already told him about Jan Baptist Dubertin and he has ordered an investigation by someone other than Dominique de Chavonnes. I am convinced those two are in it together. Did you see how the Baron hardly greeted De Chavonnes? And it wasn't that he did not recognise him; it was because he remembers him as a troublemaker in Ceylon.'

'Well, it is obvious that he respects your opinion, my dear. He seemed very impressed by your familiarity with the interior and its people. I have never met a man of such broad interests, still so curious at his age. What happened to his wife?'

Olof's face took on a curious expression. 'I will tell you what I know because, as with Cornelia Six, there is bound to be gossip about Miss Francina. She is his daughter by the only woman he ever loved, a married woman of easy virtue from Cochin. He has told the world that she is an orphan, supposedly of a carpenter called Sipkens whose family was wiped out by fever. That gives them both respectability. He has legally adopted her, treating her like his own daughter and taking her wherever he goes. He never considered marrying anyone as far as I know. That lucky young lady will inherit everything he has.'

'She looks sweet-tempered and is head over heels in love with that Maurits de la Baye.'

'Yes, I don't think the Baron likes it very much. Perhaps the fresh Cape air will put an end to the infatuation. I know the Baron intends to separate them. Don't be surprised if you are asked to entertain the two young ladies while young De la Baye and Huydecoper are sent on inspection with us.'

'I can't think of anything more pleasant,' I said sleepily.

Olof's prediction proved correct. The next morning the two young ladies arrived in the company of Jan de Grevenbroeck, Secretary of the Council, who was at that time painting my portrait. He had once been a soldier but an injury to his leg forced him from service and left him with a limp.

The painting had been commissioned by Olof who found it difficult to separate his admiration for Grevenbroeck's talents from his irritation with his effeminate mannerisms. I did not find these a problem; on the contrary, to me they were expressions of his sensitive, artistic personality.

Jan de Grevenbroeck was a helpful critic of my botanical drawings, often giving me useful hints on how to improve my work and correcting the Latin nomenclature. Marie and I both enjoyed his sense of humour and he and Heinrich sometimes had long philosophical discussions on Erasmus and Humanism. He had grown up in Nijmegen,where his father and, later, his brother were directors of the Latin School. He often joked that Latin was his mother tongue and. was one of the few people who tried to learn to speak a Hottentot language.

'I come, as usual, to play when the soldier's away, Mistress Annie,' he teased as he came through the door, Francina and Sandrina right behind him. 'But this time I bring some charges with me. The Baron has cruelly deprived these two ladies of their best companions. They have taken De la Baye and young Huydecoper on inspection with them. Unfortunately Miss Catelina is indisposed and unable to chaperone these two young ladies.'

Francina came right out with it, 'My father asks if you'll show us around while they are away. He thinks by taking

Maurits away for a week he will somehow make our love
vanish. Old people forget so soon.'

'It is in your own interest, Francina,' reprimanded
Sandrina Beets primly.

I could see irritation flash across Francina's face.

'You're supposed to be on my side, Sandrina!' she said.

'Ladies!' said Jan de Grevenbroeck, trying to defuse the
situation. 'Come and see the portrait of Mistress Annie.'

He lifted the cloth that was covering the half-finished
work on the easel. There I am, standing next to a table
showing a fruit bowl and a candleholder. In my right hand
I hold an apple and in my left hand a fan. I am wearing my
blue silk frock, the skirt pulled back to show my braided
petticoat. Above the fine lace collar you can see my single
string of pearls. My hair is fashionably done in bunches of
ringlets above each ear and a few tight, short little locks to
the side of my brow.

'What a good likeness!' exclaimed Sandrina.

'I look a little too severe. I should like it much better if
Jan could capture my smile.'

'You are a matron, my dear Annie. This is a picture for
posterity; we can't have you smiling like a child. Besides,
how long can you pose for a smile? You're constantly being
distracted by all these little children anyway.'

'He loves my children, really, ladies. It's just that he has
none of his own.'

'And never hope to have, please God!'

'There, a determined bachelor. Are you going to work on
the portrait today, Jan? I hope I don't have to change?'

'No, Annie, just bring me the frock so that I can work
on the detail of the lace. Then you can take the young ladies
visiting.'

I was happy to escape another posing session and took
Francina and Sandrina next door to see Marie and the studio. This we could enter from an outside staircase. Heinrich
had also been invited on the inspection tour of the
Peninsula and outlying districts. He was busy in the back

Anna de Koning, courtesy of Cape Archives, Elliott Collection

yard preparing bags and boxes in which to collect any new species he might find.

'Marie is in the studio. She'll be happy to see you!' he said, in his usual friendly manner.

Francina displayed a genuine interest in and curiosity about our work, but her companion seemed dejected, if not outright rude at times. I decided to ignore this and feed her as much fresh fruit and vegetables as possible to build her up after the voyage. After all this was one of our specialties at the Cape: restoring health to those poor travellers who had been living on nothing but bacon and biscuits for weeks.

Sandrina perked up, however, when we went into the house proper and she saw the spinet.

'May I try it?' she asked.

'Certainly,' said Marie. 'Do you need any music?'

She did not and, for the next hour, sat at the instrument and played the compositions of Marchand and Couperin, French composers entirely new to me. How ornate their music seemed, compared to the English music preferred by Marie. Sandrina was in much better humour after playing the spinet. Both young ladies had also brought their recorders and we invited them to join our consort.

'We could prepare a *maske* to perform when the men return,' suggested Marie.

This was received with enthusiasm and we decided to go to the Castle to discuss the project with Catelina, who needed cheering up after the departure of her beloved brother Willem Adriaen. We collected Jan de Grevenbroeck on the way and assigned him the job of set maker and chief poet.

When we went to bid farewell to the inspection party the next day Marie and I were complimented by the Baron.

'I know I leave Francina and Sandrina in good hands. You two have already distracted them, so that the one has forgotten her desire to be with one particular young man all the time and the other has abandoned her homesickness. I thank you for your resourcefulness.'

Our curtsies showed our pleasure at being thus praised and the enthusiastic goodbye kisses from our husbands showed us they were proud of us. At that moment I believed I was capable of everything and that nothing would ever happen to change my life. And for a while this remained true.

It took a whole day to select the subject of our *maske*. In this we were guided by Jan who had travelled in Italy and had seen many operas of which our *maske* would be a small form. There were many sad tales of shepherds and nymphs, but Jan said that the most popular operas these days were about women wronged, betrayed or abandoned: Lucrezia, Dido, Ariadne.

The others were as familiar with Greek and Roman myths and legends as I was with the stories of the Bible, but it was obvious no one had ever based a *maske* on a Bible story. Not enough spirits and furies, fates and destinies I suppose. I showed my inferior education by keeping quiet and trying my best to figure out which characters belonged to which stories.

Lucrezia was rejected because no one was sure how to deal with the rape, in other words whether it should be explicit or inferred. Dido and Aeneas were seriously considered, but in the end the Abandonment of Ariadne won. Jan recited a long lament in Italian from the Monteverdi opera on the subject. Here I had the advantage over those who spoke no Portuguese, and could catch the untranslatable subtleties of the expressed sorrow.

Jan did a fine translation, but persuaded those involved that certain of the sighs and sobs would be sung in Italian. This pleased Marie: she was the best singer of us all and the obvious choice for the part of Ariadne. Frans was assigned the role of Theseus, which was a tableaux part; all he had to do was balance himself in a boat on the pond in the courtyard and fend off the sea nymphs as they attack and try to sink him.

Ludovic was to be in charge of the wild beasts of Naxos who would threaten Ariadne from the 'forest' of fruit trees in the garden between the Commander's residence and the pond. It was agreed that the spectators would be seated in the walkway surrounding the pond on three sides.

Everyone got busy immediately. Jan, Marie and Catelina working on the music, I designing costumes, Francina and Sandrina making *maskes* and painting the rocks and bushes that would transform part of the pond into the island of Naxos. We held rehearsals twice a day, to the great diversion of the folk in the Castle. The Van der Stel boys neglected their work and Jan de Grevenbroeck stopped being a scribe altogether. He proved to be much more than a set designer; he was the writer, producer and director of our play.

It was during this intense time that we all spent together that I noticed Catelina's infatuation with Jan de Grevenbroeck, a man more than twice her age. She followed him everywhere, engaged him in conversation wherever she could, laughed loudly at even his most feeble jokes. It was obvious she had unrealistic hopes of romance and mistook ordinary acts of friendliness as special signs of affection and the slightest criticism as a sign of rejection.

My opportunity to speak to her about this came when I found her crying at the harpsichord early one morning.

'Whatever is the matter, Catelina? You're not still weeping for Willem Adriaen, are you?'

'You know better than that, Annie, one does not cry like this for a brother. No, I am the victim of love's cruel caprice.'

I could see the drama of our little *maske* had fired her language and her imagination.

'Come, come you must be exaggerating! What love? Whose caprice?'

'Don't tell me you don't know, Annie? It's Jan de Grevenbroeck. I am crazy about him and he tosses me around like a toy. One moment I think he's serious with his compliments and flirtations and the next moment he ignores me or, worse, criticises me over nothing. He left here just now saying my figured base is hopeless and my ornamental passages feeble. Yesterday he praised the exact same performance!'

I was only five years older than Catelina, but suddenly I felt wise.

'My dear, Jan is an attractive man despite his limp, but why do you think he is not married?'

'He just hasn't found the right person. And he has a financial obligation to his mother in Nijmegen, which prevents him from setting up a home for himself. He told me so himself.'

'Has he told you that he ever considered marrying?'

'Not in so many words.'

'No, and if you listen carefully you'll notice that he has many critical opinions of matrimony, the supposed tyranny of wives over their husbands, what a nuisance children are. No, my dear, I don't think our Jan is the marrying kind. Look, he is the same age as Olof.'

'Well, Olof was over thirty when he married you,' she said ignoring the important part of my statement, 'and he's turned out to be very much the marrying kind.'

'Yes, but Catelina, Jan is different. He's artistic, scholarly. Olof says it's a blessing in disguise that his injury put an end to his career as a soldier, judging from his lack of courage at the hunt.'

'Oh, well, Olof judges everyone by his own prowess.'

I knew she was not going to catch any of my hints, and decorum dictated that I keep my opinion about Jan's disinterest in women to myself. I would not be the one to start that rumour especially since I knew it was bound to sprout a twin rumour about his possible interest in his own sex. Our society had many taboos of which this was probably one of the greatest as was reflected in the severe punishments for sodomy. We all knew it existed and recognised it in certain individuals, but one did not go around implying its existence lightly. Such an insinuation would have constituted the most malicious of scandal-mongering. All I could do was to warn my friend in the most general terms.

'All I'm trying to say, Catelina, is don't put your heart on this romance.'

However, the next time I posed for Jan, I raised the matter.

'Do you know Catelina is in love with you?' I asked directly.

'It's hard to miss, Annie. No matter what I do, she takes it personally. It is so difficult because she is the Commander's daughter and I have to pay her attention. She is young and sweet and I don't know how to make her understand that I am not the marrying kind. You know that is true, don't you, Annie? Help me. What am I to do?'

He gave me a look that sealed the unspoken confidence between us.

A brilliant plan suddenly came to me.

'Finish my portrait and we will convince the Baron that you need to go with him to Batavia to paint Francina. Those two are not in love with you. You'll be safe and Catelina will have time to forget you.'

Little did I know that this plan would make Catelina van der Stel hate me forever. I often wonder if she would have hated me less had I told her the truth.

We surprised the returning inspection party with a brilliant performance of 'Ariadne Abandoned'. It was the first time that the courtyard had been turned into a theatre and everyone agreed that our use of the pond as the ocean was ingenious. I received many compliments on the costumes and masks. Marie's voice carried well in the open air and moved many, including my mother, to tears

Mai Angela had been invited as my special guest. Not many burghers were included in the functions at the Castle.

'Oh, Annie,' she said, still tearful after the play, 'that could have been me! Will I ever forget?'

The Baron approached us. He greeted my mother with a special warmth. 'So you are Annie's mother? Angela van Bengale? Do you remember me from eighteen years back? They tell me you are married now and a respected member of the community.'

'Life here has been good to me, Sir. Yes, I remember your visit in '57. You don't look a day older,' she replied, her flattery obviously pleasing to him. 'So much has happened to me since then but, though I'm now free, I still have many friends in bondage. What a miserable life it is for some, especially in the winter or when food is in short supply.'

'I should like to hear more about that, Mistress Basson. I am making an inspection of the slave lodge tomorrow. Would you care to accompany me? After all, you have known this place almost since its beginning. I think your thoughts and ideas on the subject would be most valuable.'

My mother agreed enthusiastically. If there was anything she could do to improve the lot of the Company slaves, she would do it. We knew that they were inadequately housed, clad and fed, but unless there was an official order to provide funds for improvement, nothing could be done. We were not encouraged to give the Company slaves charity, although many of us did this through our own domestic slaves, instructing them to share old clothing and leftover food with their friends in the Lodge.

All were agreed that the Company needed to adopt a more caring attitude to its slaves, but slaves, it seemed, were not high on the agenda of Simon van der Stel who was so busy expanding the Colony. Conditions for the slaves could only improve on directives from a man like Lord Mydrecht, and my mother was very happy that her opinion would be considered.

I was impressed by the way the Baron treated my mother. It was evidence of the way in which he considered humanity over rank and social position. Olof confirmed this when we talked about the inspection of the Peninsula later that night.

'The man is so acute in his observations and enquiries. He does not miss any detail. He wants to know everything from the names of plants to what the Hottentot are saying. Heinrich and I could help him quite a bit in those two areas. He agrees with Heinrich that the custom of calling indigenous trees here by European names is inappropriate and confusing, though how this habit can be changed I don't know. It's not exactly the subject for a *placaat*, is it?'

'Did he consult you on anything else?'

'Oh, yes, we spoke at length about the interior and whether Vigiti Magna was real or merely the figment of some geographer's imagination. But we also spoke about corruption, particularly about the way in which Jan Baptist Dubertin is filling his pockets. I told him how I had seen with my own eyes the hoard he has in the old Goske house, and how I suspected De Chavonnes was under orders to turn a blind eye to the traffic to the ships at night.'

'You did not implicate the Commander or Van Goens, did you?'

'I did not have to. Van Rheede is a shrewd diplomat. He is pretending he knows nothing and has ordered Captain Cruse to conduct an investigation. But my reward, if my story is found to be true, will be promotion to lieutenant in place of Dubertin.'

'I thought De Chavonnes was promised the same by Van Goens?'

'Yes, but I am sure in this case Van Rheede will overrule Van Goens. The Garrison can only have so many lieutenants.'

'That will certainly make De Chavonnes our enemy.'

'But subordinate,' said my confident husband.

Before the inspection of the colony went inland to Hottentots Holland, Stellenbosch and the valley of the Berg River, a most unusual party of travellers visited our town. Two French ships, the *Oiseau* and the *Maligne* arrived on the last day of May, carrying ambassadors and missionaries to the court of the king of Siam. The ambassadors were officially not allowed to come on shore and were represented by Jesuit fathers bearing gifts and messages.

These priests were mathematicians who apparently had on board all kinds of sophisticated equipment to study the stars. Their present investigation was concerned with longitude. Olof tried to explain the importance of this to me but my intelligence failed me. All I knew was that everyone from the Baron downwards was excited about having the astronomers in town.

Protocol was abandoned and the priests were given the use of the little pavilion near the guesthouse in the Gardens. The open balconies were turned into a temporary observatory as they set up their mathematical instruments, pendula, small telescopes and an enormous twelve-foot telescope. They were a cheerful bunch and very understanding and co-operative about the restriction put on them by the authorities: they were not to celebrate mass or give the host to anyone while on shore.

Every bag and box of equipment was carefully searched for a portable *hostie*. However, the Jesuits were not forbidden to hear confession or intercede, and many people who were still secretly Catholic – many of them slaves who had been forced to adopt that religion – went in and out of the pavilion, ostensibly with gifts for the fathers but in fact to make their confession. My own mother confided later that she had gone to ask for a prayer of intercession for Domingo, who had been hanged for stealing a sheep, ten years before.

The most cordial and talkative of the six Jesuit fathers was Father Guy Tachard, who soon became friendly with Heinrich. Apart from astronomy, he had a keen interest in botany, geography and anthropology. The two of them soon struck a deal: Heinrich would part with some of his engravings of Hottentots, as well as some botanical illustrations, in exchange for a splendidly sensitive new microscope from France.

Marie was asked to make a good copy of the map of Namaqualand, drawn by Heinrich on the expedition on which he had gone with Olof. It did not strike me at the time that all this had happened without Olof's knowledge. I knew the French were not our friends, but at that point they were not at war with us. Besides, Father Tachard was a missionary, not a spy.

We were all invited on the Tuesday night to view the planet Jupiter with its bands and satellites. This was in all my life a unique experience, never to be repeated. The magic of having such a tiny dot in the sky brought so close left me speechless with wonder and made me feel exceptionally insignificant in the vastness of creation.

The next evening we were shown patches of an infinity of stars in the Milky Way and examined the stars of the Southern Cross. I was at a disadvantage, never having seen the stars of the northern hemisphere, but most in the company agreed that the southern sky was in many ways more spectacular.

In the short week they spent amongst us, the Jesuit fathers made an indelible impression on me. Not only was the night sky altered forever, but the Catholic religion, which had been so remote in the religious galaxy, had come into close focus. It seemed to me these fathers were full of kindness and had a particular spirituality not found among the Protestants I knew.

I discussed this with Marie. It was her opinion that Catholics seemed more spontaneous in their interaction with other human beings and with nature because they have not been inhibited by the austerities of Puritanism.

'Beauty in all its forms is encouraged in the Catholic religion. The reformed religions discourage the practice of aesthetics in all forms except music, and even in that sphere there are restrictions. This is what stifles the spirit.'

I knew exactly what she meant and could not have agreed more. When I confided this to Olof, he said I should keep in mind that the fathers were enlightened scientists. There were probably just as many narrow-minded Catholics as Protestants.

'If a person is inclined towards spirituality he will seek it anyway. Look at you, Annie, you are a lover of beauty with a spiritual side of your own that cannot be bridled by man or faith.'

My husband knew that this kind of flattery kept me in the palm of his hand.

Baron van Rheede made his second inspection trip shortly after the French departed. This was Commander van der Stel's opportunity to show what could be achieved when the pioneering spirit of courage and endurance was combined with good agricultural land. Stellenbosch was already recognisable as a community separate from Cape Town and in need of a civic administration.

The Baron was quick to recognise this and made many recommendations on the appointment of a four-member town council and bailiff. He agreed with Simon van der Stel that the valley of the Berg River had good agricultural potential and would be ideal to accommodate the growing number of French Protestants fleeing a new wave of persecution in their native land.

Holland was finding it difficult to absorb the refugees, and a new beginning in a new land could be the solution to the problem. The Baron was persuaded to declare the Berg River Valley a new district to be settled as soon as possible. When Baron van Rheede left for Batavia in the middle of July, it seemed as though all our lives had been touched either by improvements in the administration, the uprooting of corruption or the granting of personal favours.

The Commander was given his dream – the land below the Steenberg where he could build a mansion and produce his own estate wine. He would call it Constantia. It is a place I will think of with great ambivalence until my death. But at the time, a happy Commander meant a happy Colony.

Olof had been promoted to the rank of Lieutenant in place of Jan Baptist Dubertin, who had been found guilty of profiteering and banished to Mauritius. He was mercifully spared a public flogging. Dominique de Chavonnes was implicated in the same scandal on suspicion of omission rather than commission. He displayed open bitterness at Olof's promotion, but was pleased to be chosen as part of the Commander's expedition to Namaqualand. On this expedition the Commander would take Olof's expertise, but not his person. Heinrich was the lucky one who was invited along.

Jan de Grevenbroeck left with the Baron, ostensibly because of his beautifully legible handwriting and his knowledge of Latin, to serve as editor of the *Hortus Malabaricus*. Catelina van der Stel, however, suspected a conspiracy to cure her of her infatuation.

I found myself being dropped from the Castle music club while Marie continued to be invited. I was too hurt to ask the reason for myself and Catelina was too cowardly to tell it to me to my face. From Marie I learnt that Francina had told Catelina before she left that it was my plan that Jan de Grevenbroeck should go along to Batavia to paint her portrait.

'You tell Annie Bergh that I will never forgive her, just as I will never abandon my love for Jan.'

A storm in a teacup, I thought at the time, not realising that Catelina could be as stubborn as her father.

CHAPTER SEVEN

Nossa Sehnora dos Milagros

IT ALL BEGAN WHEN the first Portuguese survivors, ragged and emaciated, arrived at the Cape with the tale of their shipwreck. The *Nossa Sehnora dos Milagros* had run aground near Cape Agulhas. It had taken the captain of the ship, Manuel da Silva, and the Portuguese members of his crew three weeks to reach the outpost at Hottentots Holland.

The overseer at the outpost, Jan Herbst, with the help of some burghers, had loaded the Portuguese on wagons and brought them to the Castle. With them were also some Jesuit and Augustinian priests, but the Siamese ambassadors, their most important passengers, had gone missing in the wilderness.

It was Olof's opinion that the Siamese mandarins had been lost on purpose in order to take possession of the treasure in diamonds and jewels they were taking as gifts to the Kings of England, France and Spain. The Portuguese were at pains to display some of these riches on arrival. The merchant João de Paiva carried with him a casket with diamonds worth 500 000 rixdollars, a fortune.

This the Portuguese posted as surety against their stay at the Cape and the salvaging of the wreck, which they said contained more riches by far. It was not clear whether the casket that De Paiva guarded with his life belonged to him or the Siamese ambassadors. Sensing duplicity, Commander van der Stel immediately sent a sergeant and six soldiers to go and look for the ambassadors. Officially this was done as a gesture of goodwill to the King of Siam.

The Portuguese were given an allowance to buy new clothes and stayed in the empty hospital while the guest houses at Rustenburg and 't Rondebosje were prepared to accommodate them. Captain da Silva had lost his son on the way to the Cape and was filled with grief, incapable of making decisions.

The Commander, in the meanwhile, persuaded De Paiva and three other officers, Cardoso, De Sousa and De Caravallo, to sign a document relinquishing all claim to the cargo. It was not difficult to convince them that even if a salvaging party were to reach the wreck, much of the cargo might already be at the bottom of the ocean. The cargo was thus relinquished without consulting the two Siamese ambassadors, who arrived some time later with their servant.

Haggard and emaciated from thirty-one days in the wilderness, where they were forced by hunger to eat grass, the mandarins nevertheless presented a dignified sight as they entered the Castle in their cone-shaped ceremonial hats. The small house on the Heeren Street between the Cruses and the Meyers was empty at this time and, at the suggestion of the Commander, it was rented to the Siamese ambassadors to recuperate from their ordeal and sort out their affairs. As far as the Portuguese and the ecclesiastics were concerned, they were happy to cut their losses and get home as soon as possible.

The Siamese were now our close neighbours and, since Olof and I were the only people in the vicinity who spoke Portuguese with any fluency, we were the ones best able to show them hospitality and Christian charity.

And so it was that I first met Occum Chamnam.

It was one of those stormy Cape days when the wind and the rain blow the cold and damp through bone and marrow, endlessly rattling windows and knocking on doors. I went in person to take our new neighbours some soup, fresh bread and ale. Occum Chamnam came to the door. Despite his noble bearing, he was pitiful to behold.

There he was, his coat of silk brocade filthy and tattered, not a button in sight. His cheeks were hollow below the high cheekbones, the soulful almond-shaped eyes perplexed and worried, his cleft chin most pronounced. Without the distinctive hat, his matted hair added to his look of desperation.

I could see he was making a superhuman effort to maintain his dignity. His smile began with a pucker of the lips before it lit up his face. Bowing gracefully, with his hands upwards and together in front of him, he politely invited me in.

'I have brought you some soup, Sir. And to ask if you want for anything? I see they gave you some firewood, but did they give you enough blankets?' He seemed relieved to hear a familiar language.

'You are most gracious, Lady. After what we have suffered, this is luxury indeed.' His accent was strange and I had to listen very carefully, but thought that by applying my powers of deduction I should be able to understand the gist of what he was saying.

He introduced me to his companions who were huddled in front of the hearth in the kitchen. The foul weather made it dark indoors and their faces in the flickering firelight appeared like those of characters from some ghostly tale. I had to remind myself that it was eleven o'clock in the morning in the Cape, just around the corner from my house.

Occum Chamnam motioned his servant to take the provisions from me, but I stopped him. Bravely I poured them some ale and they drank with great alacrity.

'I shall send my slave woman, Helena, to help you until you are stronger. She understands some Portuguese. My husband and I will visit you soon.'

Thus a bond was wrought between the Siamese, Olof and me.

Two years later, the whole world was able to read Occum Chamnam's account of how the *Nossa Senhora* was wrecked and he and his companions reached the Cape. They had been forced to desert the head of their mission, and had been abandoned by the Portuguese, discriminated against

by those Hottentot they encountered and finally, mercifully, had been shown the way over the mountains to the outlying district of Hottentots Holland.

The story appeared in Father Tachard's account of his second voyage to Siam. Yes, the same Jesuit father who showed
us the satellites of Jupiter in 1685, and had made it known to
the world and to Simon van der Stel that Heinrich Claudius
had given him a map of the interior. This revelation had bitter repercussions for Heinrich and Marie.

What was clear to us, when first told the story by Occum
Chamnam, was that the Portuguese had done their best to
get rid of the Siamese mandarins in order to keep for themselves the treasure they had already taken from the ship,
They also feared that the Siamese would reveal to the world
that the ship was wrecked not because of bad weather on
that notorious coast, but because of a miscalculation by the
pilot who turned the ship right onto the rocks.

It was just as well that the Siamese and Portuguese were
kept apart because as the mandarins regained back their
strength, they threatened all kinds of action against Captain
da Silva and his crew. They also became more insistent in
their demands that an attempt be made to salvage the
Nossa Sebnora.

The rain did not seem to stop for a whole month, but at
last the weather seemed fit for a search party to set out on
the difficult route to look for the third Siamese ambassador
and to find the wreck near Cape Agulhas. Olof knew exactly
how taxing such a journey would be; he had made several
cattle-bartering trips to the same region beyond the mountains of Hottentots Holland.

The Portuguese sold their slaves at the Cape and sailed
for Batavia, having left instructions for the recovery of their
runaway slaves. Now the Commander had only the Siamese
to contend with. On the day Olof received his order to set
out on the salvaging expedition, the Commander called
him, Fiscal Johan van Keulen and Assistant Willem
Wederhold into his office for a special meeting.

'I am sending you on this mission because you know the route, but also because I can trust you to keep everything about the operation secret. Under no circumstances are the Siamese ambassadors to know what is brought from the wreck. The Portuguese signed the cargo over to the Company and every single thing salvaged from that wreck belongs to the Company alone. I want that clearly understood.'

'Are the Siamese not entitled to their personal belongings, should we recover any of these, Your Excellency?' asked Olof.

'No, they lost everything when that ship ran aground and they abandoned it and separated themselves from the Portuguese.'

'As always there are two stories, Sir. According to the mandarins they were abandoned by the Portuguese who shared with them no food or water bartered from the Hottentot. His Excellency Occum Chamnam told me himself that the Portuguese on one occasion gave them the skins of one of the animals to eat.'

'I don't feel sorry for the Siamese, Bergh. They have been treated well by us and they may have bartered all their gold buttons away, but they still have pockets full of diamonds sewn into the insides of those comical hats.'

Everyone chuckled at this. The fact that the Hottentots refused diamonds as payment for a sheep, but accepted gold buttons and other trinkets after one of the Siamese had displayed one such trinket in his hair caused much amusement in homes and taverns alike. It was a story told to exemplify the foolishness of the tribesmen and the ingenuity of the mandarins.

'They feel strongly about the musk left on board, Sir. It is apparently the genuine article obtained from *kasturis* high in the Himalayan mountains.'

'If the musk can be salvaged, so much the better for us,' Commander van der Stel insisted. 'You will say nothing to them about musk or anything else and you will keep a close eye on the men. Everything from that ship comes back to the Castle and belongs to the Company. That is an order.'

96

Simon van der Stel knew that Olof had spent many hours talking to Occum Chamnam, finding out about the position of the *Nossa Sehnora* and the location of certain items in the hold. It was his job to find out as much as he could in order to salvage as many valuables as possible.

At that stage the order for secrecy had not been issued and we assumed that the Siamese would be able to regain possession of their personal belongings, should any be retrieved. Occum Chamnam had described to me in detail some plates and cups in gold and silver.

'They are of exquisite craftsmanship, Sehnora, of the fine filigreed embossing found only in my country. When your husband brings them back I will give you some pieces to thank you for your kindness. And the musk, you must have some of the musk.'

The night before he left for the coast, Olof repeated to me the Commander's instructions, agreeing with me that they were grossly unfair. He confided that he thought the Commander meant to see the Siamese on their way home before any of the salvaged goods ever came back from the wreck. I, in turn, raised the possibility that we might hold a few precious objects in safekeeping until the Siamese should call at the Cape on a future mission to Portugal.

'Occum Chamnam tells me that his plan is to go home and recover from his ordeal and then proceed on his original mission. He is determined to get to Europe.'

'Don't even think about it, Annie,' said Olof. But I was not convinced that he had dismissed the idea entirely.

Olof, the Fiscal and Assistant left on 9 July 1686. They took with them a wagon and several men, including Arent and Willem Hendricks. They kept a journal of this journey and sent regular reports of their progress to the Commander, who personally kept me informed.

I quote from their journal:

'July 10th: Passed the Company post 'de Cuylen' and went on to lunch at the farmstead of Henning Huysing.

Pressed on to reach Hottentots Holland at nightfall.

July 11th: Crossed the Hottentots Holland mountains at the 'Cloof' and reached the 'Wild Palmiet River'.

July 12th: Camped at the 'Botter River'

July 13th: Reached the 'Swarte River' and camped near the kraal of Captain Claas.

July 14th: Followed the 'steenbok River' until we came to the 'Casten River'.

July 16th: Passed the 'Casten River' where we saw three lions.

July 18th: Passed 'Soetendaals Valley' and arrived at sunset at the place where the Siamese gentlemen had camped. Having pitched tents the Fiscal, Lieutenant and the Assistant rode to the sea shore, and after many delays saw the hulk of th: Portuguese ship lying amongst the breakers, when, hast. .d by nightfall, they returned to the tents.'

What happened then was described in a long letter from the coast north of Cape Agulhas. I shall summarise it for you:

The first thing Olof and the others saw was a cask afloat but attached to the wreck by a rope. They sent one of the men and a Hottentot helper to try and bring the cask ashore. Olof saw them struggling to do this and, disregarding the danger of sharks, swam across to the wreck himself. The Hendricks brothers and three others had meanwhile made a raft and followed. (Van Keulen later claimed to have been unaware of this, though it was clear that he was aware that one man drowned in the process.) On board they found a young slave boy, Antonie of Mozambique, guarding the possessions of his master, Father Joseph de la Gratia, the General of the Augustinian monks. The poor boy must have lost count of time. He said he had been on the wreck for three weeks.

Arent Hendricks confessed later that this was the day that Olof allowed him to break open a small floating casket and pocket the jewellery he tried to sell a year later. There were, indeed, a few caskets floating around, but most had been opened already by the runaway slaves of the Portuguese. The rest of the cargo in the hold was completely immersed and inaccessible. The ship had split in half and the saloon and gunroom had been battered to pieces by the sea.

The sea was rough and, since there were some provisions and water on board, Olof stayed on the wreck for twelve days supervising the recovery of the following: eight small cannons weighing no more than twelve pounds, three anchors, new cables, some porcelain, and bales of cinnamon found on deck. This was all they could get ashore. At that point they sent word to the Castle asking whether they should blow up the wreck or wait for they sea to break up the hold. If they were to stay longer and wait, they would need more provisions.

The Commander decided to send more wagons with Ensign Schrijver to collect the salvaged goods. Only Olof and Fiscal van Keulen were to return to the Castle. The men, who knew what had been found at the wreck, were to be kept away from the Cape until after the departure of the Siamese.

Olof recommended to Simon van der Stel that another attempt at salvaging the cargo in the hold be made from the sea, but this plan was also postponed until the Siamese had left. The mandarins were understandably disappointed that nothing from the cargo hold had been recovered. The Commander's tight-lipped account of the salvaging expedition made them suspicious that they were being deceived in some way

In private Olof assured them that this was not the case. It was then that he made a commitment that would later prove to be disastrous. He promised Occum Chamnam that if he should recover any of the gold and silver objects so carefully described, or any of the musk, he would find a way to persuade Commander van der Stel to hold these until the time of the intended return of the Siamese mission.

When the time came, I was sad to part with Occum Chamnam. During the weeks Olof was away, I had spent many hours in his company. As the weather improved and he regained his strength and curiosity, I had appointed myself as his guide. He was an keen rider and after we had explored the length and the breadth of the town on foot, we ventured further afield on horseback even though I was already six months pregnant. I shall never forget his excitement when he saw the mulberry trees in the gardens at Rustenburg.

This was when he told me about silkworms, the production of silk thread and the weaving of the very fine fabrics in his country. There was a silk industry on one of his estates.

'How I wish you could see this with your own eyes, my dear *Sehnora*. But I make you a promise: when I return I will bring you some silkworm eggs and you can have your own silk industry right here at the Cape. These trees are fine, though you'll need many more to feed all the worms you need to spin the many cocoons needed to make just one length of fabric. I suggest you start planting them in the spring in order to be prepared.'

'I wonder whether the eggs would hatch, since the seasons of the north and the south are reversed. Have you ever heard of eggs from the northern hemisphere hatching in the south after only six months' maturity?'

'I have not heard of a similar experiment conducted anywhere else in the southern hemisphere. The only places where it could have been tried is South America, but of that I have no knowledge.'

'It certainly seems worth trying. How thrilling it would be if such a thing could work here at the Cape.'

In early September, we bade the Siamese gentlemen a fond goodbye in the language that promised a meeting in the future. Soon after came reports from Wiederhold and Schrijver that the wreck was breaking up and chests from the cargo hold were beginning to surface. These would best be recovered from sea rather than from land. The bales of fabric, canvas and clothing that had washed ashore were damaged and would need to be washed.

Sergeant Henning was sent on the sloop *Jupiter* to attempt the salvaging of the chests, but the vessel beached on a sandbank near Struijs Bay. Olof was then sent on the yacht *Jambi* to float the *Jupiter* and recover the chests. He took with him a carpenter, Werner Sijbranz, who was to close any broken chests and build containers for loose objects.

Olof returned to the Cape in late November with a number of chests and a blue canvas bag containing caskets of the precious musk of which Occum Chamnam had spoken. Each casket was individually wrapped in its own little canvas bag. He had also found some gold cups and a silver saucer. These had been carefully packed in a small crate by Werner Sijbranz.

Olof presented me with one casket of musk and the small wooden container.

'Did you get permission to keep these?' I asked anxiously. 'I thought the Commander was away at Constantia? You know how particular he is about Company property'

'I reported to him before I came home. I told him about the open chests and the open bag of musk. He was tired and very excited about the completion of the house at Constantia. He agreed to us keeping these safe for the Siamese to collect on their return to Europe. I must write my report before I go to bed.'

We buried the musk in a cool place in the garden, as instructed by Occum Chamnam. Musk is very sensitive to heat and loses much of its healing power when exposed to the high temperatures we experienced in the height of summer. The gold cups and silver saucer we displayed on the mantelpiece for all to admire.

But Dominique de Chavonnes saw these beautiful objects and a plan began to form in his jealous bosom. From their days in Ceylon, Olof had been his rival; both had their

101

heart set on succeeding Hieronimus Cruse as Captain of the Garrison, but Olof had been promoted over De Chavonnes by Baron van Rheede and would be the obvious choice for the post. If he could be discredited, the way for Chavonnes would be clear.

De Chavonnes saw his chance the following April when our neighbour, Frederick Russouw, began to brag about the gold cross with eight diamonds, a silver filigree scent ball and a coral rosary he had apparently bought from Willem Hendricks. It was also rumoured that the same Willem Hendricks had sold some gold jewellery to the minister of our church, Dominee Overney. This the Dominee denied from the pulpit, but De Chavonnes reported the rumour to the Commander and insisted on an investigation by the Fiscal, Johannes van Keulen.

Late one night, in early April, Arent Hendricks arrived at our door in a panic. His eyes were wild, his appearance dishevelled.

'Where is the Lieutenant?' he asked.

'In Stellenbosch with Baas Arie. He's supervising the building of the new Council Chamber. Why, Arent? You look awful, what's wrong?' My heart was pounding.

'They've taken my brother Willem into custody. The Fiscal and De Chavonnes searched his house and found the jewellery from the *Nossa Sehnora*. They are now searching the house of Sergeant Henning and will probably arrest him also.'

'Why? Did Willem really steal from the wreck? And Sergeant Henning?'

The expression on his face turned from panic to malice.

'We're all in it together, Mistress Bergh. Your husband knew about the jewellery. He was the one who encouraged us to take a little on the side. I can still hear him say: 'Such hard work for so little reward; the Company will not miss a little something here and there.'

'I don't believe it! Lieutenant Bergh would never encourage dishonesty!'

'No? And what about the gold and silver in your own

house? I hear the Commander is furious and has ordered a search of your house and garden. Dominique de Chavonnes is spreading all kinds of rumours discrediting your husband. He has told Commander van der Stel about the past in Ceylon. How your husband showed the enemies of the Company how to use gunpowder, how he murdered the husband of his lover and blackmailed the Council into granting him a pardon.'

'The Commander has more sense than to believe such slander. He trusts my husband, they are good friends.' I said this more to convince myself than the man at the door. I could see that he, like everyone else, was ready to believe anything that would deflect guilt from themselves.

'In any event, my husband must be warned. I will pay you to ride to Stellenbosch at first light and inform him of what is happening. You'll see, we have nothing to hide.'

The fact that Olof took his time coming back from Stellenbosch was proof to me that the matter was not serious. This soon changed when, on his arrival, he was placed under house arrest. The front and back doors of our house were placed under guard and only I was allowed to come and go. The next day Olof was taken to the Castle to be questioned by the Council and the visiting Commissioners headed by Admiral Daniel Braams. I was given permission to attend the interrogation.

The Commander himself took the chair, determined to show the visiting dignitaries how conscientious he was in routing out crime against the Company. He had the stern look of a man who was willing to believe the worst. He was careful to avoid any eye contact with me.

'Lieutenant Bergh, we now have confessions of theft from Christoffel Henning, Werner Sijbranz and Willem Henning. These men were under your supervision. How is it that this could have happened?'

'Your Excellency will appreciate that I was not in a position to watch every move of every man. We were working in dangerous conditions in rough waters. Many of the chests we recovered had already been opened and looted by the

Portuguese slaves. It would not have been difficult for anyone to pocket some small pieces of jewellery unobserved.'

'The carpenter Sijbranz testifies that you instructed him
to open some of the chests. What were you looking for?'

I could see Olof flush with anger. He made a concerted
effort to control himself.

'Your Excellency may remember that in my verbal report,
on my return from the wreck, I told you about that. We had
to open some chests to discover whether the contents was
worth salvaging. You told me yourself not to mention that
in writing. You also gave me permission that day to hold
some objects in safekeeping for His Excellency Occam
Chamnam, the Siamese ambassador.'

It was obvious that Olof's confident defense upset the -
Commander. Suddenly he developed selective amnesia.
And that doomed us.

'I remember nothing of such a conversation. All I have as
evidence is your written report. Admit, you are as guilty as
the other men. You abused your position of authority by
allowing this theft and taking part in it yourself. I am now
ready to believe that you incited the other accused to take
what was not theirs by your loose talk about insufficient
reward. I am also ready to believe all I was told about your
conduct in Ceylon. You are a fine actor, Olof Bergh. I was
a fool to be taken in by you.'

I could feel the collective agreement of the Council
members. I saw Dominique de Chavonnes sneer victorious-
ly and I wished I were invisible.

But Olof persisted:

'I must speak in my own defense, although I doubt it will
be recorded for posterity. Hendrik Hoogeboom died in a
shooting accident in Ceylon and I was not his wife's lover. I
happened to be present at his death and was cleared of suspicion of murder without blackmailing anyone. To that
Baron Isaac St Martin could testify himself, were he here.
Certainly, you may recall that during his recent visit he did
not treat me like the rascal you make me out to be. He

would also tell you that I showed some of the Raja's men how to use explosives in construction, not in warfare. The man who is spreading these rumours is right here in this room ...'

He was looking straight at De Chavonnes, but the Commander interrupted him.

'Enough, no more! Your guilt in the matter of the Portuguese wreck is self confessed and obvious to all. I am ordering the confiscation of the gold and silver from your house, and the musk shall be dug up from your garden. I recommend to this Council your immediate removal, under close guard, to Robben Island until such time as a sentence arrives from the Council of India.'

'And I will appeal this gross injustice to the Lords XVII themselves!' shouted Olof, angry, but undaunted. 'My life is not over! I shall fight to the bitter end.'

I rushed forward to embrace him as the guards led him away, but they would not pause to allow me even to touch him. He looked back at me, his blue eyes dark with emotion.

'*Ate logo*, my love. I count on your courage!'

CHAPTER EIGHT

Wreck

FOR YEARS I DID NOT want to think about it, let alone talk about it.

As many innocent sources combine to make a mighty river, so did several incidents combine to form that bitter stream that was to sweep away my cosy life and cast me out to sea. There I was, adrift with four small children, our protector incarcerated on unfair and flimsy charges while the winds and waves of rumour and ill will raged about us. When they came to confiscate our house, I knew for sure that we were totally ruined.

Have you ever had two men and a slave take your whole house apart, inspecting and describing your every possession for their inventory? This usually happens after one is dead. But I was alive. I had to show them everything, even my most intimate garments while they checked off the few things the Commander had allowed me for my personal use.

Dominique de Chavonnes arrived first with a look of triumph on his face as he looked around my living room.

'What a fine sale we will have! Everyone is looking forward to buying these fine things that you and your husband have so greedily been hoarding, Mistress Bergh.' He fingered Olof's swords covetously. 'What does a man do with nine swords, I ask you?'

'Don't count your chickens before they are hatched! You know as well as I do that nothing will be sold until final word of sentencing comes from the Lords XVII. And that may take a long time during which we will prove that what you say are stolen goods were gifts received in good faith. I will not defend myself against your accusations of greed, Sir, for I know your judgment of me is so rooted in envy and prejudice that anything I say will be entirely useless. But I insist that you refrain from making insulting and sarcastic remarks until Mr Linnes arrives.'

I was not going to call him 'Lieutenant'. That was my husband's rank into which he had stepped so conveniently. It was almost unbearable to be in the same room with him, Olof's accuser, this man who had left no stone unturned to produce so-called evidence against Olof and to poison the Commander's mind with trumped up charges about Olof's past in Ceylon.

I looked at his weak fish face, the puffy lips pursed in contempt, the shallow blue eyes opaque with malice. He was the source of all rumour against us, the interrogator of Arent and Willem Hendriks. It was he who cracked the loyalty of Christoffel Henningh and twisted his words in order to implicate Olof.

'Your haughtiness surprises me, Mistress Annie Bergh. Your husband is at least humbled by his punishment. But we all know that it was you who instigated the looting and fabricated the convoluted stories about supposed gifts and safekeeping. Did you honestly believe that such feeble explanations would deflect us from the reality of your husband's blatant part in the conspiracy to deprive the Company of valuable goods? You instructed him to steal that gold and silver, to break open box after box until he found the casket of musk. You are the one who should be punished.'

'And what do you call this? Is this not punishment? First you incarcerate and banish my husband and now you confiscate all my possessions. Is such a living death not punishment enough for anyone? But don't expect me to be humble. I still have much to be proud of: my children and my work. This will not destroy me.'

This brave talk was not convincing me or the despicable man before me. The sarcastic curl of his thick lips showed nothing but contempt for my little speech.

'Work, what work?' He pointed with a sneer to my water-colours on the wall. 'Are you referring to this little hobby? There's not a living to be made out of painting plants, you know. No, your best bet would be to use the feminine charms God gave you and find yourself another protector.'

His sword jangled as his protruding belly filled the space between us. I was sorry I had sent the children away to be with my mother. The implication of his words was obvious and soon his pudgy hand would be on me. My head spun as I quickly moved towards the window from where, to my relief, I saw Mr Linnes mounting the steps.

I rushed to open the door for him. With him was his slave, Claes, a man who was well known to my family but today was keeping his eyes on the ground.

'Come in, Mr Linnes, we have been waiting for you.' He saw my anxiety but did nothing to reassure me.

'I'm a busy man. This inventory comes as an added inconvenience. Shall we get on with it? Here is the list of items you are allowed to keep. The Commander is graciously granting you the use of one bolt of fabric and your sewing equipment. You are not allowed to take any furniture. Your husband may have his bed and bed linen, but you will have to have to look to your family to provide these for you. The Commander made it very clear that you were to have no luxuries.'

He knew all about confiscation and exile. I remember well when he was sent to Robben Island for embezzlement. His wife suffered the same humiliation, but long before his twenty years were up there was a change in command and back he came. He was now a prosperous man. His story was a small ray of hope in the darkness of my misery.

'Let's get started,' I said, holding back my tears.

They began in the living room. Claes was instructed to take everything off the walls: Olof's swords, canes, guns and other weapons, my little watercolours, my portrait (thank goodness I had rescued Olof's half-finished portrait from the Claudius studio before they left). Then they listed the furniture and everything on display. When De Chavonnes saw Olof's collection of snuffboxes, he said:

'That reminds me. Bergh already took a big tin of chewing tobacco to Robben Island with him. He'll have to compensate the auction for that.'

The word 'auction' made me cringe. I reminded him that nothing could legally be sold until the final confirmation of sentencing had come from Holland. Linnes noted this without comment.

Then the real invasion started. I stood by as the slave unpacked bolt upon bolt of fabric and sewing equipment, my large stock of silver and gold buttons. I watched as my dresses were taken out of the cupboard one by one and laid on the bed in the corner. Stupid men, they did not know much about women's clothing. I had to tell them what many of the garments were called. I asked to unpack my underwear but they would not have it.

'My orders were not to allow you to touch anything, Mistress Bergh. Will you kindly stay back and allow the slave to do his work!'

In the bottom drawer of the chest, they found our cash box and the bundle that contained the 1 400 guilders paid by Frederick Russouw as the first installment on the house. He was to occupy it after I was kicked out.

'I am allowed to keep the money. It says so on the Commander's list.'

'Let me see that!' De Chavonnes grabbed the list from me and made a myopic inspection of it.

'The money in the cash box you can keep,' he said, counting it carefully for the benefit of Linnes's accurate record. Yes, let's see. Exactly 177 guilders and 10 stuivers in change. Not what I would call a fortune with which to feed and clothe four brats, is it? The installment on the house goes straight into the bailiff's strongbox.'

He looked triumphant, but I could see he was still not satisfied.

'Let's go and see if anything interesting is hidden upstairs.'

'The Fiscal turned this place upside down. I doubt you'll find anything of interest.'

They found nothing in our bedroom, but when they started poking around the small storeroom upstairs, De Chavonnes suddenly cried out:

'Here it is! The final incriminating evidence we need!' he shouted, holding in the air a little blue canvas bag as though it were made of pure gold. 'Isn't this exactly like the bag of musk we sealed a year ago, Linnes?'

He was very excited. 'There, Mistress Annie, can you deny that this bag contained the musk buried in your garden? Look there is still soil on it! Why did you not hand this over to the Fiscal?'

His pettiness exasperated me. He took such perverse pleasure in having his own insignificant piece of the action.

'No one ever denied that the musk was in the garden or that the casket was inside the bag. They took the casket and left the bag. It is obviously worth nothing.'

'We should make special note of this, Linnes, in case the Fiscal needs it,' he said importantly.

The last rooms in the house to be inventoried were the kitchen and pantry. I was allowed to take all the dry goods and a small number of dishes, pots and pans and a laundry iron. We loaded these into a basket. Then Linnes and I went upstairs with another basket to collect our clothes. He checked off every item as I packed; it was meant to impress on me that I was receiving the Company's charity and that nothing in the house belonged to me anymore.

'May I take one small mirror?' I asked faintly.

'Not on the list, is it?' he answered firmly.

I could hear De Chavonnes and Claes fitting the bolts to the outside of the doors. Linnes gave me no help carrying the basket downstairs. I took from the chest in the living room the bolt of chintz I was allowed. I struggled to get the basket outside. Linnes just watched.

Silently they secured the house, closed all the shutters, bolted the doors from the outside and placed huge brass locks on the bolts. My house and earthly possessions were handcuffed and shackled, properly taken into custody. They left without another word.

I found a corner in the shed where no one could see me. I knew the neighbours were watching from behind their curtains. How I missed Marie and Heinrich. They would have been here with me during this humiliation as I was with them but a few weeks before when the Commander discovered that Heinrich had given Father Tachard sensitive information bearing on the security of the Cape. I alone stood by them while others called them traitors and applauded their sudden and brutal deportation.

I do not blame my neighbours. They had to survive like everyone else and had already surreptitiously done their best to help since our troubles began. Aaltje Elberts sent soup and cakes and Baas Arie offered transportation, but physically they kept away.

I looked at the two baskets containing my worldly possessions and began to weep. Every muscle in my body ached and I felt my head would burst open. Surely this was how those poor shipwreck survivors felt on the shore near Cape Agulhas.

Visions of Occum Chamnam's survival in the wilderness flooded my memory and made me howl in panic. I lost control as I tossed my body this way and that, pulling my hair and banging my head against a post. This was how my half-brother, Willem, found me.

He put his strong arms around me and held me firmly. He spoke to me as I had often heard him speak to an animal he was trying to tame.

'There, there, softly, gently, softly, gently.' He repeated this incantation with such confidence and reassurance that after a while my sobs subsided and I felt my body relax in his firm grip.

'Willem, what are you doing here? I thought you were at Drakenstein?'

'I came for supplies and more cattle to take back.'

A brilliant plan flashed through my brain. I saw my escape clearly before me.

'Take us back with you, please, Willem? I promise the children will be no trouble and I can keep house for you.'

I knew this was a big thing to ask and I watched him closely for any hesitation, but he did not flinch for a moment. Perhaps the idea was not new to him.

'That is a good plan. You need to get away from here for a while, at least. Mother and I had discussed the possibility. You know it is completely wild out there? But, Annie, it is incredibly beautiful and I have built a basic house. We can easily add a room for you and the children.'

'You are the best brother a sister could wish for, Willem Basson. I will not be a burden, I promise.'

He hugged me tightly. 'You have been a loving sister to me, Annie. In times like these a family should stick together.'

I began to cry again, but in a less frenzied way.

'That's good,' said Willem, 'get it out of your system. You need to be strong for your children.'

Baas Arie van Brakel appeared in his back yard.

'Do you need any help, Willem?' he called. It was obviously all right to speak to Willem. 'Would you like to borrow the horse and cart?'

'Yes, thanks, Baas Arie, may we? You go on to mother's house, Annie. I'll bring your things.'

My children saw me coming and ran to meet me; little ducklings instinctively seeking their mother. Christina, now almost eight years old, was carrying little baby Polla while Maria held my blond curly-headed Pieterke by the hand. As I forced back my tears, I felt my courage rise. There in front of me were four very good reasons why I should be strong, why I should ride out this disaster.

I gathered them all into an embrace and held them there for a long time. I resolved then never to let them see me cry. I would save that for the middle of the night when I could be sure I was not observed. Without a father, they needed a mother who could at least pretend to be strong.

My mother saw my tear-stained face, but when we looked at each other, I could see her relief. When she spoke it was like a general leading his troops to battle, transferring her strength to me.

'You are going to be all right, Annie. I can see the determination in your eyes. Hold your head high. Stiffen your spine. No child of Angela of Bengal will allow herself to be destroyed by circumstances. Think of the obstacles I overcame; think of your own challenges. We are strong people; your father was no coward. Be brave and make us proud of you!'

Willem and I and the children left the next day for Drakenstein in an open wagon provided by Baas Arie, who had also lent us a slave to get us to the farm and bring back his wagon. We loaded the two baskets and the small chest given to me by Heinrich and Marie on their hasty departure. It contained a set of recorders, some music, reams of folio paper with the watermark of the City of Amsterdam, two complete folios of drawings, a few good brushes and the necessary pigments to make my own paint.

The weather was perfect and Willem and I pretended to the children that we were going on an adventure of endless picnics. We convinced Maria and Petrus, but little Polla only cared about feeding and sleeping and Christina stayed very close to me. She was totally aware of what our flight into the interior meant. The second night when we stayed with friends near Stellenbosch, she waited until the others were asleep and, snuggling up close to me, said:

'Poor Pappa, he must be very lonely. When will we see him again, Mamma?'

'Who knows, *skatje*, perhaps sooner than we think. But if we really concentrate and think of him together, we might visit him in our dreams'

Willem's farm was called Paradijs. Like all the engravings you have ever seen of paradise, it was a wilderness filled with a multitude of wild animals and rampant plant life. Willem had built his little pioneer's house close to the banks of the Berg River. This river had been named long before Olof ever set his foot on African soil, but Christina insisted that the river belonged to us. A wooden palisade surrounded the house with a gate leading to an equally fenced kraal.

The valley was flanked on three sides by high mountains that changed colour through the course of the day. The place was indeed so stunningly beautiful and imposed such an overpowering order of its own that one soon forgot about the feeble attempts of mankind to organise itself in towns and cities.

Danger from wild beasts and people seemed part of the cycle that swept us into its rhythm of sunrise and sunset, of fair and foul weather, of the inevitable progress of the seasons. There existed a simple certainty, an absence of social pressure, a freedom to be oneself. Slowly, I felt the confidence of my childhood return, my damaged identity restored.

For nearly a year I did not look in a mirror, burnt my skin as brown as a berry and wore two identical frocks alternately. We all dressed in the same chintz. Willem and I joked that the Hottentot might mistake us from a distance for a new kind of animal. Life was not too hard. With one female and two male slaves on loan from my stepfather, I had as much time as I wanted for my drawings and to enjoy my children.

Christina was reading quite well now and I spent some of my time with her on her schoolwork. We worked together on a bestiary called Beasts of Paradise, sketching and describing the animals around us in the valley and imagining fantastic beasts that lived in the mountains.

We picked one kloof opposite the entrance to the house as the habitat of Lord Dracus, our own special unicorn. Of course we never saw him, but we greeted him every morning and wished him goodnight. He shared responsibility with the good Lord to watch over Olof on Robben Island and make him dream good dreams of us.

Sometimes we invented such fierce creatures for our bestiary that we managed to scare even Maria, who had a reputation for fearlessness. It was she who persuaded Willem to adopt the abandoned baby rhinoceros, Jochem, and collected every insect and lizard she could lay her hands on. Petrus followed her everywhere and copied everything she did, which meant that their vocabulary was also identical. Polla thrived and began to crawl, stand and then walk.

I taught Christina to play the descant recorder and soon the strains of La Folia could be heard miles up the valley where our distant neighbours lived. The humiliation I had suffered in Cabo began to recede. I began to forget the wagging tongues and the spiteful faces.

But my longing for Olof was with me daily like a dull, persistent pain. I had one message from my mother saying that he was reported to be well on Robben Island. That was all, until a letter in Olof's own handwriting came, almost six months later.

'Annie, my dearest wife,' it said, 'I am back in the Castle. The Commander, now called Governor, has brought together every able-bodied soldier in case of a French attack. The usual exaggeration and paranoia on his part, but this time to our benefit. Come back to the Cape, dearest! I am told you would have visiting rights. Is your body longing for me as much as mine is longing for you? Kiss our dear children for me.'

My heart pounded and my legs felt weak. I knew I would brave any social humiliation just to be with my dear Olof once more.

CHAPTER NINE

Exile

THE CASTLE HAD NEVER seemed so close and yet so far, its walls solid and forbidding. Inside was Olof, outside his family; the distance between determined by the conditions of his confinement. We were granted permission to visit him once a week at his quarters; there would be no spontaneity, no rushing into his arms as I had dreamed.

We acquired new clothes and marched in a dignified little group past the parade ground to the Castle gate. Everyone on the streets knew where we were going. On my return I had found the general air of spiteful triumph towards us had turned into pity. I do not know which was harder to bear. I returned the stares of silent commiseration with my own brand of constrained humility.

The time at Paradijs had healed the immediate wounds caused by the initial humiliation. I was ready to manage my life as my mother recommended, with a stiff back and unclouded vision. Come what may, the sun rises every morning. Fate deals its cards and we poor mortals have to play our hand as best we can.

The guards at the gate were friendly: Olof had always been popular with the men. He had a reputation for being exacting but fair, of listening before jumping to conclusions. He always maintained that rank marked a position in the orderly management of security and conflict and was not to be used as a point of power over men.

I knew there were many soldiers under his command who believed that Olof had been unjustly accused. The Commander, now Governor, also aware of this loyalty, brought him back to continue in his professional role though he received no pay for this. Had it not been for Olof's small, irregular and frugally managed annuity, we would have had to live on only the uncertain income from my sewing and drawings.

Olof was waiting for us at his quarters. He had lost weight and looked fit and handsome in his white shirt and narrow trousers. He gave me a cursory hug and turned his attention to the children, particularly Appollonia whom he had last seen as a baby. My heart was in my throat: there was not only the Castle wall between us. But I drank tea and pretended to be content answering questions, listening to his chatter about life in the Castle.

Then Jan de Grevenbroeck appeared. He exchanged a look with Olof that told me his appearance had been planned.

'Annie, it's so good to see you again! And look at your brood!' said Jan with his customary scorn for the products of marital bliss.

'I heard you had come back from Batavia, Jan. Was Francina's portrait a success? It seems Catelina gave up hope and returned to her mother.'

'I finished the portrait just before the Baron died. He was very pleased. I have a long letter for you from Francina. She was devastated by her father's death, but young Maurits de la Baie is doing his best to comfort her. But more about that later; right now, Uncle Jan is going to take all the little children away for an hour to walk in the orchard and watch the dolphin fountain.' He gave us a big wink.

As soon as the door closed behind them we fell into each other's arms. Furiously and passionately we made love, making up in intensity what we had lost in frequency. Rapture released the tension of a whole year and as my muscles relaxed, tears overwhelmed me.

At first Olof held me silently, stroking my trembling shoulders, my dishevelled hair, but then I felt his body begin to shake. Olof was crying; that brave Swede, my hus-

117

band and hero was crying! We held on to each other for a long time until the sobs subsided.

'It's not over, Annie,' he said sadly, but not desperately.

'It may never be over!' I said ready to start crying again.

This spurred him on. 'We must be brave, my love! Not only that, we must be ingenious. We must apply military strategy to every plan we make. And I predict in the end we will win. De Chavonnes may think he's done me in, but I will get my chance for revenge. As for the Governor, he may know all about wine-making, but he knows nothing about cunning.

'I promise you, I will devise a plan that will ensure for us and our children position and property in this Colony second to none. The day will come when we will soar above those who now applaud our downfall and misfortune. But you have to be patient and trusting. Above all, you have to be strong and carry on without me as if that were the normal way of things.'

He lifted my face towards him and engaged my eyes. 'Do you think you can do that, my lovely Annie?'

'I can try,' I said, attempting to enter into the spirit of his optimism.

We had just enough time to recover a respectable appearance when who should arrive with Jan and the children at the door, but the Governor himself. He greeted me with a cordiality entirely opposite to the cold disdain he had shown me a year ago. Olof's apparent friendliness towards him surprised me until a sideways look from Olof made me realise that this was an act with which I was required to go along.

'You look well, Mistress Bergh! And so do your lovely children,' he said, extending his hand.

No thanks to you, I thought, but accepted the kiss he planted on my ringless fingers.

'Thank you, Your Excellency. I have enjoyed my sojourn in Drakenstein. My brother is building a fine farm in that wilderness.'

'I am told you have continued your drawing over there. I

would be very interested in seeing your work. Requests for plants and drawings arrive on every ship from my cousin Huydecoper. It seems our Cape plants are in high demand in every new herbarium and exotic herbal in Europe. Commelin is becoming famous for his foreign collections.'

Was he offering me business? In that case there would be a reason to be civil towards him.

'Your Excellency would be most welcome to inspect my drawings. I have many copies, but also originals of plants I found in the valley and mountains around Paradijs. I have also dried some plants and collected seeds and bulbs.'

I could see relief in Olof's face.

'I congratulate you, Annie,' said the Governor familiarly, as though he was speaking to a child. 'I will come to your mother's house later this week before I go back to Constantia.'

'I am actually staying with the widow Cruse, Your Excellency. It is closer to the Castle for visiting purposes and Aaltje needs to be comforted after the sad passing of her husband.'

I wanted him to know that old and important friends had not deserted me, that he was not to patronise me with this new affability.

'I shall come tomorrow then, since it's so close.'

He knew I would not refuse. We were in his power; one word from him could remove Olof to Robben Island within hours. I was forced to play by his rules. I disguised my disgust with concerted effort and buried my hatred for him deep in my heart.

For a year we settled into a routine of weekly visits and the odd glimpse of Olof on the parade ground. It was as though Jan de Grevenbroeck had marked our visits in his diary, for he turned up without fail to amuse the children while Olof and I spent some time alone.

Inevitably I became pregnant again and little Carolus Erlandt was born in the winter of 1689. But it was as though the little fellow knew his timing was bad. He did not even fuss; he just failed to thrive and died quietly three weeks after his christening. I am still surprised at the equanimity with which I took his death. Perhaps the small creature conveyed to me that it was not worth fretting; perhaps I was beginning to accept adversity as my lot.

When both the Governor and Captain de Chavonnes (oh yes, he had been made Captain of the Garrison after a mysterious fever took Hieronimus Cruse the year before) happened to be absent from the Castle, we extended our visiting hours to take supper together. Sometimes these occasions included the two princes from Macassar, Dain Mangale, brother of the King of Macassar, and the aged hostage, Dain Manjampa.

Dain Mangale was himself a victim of plotting and false accusations. His brother had contrived his exile to remove him from the court of Macassar where he had mounted an armed resistance to challenge his brother's complicity with the Dutch. He came to the Cape in 1681 and had tried ever since, by appealing to various authorities, to be repatriated.

Baron van Rheede heard one such appeal in 1685 and acted on Dain Mangale's behalf in Batavia, but to no avail. It was also because of recommendations by the Baron that Dain Mangale's allowance and living conditions in the Castle improved. Simon van der Stel even took him on his expedition to the interior in 1685.

It seemed that Olof had formed a firm friendship with Dain Mangale and Dain Manjampa. He spoke their language and shared their enthusiasm for *sirih*. Even during serious discussions they would lapse into Malay to crack a joke or exchange some witticism. They were friendly by nature and exile had eroded their vigilance, mellowed their initial hostility.

Privately, Olof confessed to me that he was getting information from them that would be useful in future. The princes knew the power structures of the Indonesian islands; they knew who had influence to sway opinion in favour of the Dutch, whose struggle to gain trading monopolies in the East continued. It was possible to gather all kinds of detail about territory and personalities during those friendly sessions of *pinang* and politics.

The dignity and good humour with which the princes suffered their exile and confinement was an inspiration to me. Patiently they countered each rejected appeal with another request to a different authority. Tirelessly, they petitioned every visiting dignitary in the hope of building support for their cause. I counted myself lucky that my husband was at least accessible and that I was able to live in my own country, albeit in reduced circumstances.

I became hopeful that things might change for us when Dain Mangale was finally repatriated in 1689. The Governor had somehow become convinced that such an important prince should have a high-ranking escort and sent Captain de Chavonnes with him on the *Nederland* to Batavia.

I suspected Olof had something to do with this, but when I questioned him he became vague. That was just the beginning of his secretive behaviour.

Olof had sent his own appeal to the Lords XVII, but it was not until April 1690 that a reply was sent. It arrived in September on the same ship, the *Zwarte Leeuw*, that brought my first real payment from the Botanical Gardens in Amsterdam. The news of Olof's release, however, quite overshadowed this personal achievement.

Olof had arrived triumphantly at Aaltje's doorstep that afternoon, waving the letter in the air like a flag.

'I'm free!' he shouted, 'listen to this! The Lords XVII think I have been punished enough! I can stay at the Cape as a Free Burgher or go to Ceylon or Batavia with my rank reinstated!'

It did not occur to me for a moment that he would choose the latter. He loved this country as much as I did. In all our conversations about the future, the possibility of moving anywhere, even to Sweden, had never arisen. I hugged him in the full confidence that our life would soon be normal again.

I insisted on helping Olof to move his personal belongings from his quarters in the Castle to Aaltje's house where
he would stay until we found a place of our own.

'You sort out your clothes and weapons to take and I'll
deal with the stuff on the desk,' I said.

His reaction surprised me: he moved quickly to the desk
as though there was a snake inside. I managed to catch a
glimpse of a page in fine feminine calligraphy lying on top
of a pile of letters.

'No, I'll do the desk, you do the clothes.'

'What are you hiding. Olof? You know I have never read
your diary. I am perfectly capable of packing your papers
without snooping.'

I pretended to have seen nothing, but my curiosity had
been aroused and a small seed of doubt was planted in my
brain. When Olof announced that he was taking the option
of exile in Ceylon, it grew into a weed of suspicion.

'Why Ceylon? Why exile? I don't want to move. I love it here;
this is where my family is. I can't leave my mother all alone!'

'I'm going alone, Annie.' His voice was distant, his
expression uncomfortable.

I was speechless with disbelief. The weed of suspicion
became a wild flaming bush of distrust and anger. He saw
my astonished fury and tried to calm me.

'I have to. There is work to be done. It would not be wise
to take a family.'

'Work, my foot, it's a woman. It's Christina Hoogeboom.
Don't think I didn't see that letter! To think of all I suffered
on your behalf and now, when everything can be normal
again, you betray me in this way!'

He tried to embrace me, but I pulled away violently:
'Don't touch me! Traitor!'

'I am not a traitor. I am not going back to be with
Christina Hoogeboom. There is work to do and the less you
know about it the better.'

'Secrets! There is only one secret, and that you have not
kept very well!'

My ranting was annoying him. His eyes turned icy blue and he looked dangerous. He lifted his hand to strike me but controlled himself with great effort.

'I can see you are determined to believe your imagination. Have I ever given you any cause to doubt my fidelity? Better men have failed in this respect, but I have in all these past difficult years never given thought to anyone, but you. Is this how you reward me? By jumping to base conclusions, by accusing me of the stuff of which vulgar gossip is made?'

His speech calmed me somewhat, but I persisted.

'Then explain to me the real reason. I can keep a secret. If I have to face down a whole new wave of gossip and rumour after you're gone, I have to know the real reason. With doubt in my own mind, I would not have the strength.'

And this was how I knew Olof really loved me. He told me about the plan to capture the Hadji Shaykh Yusuf of Macassar. This man was a strong leader in the armed opposition to the Dutch monopoly in Bantam. Olof had learnt much about the Shaykh from Dain Mangale and would be part of covert operations to bring this enemy of the Company to justice.

'This is the most difficult choice I have ever had to make. To leave my loved ones behind for the sake of another mission in service of the Company. But I have been asked to do this by St Martin himself. If this is successful, my honour will be restored and I will be in a position to demand the ultimate promotion from the Company. How would you like to be wife of the Captain of the Cape Garrison?'

And this is how Olof knew I loved him. I told him that the Christina Hoogeboom story was a good cover and that I would be prepared to act a little longer. This time I would play the abandoned woman, Dido and Ariadne in turn. I would encourage the rumour by my dejected behaviour here and sad letters abroad as long as he swore to me that all he would ever do with Christina Hoogeboom was to take tea with her!

Relief flooded his face as he put his hand on his heart.

'I swear, my dearest. I will return with the spoils of war as soon as possible!'

Although the role of the forsaken woman appealed to my romantic soul, it was clear to all that Olof planned to return.

Before he left, he bought the property on the Heerengracht next to the Cruse property on the corner of Heerengracht and Heerenstraat. Of all the streets in Cape Town, the Heerengracht afforded the most beautiful vista of the meadows and pond, the Castle and the Bay. One had a splendid view of the Devil and Table Mountains, and on a clear day one could see all the way to the other side of False Bay.

For years, first from my back garden on the opposite side of the block and then from Aaltje's house next door, I had watched the modest house on this desirable piece of land fall into disrepair. Olof delayed his departure for Ceylon in order to supervise the renovation of the house and reorganisation of the garden. The Governor, relieved by the decision of the Lords XVII to reinstate Olof, assumed his former friendliness towards us and assisted us in any way he could to convert the dwelling into an elegant gabled townhouse with high ceilings, large windows, ample rooms and an attic.

Simon van der Stel made available to us, at a price, of course, some of the precious building materials left over from the building of Constantia: rafters and floor planks of imported seasoned wood. He allowed us to use the slaves who plastered his mansion to fashion for us a particularly fine little 'Italian' gable over the heavy wooden front door.

Two sets of steps met at the top of a wide stoep in front of the house. Olof joked that he would be back before the vines had time to cover the pergola.

We built new stables and a cowshed at the back of the property since we owned that part of the block that became known as Bergh se Gang, an alleyway with an entry from Olifantstraat. We also built some comparatively luxurious quarters for our slaves.

I managed to rent the studio originally used by Heinrich and Marie. It had fallen into disuse after their departure and needed fixing up, but the light was excellent and gave me a view of my own back garden. Olof did not talk about leaving until the house was completely comfortable and the studio ready.

The time for his departure arrived shortly after Christmas in 1691.

That last morning, as we watched the sun rise over Table Bay, the summer warm and golden around us, I wondered if I would ever see him again. Would the Indian Ocean swallow him as it did my father? I did not voice my fears, but channelled them into kisses and caresses and sharing with him the news that between us was a living unborn bond, a small being that would bear witness to our love. We decided that if it were a boy, he would be called Olof, and if a girl, she would be Johanna.

The children and I went down to the quay with Olof and lingered until the last moment to wave and watch while he boarded his ship. Then we went home, collected our kites, scrambled up the tail of the Lion Mountain and flew them for hours, extending our farewell until the small fleet bound for Ceylon was out of sight.

Thus my single life began again. It would be four years before we resumed life as a normal family.

CHAPTER TEN

Grass widow

MY MOTHER MOVED IN with us shortly after Olof's departure. She left my half brother Gerrit in charge of the house she built when she was manumitted. That simple dwelling in the garden against the Lion's Tail will always have a special place in my memories of childhood. That was a time of treasured closeness when I grew to admire my mother's determination, share her ambition, emulate her kindness and imitate her sense of humour. Her marriage to Arnoldus Basson had put a temporary distance between us, but now that she was a widow, the old ease of being together returned.

Once again her absentminded humming enhanced the feeling of well-being in the house. At cooking or at sewing, she sang the songs from her childhood. Like a river running over rapids, Bengali folksongs poured forth, rising and falling through microtones never heard in the Western world. This was the voice that sang me to sleep; these were the complex sounds that nurtured my original love for music.

How plain the diatonic compositions of Europe seemed compared to these highly ornamented songs. It could be likened to the difference between Eastern and Western food, the first infinitely variable in its distinctive blend of spices and textures, the other bland and uncomplicated in its components and preparation. As with the music, the food of my childhood came back and soon my children developed a pleasing enthusiasm for *beryanis* and *samosas*.

Mai Angela was in her early fifties, as fit and good-humoured as she had always been. She could still tell a ghost story that would make your hair stand on end. The children could not get enough of this entertainment. Some nights the stories were so scary that I had to have both Petrus and Polla in bed with me! In her lively style of story telling, the narrative was punctuated with questions to the audience. This allowed her eager listeners to determine the details, the development and, sometimes, even the outcome of the story.

This style of narration meant that the same basic story was fresh and different no matter how often it was told. My mother conjured up dramatic moments by bending her voice this way and that, crouching or lurching, her hands extended. As she turned wild eyes to the window shouting, 'There he is!' or looked straight at a corner of the room, saying enigmatically 'I feel the presence of the Banshee', her audience would freeze in their seats, not daring to look round.

As word of the nightly story telling spread, our *voorhuis* filled with visitors. Entertainment, it seemed, persuaded many of my former critics to abandon their hostility. Jan de Grevenbroeck jokingly called my house the *odeum* as though it were a theatre or a place for public entertainment. He frequently graced us with his presence and was collecting material for his essay in Latin on the oral tradition of story-telling. Mai Angela, he said, was a classic example of how stories multiplied and survived in non-literate cultures. A special affection arose between my mother and my friend and they spent hours talking about her past.

'Her life is a book in itself,' he told me. 'It is fascinating to me to talk to someone who has adapted so successfully to so many situations in one lifetime. First a child in Bengal, then slave to a Portuguese master, a housemaid in Holland, then slave to the first Commander, then a Free Black supporting herself, then wife to a Dutchman and now a widow, still supporting herself, always busy.

'It is so incredible to talk to someone who has been here since the very beginning of the Colony, who can point out where the first Fort was, the first mill and kiln. Someone who knew all the personalities, someone who survived all the hardship and still comes out smiling. I count myself very fortunate to be her friend.'

My mother had also helped Jan a great deal in his many conversations with the Hottentot, convincing them of his good intentions in compiling a dictionary of the Hottentot language.

'You are very lucky to have such a mother, Annie,' he said. His delicate features were all brightness, his intense eyes dark with admiration.

'I owe her much, I know. But don't think she has come through this without the scars of suffering. Have you noticed the white patches on her hands? They say that is what anguish does to the skin. She has those patches all over her body. Nobody sees it because she is so well covered. And she is lucky not to have them all over her face. She puts it down to many pregnancies, but I know it is because she turned her hardships inward on herself.'

At close quarters I noticed some changes in her. For instance, she had reverted to sitting on the floor whenever possible. When asked about this she defended herself in an off-hand manner.

'Ag, chairs? Who wants to sit on chairs? God gave us the ground to sit on. If He had meant us to be so high above the ground, He would have shaped us in a very different way. Look at all the European women my age, stiff in the knees, unable to walk properly from sitting in chairs so much. No, give me the ground any day!'

I noticed another change, subtle, but disturbing: the scarf she had abandoned for a bonnet during her years as a proper Dutch wife had reappeared and she would retreat at regular intervals during the day. I noticed that she would slip away on Thursday nights, accompanied by my slave, Helena of Macassar, who had persistently refused to adopt the Christian faith. It was rumoured that there was a *hafez* who held secret meetings in town to recite the Koran.

On Sundays my mother would volunteer enthusiastically to stay with the younger children while Christina and I went off to church. It seemed as though she relished having an excuse not to attend services herself.

One morning, before sunrise, I heard her reciting an incantation and realised that she was praying. It was not Dutch or Latin; no, it was unmistakably Arabic. I distinctly heard '*Allah Akhbar*'. My mother was performing Muslim devotions in my house! I tried to confront her gently; I was hoping not to have an argument.

'I heard you pray this morning, Mai. It was not a psalm or a hymn I heard.'

She gave me a defensive look: 'No, Annie, it was a prayer to Allah. I thought everyone in the house was still asleep.'

'Old habits die hard, don't they? For years you have sat in church every Sunday confessing your belief in the Christian God! What is happening to you?'

Her face took on a determined look:

'Now, you listen to me, Annie. I am fifty-four, though it feels as if I have lived many lives. The Christian religion was forced upon me along with slavery, first as a Catholic, then as a Protestant. Every time it was like learning a new dance to please my masters. It was practical to be a Christian, but it never felt normal.

'While Arnoldus was alive and I was raising his children, it was necessary for me to profess his faith. Now I am alone, all my children grown up, now I am at last free to return to the religion that comes most naturally to me. That religion is the religion of Islam, the ways of prayer and devotion I learnt as a child.'

'But Mother, there are my children to consider. Olof and I mean to raise them as Lutherans even though they have been baptised for convenience in the Dutch Reformed Church.'

'Well, exactly. You have done the practical thing too.'

'Only in a small way. There is a huge difference between what you are now professing and the Christian faith. You know as well as I do that Christianity and Islam are traditional enemies. I hope I can count on you not to confuse the children with this newly-found Muslim religion of yours.'

She was rarely angry, but now her dark eyes widened and flashed.

'My newly-found Muslim religion? It has been there all along, Annie, and it did not confuse you, did it? You and my other children are living proof that I can raise children in the Christian faith in loyalty and obedience to the wishes of their fathers. I will do the same for your children. But now that I am free from the yoke of submission to a husband, personally I will follow my own faith.'

I had no choice, but to accept that. She had sacrificed so much, why should she not follow her heart now? She had every right to her personal choices and I had to make room for her. The conversation had brought a new understanding between us. When she disappeared sometimes, without explanation, I knew it was to attend some gathering of her fellows in faith whose religious practices were tolerated, but not officially permitted.

At Ramadan I explained her fasting to the children and saved dates especially for her *Ta'jil* tea, the meal that breaks the fast during that month. In some of the protracted discussions we had, especially in those last introspective months before Johanna was born, she explained to me how her faith was providing her with spiritual comfort in a way the Reformed religion had never done.

'The Dutch religion is one of straight lines, dividing black and white, logical and rational; our religion comes in curves of comfort with the solace Protestants only find in dreams. I often wonder if poor Eva would have lost her balance the way she did if she had had a faith like mine to rely on, something deep inside that holds you together no matter how things change on the outside.'

'It is straight lines and rational thinking that has changed this Cape of Storms into the Cape of Good Hope, Mai. But I know what you mean; that is why I take my music so seriously. It puts me on another plane altogether; away from words and confused meaning.'

'I wish only that you could hear a sitar, Annie. You would be transported.'

But that was never to happen; and I had to be content with my recorders and the viols of others.

Viol music was the attraction in an invitation that came from Governor van der Stel a year after Olof left for Ceylon. The quality of music at the Cape varied with the accomplishments of the players who came and went. There was a small band of slaves who played dinner and dance music, and there were amateurs like me who persisted on our various instruments, met regularly to play and taught our children what we knew.

But on rare occasions a really excellent musician would call on his way to the East and play the latest music from Europe, delighting us and recharging our enthusiasm. Such was the case when Egbertus Wieland, a surgeon from Utrecht, put into port.

At that time Jan de Grevenbroeck was teaching Christina Latin. Twice a week he would come to our house for breakfast and tutor her for an hour before she went to school. This was my opportunity to formalise my knowledge of the language that I could read but not write very well.

Without asking permission, I sat in on the classes, listened to the explanations and did the exercises. After a while Jan started calling me the 'invisible pupil'. He would question Christina and then ask the 'invisible pupil' to conjugate or translate. It was a game we all enjoyed and it gave me the option to disappear if I wished.

I never did. Not surprisingly, Jan was an excellent teacher: he came from a long line of Latin teachers from Nijmegen. He was also becoming my best friend.

One morning he arrived at the door for a Latin lesson in the company of a stunningly handsome young man carrying a large viol case.

'Annie, I want you to meet Doctor Egbertus Wieland

from Utrecht. This morning there will be no Latin. Give us some breakfast before you listen to the most divine music you have ever heard.' There was passion in his voice and it occurred to me that my friend could possibly be in love.

I scrutinised Doctor Wieland's person: the dark eyes, eyebrows, nose and chin in perfect proportion, the mouth strong and sensual. He wore an ample curled wig, his clothes more frilled and beribboned than our backwater was used to. It struck me how fashion had changed even in the few years since the Baron van Rheede had visited.

'Utrecht? I have a friend who lived in Utrecht, Francina van Rheede? Did you know her? She has since moved to Ceylon where my husband is at the moment.'

He kissed my hand, his smile ambiguous.

'I knew her well, but I knew her cousin Maurits de la Baie even better.'

'They have recently married, did you know? My husband went to their wedding in September. He says they look very happy. Where did you study music?'

'In France of all places,' answered Jan, 'at the court of the Sun King! Show them your viol, Egbertus. It has seven strings, a modification made by the teacher of Marin Marais, the man who taught him. It produces the most amazing sound, especially with the different kinds of tuning.'

'Patience, Jan. Let's have some breakfast. Then all will be revealed,' said the Doctor.

We talked about Francina and Maurits and the dear departed Baron. Doctor Wieland told us about Utrecht and Paris and, after they had had their fill of ham and ale, he opened the case and began to tune the viol. It was indeed strange to see a viol with seven strings and the tuning sounded different from anything I had heard before. Apparently this was also a specialty of Master Marais.

'I will play the most difficult first,' he said, '*La Reveuse*, which the maestro wrote for a most particular lover.'

The rich tones of the instrument seemed to massage the seductive melody. The physical effect on me was instantaneous: it produced in me an almost unbearable longing. First I thought only of Olof, but as the music progressed I sensed with alarm that my emotional focus was shifting.

I watched the long fingers on the strings, the elegant hand bowing, the intense face willing the music to express deliberate and explicit passion. Was I confusing the intent of the composer with that of the performer? The interpretation of beauty serves to complement the needs of the interpreter. This was so true for me that day.

There was a long silence after the music stopped. We were all staring at the floor.

'Beautiful,' I said. 'We seldom hear anything so exquisite!'

He played more and stayed after Jan reluctantly went to attend to the secretarial needs of the Governor who was in town, for a change, instead of at Constantia. After some particularly fine variations on La Folia, Christina and I were persuaded to bring out the recorders and play our modest duets. Doctor Wieland gave us genuine applause.

'You are a pleasure to listen to. I will propose to the Governor that you be invited to Constantia next week. It promises to be a jolly party. His Excellency has some important visitors to entertain and wishes me to fill his new house with the strains of my viol. We could practise together and vary the programme a little.'

I knew he was creating a pretext and I should have refused the proposition right away, but La Reveuse had weakened me and I allowed myself to be flattered.

'If you really think two such middling players will not depreciate your talent. Christina has not seen Constantia.'

My heart was racing when I said good-bye to him. I sent Christina off to school with the other children and ran to my bedroom to calm myself. What was happening? Here I was, mother of five children, a married woman with never a thought of infidelity. To be sure, I was in my early thirties, attractive and often complimented by men, but I had always imagined myself immune to the afflictions of romantic whims.

I was skilled at diverting flirtation into friendship. I now knew that none of those flirtations were ever tempting enough. The thought of those long hands caressing my body, his mouth kissing mine, filled me with longing. I stopped myself. This temptation could lead me into uncharted waters. I resolved to control myself, for my own sake as well as that of my children.

I tried to refuse the invitation to go to Constantia by using Johanna as an excuse. The Governor surprised me by insisting personally that I attend:

'It is only for a few days, Mistress Annie. Your mother tells me that the little one is weaned. Leave her with her grandmother. You know she will be well taken care of.'

I could not turn him down. Christina and I packed our best clothes as well as our recorders and set off early one morning in convoy with those bound for Constantia.

I had only once been near the site of Simon van der Stel's pride and joy and that was when I went with Olof to the forest called Paradijs. Then all had been wild along the Steenberg. Now there was a decent track leading up an avenue of young oaks to the entrance of the elegant mansion. From far away we could see the gables and four chimneys of the house, vineyards stretching up the slopes of the mountain behind.

We passed the stables and servants' quarters and were greeted at the top of the double stairway by Simon van der Stel himself. He seemed very different from the stern administrator we knew in the Cape. His jovial and informal manner matched his simple coat and jacket. He was not wearing a periwig and his stylishly curled, evenly greying hair made him look quite distinguished.

'Welcome, welcome,' he shouted as we descended the carriages. He addressed everyone by their first names.

'No need for formality. Here at Constantia we are all friends, all equals.'

He was obviously not including in this description the tradesmen hard at work in their little workshops on the lower floor and the large number of slaves going about their duty.

Most of the visitors, including Jan and Egbertus, were housed in the guesthouse to the north of the avenue. Christina and I were considered specially privileged to be offered accommodation in the manor itself. I was relieved since it distanced me from Egbertus whose attentiveness was putting my resolve in jeopardy. His behaviour had not escaped the notice of Jan or the Governor, and Jan had already remarked on it on the way to Constantia.

'The Doctor fancies you, I see. Be careful. I am told he has broken many hearts without remorse.'

'I can look after myself, Jan. But can you? You cannot hide from me that you are totally smitten.'

Regret flashed across his face. 'If the world were different, my dear Annie, and I were a woman, I would gladly suffer a broken heart for a little love from him. But we know the upside down world in which I live; it demands from me super-human control and constant discretion.'

'It demands no less from a grass widow such as I. Let's not be rivals, my dear Jan. This charming man is here today and gone tomorrow. It would be much more sensible to forget this nonsense about infatuation and concentrate on the lovely music he plays.'

The frankness of this little interchange seemed to move our friendship to a new level of intimacy. There was no such forthrightness, however, when the Governor explained to me why he had given a room to Christina and myself next to his own bedroom:

'I have an obligation to my friend Olof to protect you from unwanted attention as much as I can. Just in case those young men in the guesthouse forget their manners and harass you. Here I can keep a fatherly eye on you.'

What was it in his manner that prevented me from entirely believing him? Was it that his eyes on me were flattering rather than fatherly or was it just that I was in a vulnerable frame of mind, apt to interpret any male attention as sexual? From a distance of thirty-four years it looks extremely silly, a temporary madness, but then it was very real and caused me much anxiety. Outwardly I tried to behave with dignity and charm but my thoughts and feelings were in turmoil and I carried on in a state of perpetual lightheadedness.

We were taken on a tour of the estate, inspecting the out buildings and wine making on foot. Then we were conveyed on carts to view the vineyards. On the second day we were up at dawn to make an expedition up the mountain beyond the vineyards.

We watched the sun's first light: bronze, then pink, on the white buildings of the manor below us. Beyond we could see False Bay, the mountains of Hottentots Holland faintly distinguishable in the morning mist. Egbertus stood close to me on the right, Christina on the left.

For a foolish moment I wished she were not there, but maternal instinct triumphed and I said pedantically:

'That is the Indian Ocean, Christina. If we climb right to the top of this mountain, we might see the Atlantic. Your Papa has been right to the end of the archipelago where you have a view of both oceans.'

It worked. Jan took over and a general conversation about oceans and the topography of the Peninsula followed. After breakfast on the mountainside we descended, Egbertus constantly at my side to offer a steadying hand.

I told myself this was harmless chivalry and that I should enjoy it. Just once, when we were a little behind the rest of the party, did we stop to look at each other. The conversation that ensued still makes me blush a little. How could I have been so brazen? Or is it loneliness that makes us all vulnerable and therefore reckless?

'When will we embrace?' he asked. 'When can I come to you?'

136

His meaning was clear, my longing obvious, my protest feeble.

'It seems impossible; I am surrounded by servants, children, friends, respectability!'

'But I know you want me.'

'I do. I find you most attractive, but I would have to be out of my mind to give in to this. Don't make it more difficult.'

'All I'm offering you is pleasure, a bunch of grapes, a glass of wine.'

His tone was casual and his manner completely carefree. I was disconcerted.

'Such hedonism is fine for a man like you, a ship passing in the night. I am the one that will have to live with a ruined reputation!' I moved quickly to catch up with the rest of the party.

But the madness inside me persisted. That evening when I was mellow with music, and he daring with wine, we met in the dark just beyond the lights of the porch. We embraced passionately, charged with lust and longing. I would have given myself to him there and then were it not that a clearing of the throat made us aware that we were being observed.

I turned and saw the Governor at the edge of the porch. He stared into the dark, then turned and went back into the house.

Panic poured over me like cold water. 'Enough,' I said, 'no more! This is wrong!'

I kept repeating that phrase to myself in the hope of exorcising the desire that seemed to possess me. I hardly slept that night, but by morning I was determined to pull myself together. I invented Johanna as an excuse to leave before the rest of the party.

'I miss my little baby more than I can say,' I said to the Governor, watching for a sign that I had been recognised the night before. His smile was ironic, but his reply friendly.

'I understand. I will be sorry to see you go. Next time you must bring all your children.'

There was no indication that he suspected my reason for leaving, but Jan was wise to me.

'You're doing the right thing to go, Annie. He may be beautiful and a wonderful musician, but he is not discreet.'

I did not want to know what his remark implied. All I knew was that I had to extricate myself as quickly as possible from a potentially scandalous situation.

I did not see Egbertus again, but the episode taught me a humbling lesson. I was human, vulnerable, made of feminine flesh and blood, not immune to temptation. I resolved to control my desires in future and never let them get out of hand ever again.

My trouble was not over. The Governor had become attentive, paying casual visits when he was in town. His manners were always impeccable and most of his visits concerned the work I was doing for his cousin, Johan Huydecoper. Or he would show me a new herbal that had arrived. There was not a hint that he knew anything about my indiscretion.

The next invitation to Constantia was for Christmas.

'Bring the whole family this time, Annie, even your mother. You can have the guesthouse to yourselves. I am inviting the Phijffers and a few friends from Stellenbosch, but they can be easily accommodated in the manor house.'

It was a most respectable invitation, and we all set off for the estate a week before Christmas. It was Governor van der Stel's wish that we lend a feminine touch to the decorations and menu for the festive season.

Mai Angela was pleased to be included; to her it meant that I had made it up the social ladder. She proudly assumed leadership in the kitchen without displacing the housekeeper, and was flattered to hear that her reputation as a pastry chef had preceded her.

I used the extra days to hunt for specimens to draw and in this the Governor eagerly accompanied me. We scoured the kloofs and woodland for geraniaceae and liliaceae and climbed to the top of Steenberg in search of many varieties of *carduus*. Some of these flowers were given for floral arrangements in the house, but the best ones I kept for life drawings.

I set up a temporary studio in the best-lit room of the guesthouse. Memories of my temporary insanity were dissipated by these practical, work-directed activities. I began to share the Governor's fondness for this place with its balmy air and long views.

The holidays passed in a haze of company and merriment fueled by the best wine in the Cape. We spent New Year's Day on the beach at Simon's Town, grilling lobsters on open coals. Maria and Petrus collected many shells and made their own music on the *tromba* lying about on the beach.

The sun was heady and that evening I feared I had a touch of sunstroke. I was sent to bed early with a sleeping draught and told not to rise until I felt better. I had every expectation, however, that I would be woken in time for our departure the next morning.

Imagine my surprise then when I awoke to find everyone gone and the sun high in the sky. The slave who attended the guesthouse told me that everyone except the Governor, had left. I was about to get dressed when the door opened and the Governor entered. I grabbed the front of my dressing gown in order to cover myself properly.

'Excuse me, Your Excellency. I seem to have overslept and now it seems everyone has gone. Let me make myself respectable and I will be gone also.'

The look in his eyes alarmed me; his words positively frightened me.

'Try as you may, you will never be respectable, Annie de Koning! Why not admit it? The slave mentality is bred in your bones.'

'What is this? I have never heard you speak like this before. Please leave so that I can get dressed.'

'I can help you do that.' His speech was slurred and I realised he had had too much wine for breakfast.

'Please, Sir, you are not yourself. Leave now before you

say anything you will regret later. I am your guest. You are supposed to be my protector. Think of your position.'

I was confident I could dissuade him. Surely, the powers of persuasion I use with children would work on this man who was acting so childishly and out of character.

'A protector has rights, you know, especially when a protégée like you has proven herself to be of loose morals! You gave yourself to that viol player! I saw you; you did it under my nose! Why should I go away? All this time you have been leading me on and now you send me away?'

The nasty tone in his voice reminded me of the time he supported the accusations against Olof. He was advancing.

'Kaatje!' I called for the slave, but he scoffed at this: 'She has been sent about her business.'

'Think about your reputation. These things always come out.'

'No one will know unless you tell them. Admit it, you want me as much as I want you!'

He grabbed me and pushed me towards the bedroom. I struggled, but he was strong. Now I believed the rumours about his violence against his wife, the real reason why Catelina went back to Holland.

'I have no desire for you! Will you violate me against my will?'

That is exactly was what he did, leaving me sobbing on the bed. As soon as I was calm enough, I dressed, went to the stables and took a horse to ride back to town. It seemed to me the stable lad knew I had to get away in a hurry.

The drawings and specimens I had left behind me were delivered to my door two days later with a note from the Governor. 'Forgive me,' it said.

I replied: 'Never!'

I spoke to no one about the incident, not even my mother, though she knew something was wrong by the distracted way in which I arrived back home on horseback. It was, after all, a very private humiliation and I knew the standard response to rape: 'She asked for it.' Why humiliate myself further by blaming the perpetrator just to have him deny it in public? Not even Olof would know about this.

More than ever I longed for his return.

I had to wait more than a year.

On the night of April 1, 1694, the *Voetboog* put into port. As I often did when I could not sleep, I sat on the front porch in the shadows and watched the world go by unobserved. I saw the ship throw anchor and the lighter take passengers to the dock. There was no salute, no shouting; it was all rather mysterious.

As I watched, a large procession filed into the Castle. I kept watching. A cloaked figure appeared after a while and came walking up the track past the town's pond towards our street. The stature was right, the gait unmistakable. My heart leapt. Could it be true? I rose and went to the top of the steps. Olof saw me and put his fingers to his lips. He waited to embrace me until we were inside the house.

'What is this? Why the secrecy?' I asked after many kisses.

'I have delivered my precious cargo!' he said triumphantly. 'I have earned my reward!' He was carrying only a small copper-bound wooden chest.

'Your luggage will be brought tomorrow?' I asked.

His answer hit me like a thunderbolt:

'I am going on to Europe,' he said. 'No one is to know that I'm here.'

He must have seen the deep disappointment on my face for he quickly unlocked the chest and produced some documents. He put them on the table and pulled the candle closer.

'Look,' he said, 'here is the letter of Governor-General van Oudtshoorn to the Lords XVII. Not to Simon van der Stel, you realise, but to the XVII themselves. It tells them about my role in this operation and recommends that I return to the Cape as no less than Captain of the Militia. I have to deliver this myself and bring back the order personally; nothing will be left to the whims or caprices of the Governor.'

He saw my scepticism and produced a letter. It had the seal of the city of Gothenburg.

One other thing compelled Olof to go to Europe: his father had died and the estate had to be settled. He would have to be there himself if he were not to lose most of his inheritance to agents and middlemen.

'Nine more months, dearest, at the most a year and I'll be back forever. The money I bring back will buy us the best properties in this Colony!'

'How many nights do we have?'

'The *Voetboog* will take on water and supplies, that's all. Perhaps two, three? Let's make the best of it.'

It was like having a secret lover. He came around midnight and left before dawn, three nights in a row. Our meetings were thrilling and passionate, but we did not miss the humour in the ridiculous situation that would force a man and wife to behave like illicit paramours.

The morning before he left, he went around the sleeping children and kissed them one by one, leaving them each a copper *stuiver* from Ceylon. And because it was the middle of the month and I irrepressibly fertile, I was pregnant again.

CHAPTER ELEVEN

Tjantings, indigo
and beeswax

IMAGINE OUR SMALL PROTESTANT community suddenly enlarged by forty-nine souls, all professed and publicly Muslim! To the many slaves working in our homes and gardens this was a dream come true.

Overnight their eyes became brighter, their step lighter. Here in their midst was one of their own! A holy man of grand repute who represented the soul of all they had been denied. He was a Sufi who had dedicated his life not only to opposition to their Dutch masters, but was an authority in the teachings and mysticism of Islam, the religion they were forbidden to practice.

And this man was recognised by the Governor, given a monthly stipend and his retinue accommodated according to the rules of his religion: men and women quartered separately, a room for prayer set aside. Suddenly there was hope that the respect afforded the Shaykh would soon extend to the covert Muslim community at large, that a mosque would be built and prayers allowed.

Slaves, including my own Helena, found all sorts of excuses to visit the Castle just to catch a glimpse of the holy man or any of the imams he had brought with him. Although they were mostly confined to the Castle, the exiles were allowed to take the air in the Company Gardens in the late afternoon.

The first procession was a most extraordinary sight. My children, Mai Angela and I watched them as they appeared through the Castle gate: first came the men, headed by the

Shaykh, walking with the stiff gait of an old man;. The Governor, unmistakable by his costume was walking with them.

The women followed in order of importance: the two wives, the two concubines, and the daughters and wives of the sons. Completely covered in flowing black cloaks, they were veiled to the eyes, but they moved with such a sedate fluidity that seemed choreographed to some inner, inaudible music. The children came last, bobbing and skipping about as children do.

As they proceeded up the meadow past the public pond, people began to join them. The soldiers who were accompanying the party chased away as many as they could, but still a small following persisted. As they approached our house to go up the Heerengracht to the Gardens, we moved onto the porch to get a better look. The Governor stopped to greet us in a show of exaggerated joviality.

'Good afternoon, Mistress Bergh, Widow Basson!'

Simon van de Stel never missed the opportunity to play to an audience. Now he placed his one hand on Shaykh Yusuf's shoulder and pointed to me:

'That is the wife of Lieutenant Bergh who came with you on the *Voetboog*,' he said to the Shaykh. The old man stopped and gave me a penetrating look, his white beard severe. For an instant I was worried. Was I friend or foe? But then, to my relief, he smiled a kind, angelic smile and I knew Olof must have treated him well.

'My wives and daughters would like to meet you, Mistress Bergh,' he said in perfect Dutch, 'your husband told them much about you.'

I curtsied, not knowing how else to show respect. I felt a dozen pairs of female eyes curiously staring up at me through almond-shaped slits. Suddenly I was painfully aware of my arms, neck and face. It was almost like being naked. I curtsied again towards the women and saw a collective smile appear in the dozen dark eyes.

'If I have permission from His Excellency, I will come and visit them,' I said, appealing to the Governor.

'Suit your own convenience, Mistress Bergh, but it is best to come between prayer times; the ladies observe their prayers with great devotion. It may be good to bring the Widow Basson with you. You do speak some Malay, don't you, Madam?'

My mother nodded with enthusiasm; she was obviously delighted to be included in the invitation.

The Governor's ingratiating manner vexed me. Ever since that shameful incident at Constantia, he had tried to make amends with small gestures: a flask of wine, a basket of fruit. Now, with the possibility of Olof's return and his almost certain re-instatement, he was going out of his way to be attentive to me in public.

He knew I would not snub him but it was more than apparent to me that he was exploiting my mother's excitement to mollify me.

The next morning we set off for the Castle with Christina and Maria in tow. What we found there was a complete surprise. It was as though the curtains had gone up; the ladies, now with their sombre full covers removed and in their own quarters, were clothed in the most beautiful fabric I had ever seen.

The garments were familiar; our Malaysian slaves wore skirts folded from one piece of cloth with draped shirts and head scarves, but they were given the cheapest fabric. The women of Shaykh Yusuf's retinue wore *batik* fabrics of the most intricate geometric patterns in browns, indigo and white.

After the formalities of introductions and establishing which children belonged to which wife, I ventured to ask about the cloth.

'We make this ourselves,' said the senior wife, Carecontoe, her broad face filled with pride.

'Not the weaving,' explained the other wife, Carepane, when she saw my puzzled look. 'It is the patterns on the cloth that we make. If you'd like it we can show you.'

I looked at the elaborate designs and thrilled at the thought of a new foray into the world of decorative art.

'When can we begin?'

'Soon,' she said, cautiously.

It was understood from the beginning that the exiles from Macassar would be moved from the Castle as soon as a suitable place could be found for them.

It was not difficult to imagine that popular support for the Shaykh amongst the slaves could pose a threat to the authority of the Governor. He insisted on housing the exiles at a distance from any of the established communities. There was to be no easy access to these purveyors of Islam.

It took them three months to find such a place. The Company rented the farm Zandvliet from our minister, Dominee Kalden, who was using it mainly to graze sheep. It was in a dismal location at the mouth of the Eersterivier, between the sand flats and the dunes of False Bay.

It was said of this place that the wind could blow a grown man over those dunes and into the sea or bury a sheep in sand in two hours. There were few trees to shelter the very basic *opstal* on the property. A humble dwelling place indeed for such refined people, used to the palaces of Sulawesi and Bantam.

The ladies disregarded the ill reports of their future abode; all they cared about was having enough space to set up the dye baths for their *batik* and to process their own indigo dye. Although they had brought with them many cakes of concentrated indigo and jars of ground up soga bark preserved in cow dung, they were happy to see some indigo growing in the Gardens.

Carecontoe was the only one who actually knew when to harvest and ferment the indigo leaves just after blooming and how to crystallise the juice in stages to produce a strong dark blue dye. She had learnt about indigo as a child in Sulawesi.

'The others never had enough time in one place to learn about indigo,' she said. 'My husband moved us with him wherever the struggle led him, you know. At last we will have time to rest,' she said, optimistically.

I did not want to disillusion her, but I had a pretty good idea that she would never raise a crop of indigo leaves in that godforsaken, windswept place to which she was to be removed. I tried, instead to get together all the local supplies needed for *batik* making. I bought all the available plain cotton in the Warehouse, bribing the merchant's assistant to exceed my quota, and did the rounds of everyone who had beehives to buy up their wax.

Getting more *tjantings* – the little copper vessels from which the wax was poured – was a little more difficult. Red copper was in short supply and even those who had some were loathe to part with it. Carepane, the younger wife, and Seity Labibah, the jolly daughter, were the *tjanting* experts and both insisted on red copper being used for the wax reservoir and spout of the *tjanting*.

'Red copper retains the heat of the wax best. I once tried using a yellow copper *tjanting*, but the wax cooled down so quickly, I could hardly finish the outline of a *lar*.' said Labibah, as though I knew all about the tools, process, names of the designs and the dyes.

The more I learnt, the more impatient I became to actually start doing *batik*. My brother, Willem, finally found red copper in Stellenbosch. He did not even have to buy it; one of the Free Black burghers of Stellenbosch told him to take as much as he needed when he heard it was to be used in the manufacture of special tools for the wives of the Shaykh.

Now I had to persuade the jeweller at the Castle that his skill, rather than the blacksmith's, was needed to make the sophisticated little tools. Carepane was fussy about the exact size and angle of the spout and had the jeweller do the first prototype three times until it was perfect. Were it not for the fact that this man was himself a covert Muslim, she would have had to be satisfied with his first attempt.

The rains held off that winter, and I was able to have my first session of instruction soon after the exiles were moved to Zandvliet, which was fast becoming known as Macassar. I informed the Governor of my plan and to my surprise he was most amenable though he warned me that I should go by oxcart instead of a carriage since the track to the farm was rough and rarely traveled. I decided to find accommodation at the outpost at De Cuylen and go to the farm on horseback every day, confident that the exercise would be good for me during the early months of pregnancy.

Now I learnt all about the process: starting with a virgin white cloth, the basic design was sketched out in pencil. This made sense, but it took some time to get used to the concept that the part of the design that was to remain white had to be covered in wax. After a while it dawned on me that this wax resist process required reverse thinking.

In order to become skilful with the *tjanting*, I worked with the younger girls. We were given the task of outlining many millions of little 'fish scales' that formed the background of the *gringsing* design, consisting of tiny circles each with a dot inside.

The most difficult thing was to control the flow of the hot beeswax as it emerged from the tiny spout at the end of the red copper reservoir.

'Keep a rag handy to catch the drips,' warned Caresangie, the gentle, thoughtful daughter. 'Once you leave a blob on the cloth, it can never be erased. It's like a sin that can never be hidden, always there for the whole world to see.'

When she saw my concerned look, she added reassuringly, 'Don't let it worry you, we've all blobbed at one time or another. I have seen the most expert *batiksters* leave a blob or two on purpose just to show that only Allah is perfect!'

Having passed the *gringsing* test and producing a handsome scarf called a *slendang*, in white and the rich brown of the soga dye, I was set to work on a *kemben*, the name for the women's upper garment. For this we used a pattern of flowing vegetation around the very distinctive motif of the *lar* or stylised wing of the garuda bird. It was clear that my hand was practiced at drawing and the ladies allowed me to complete this cloth on my own.

The process was more complex in that I was now working in brown and blue and had to decide exactly which parts of the design should remain brown and cover those in wax before putting the cloth in the indigo dye bath. The expert eyes of Carecontoe and Carepane could see that this cloth was made by an amateur, but they praised me enough for me to attempt a *tapih*, the wraparound skirt that would complete the outfit for a Christian woman like me who had no need for a prayer scarf.

The *tapih* was to be in the diagonal design known as *parang rusak* or interlocking 'knives of the lost war'. How ironic that this design should remind the women of the defeat of the old holy warrior to whose fate all their lives were permanently tied!

Sometimes, taking a break from the concentrated but repetitive work demanded by the design, I would watch the concubines Muminah and Naimah making *katjus* for the men. These were kerchiefs used as prayer mats usually covered in verses from the Koran.

Muminah and Naimah used sayings from the writings of Shaykh Yusuf himself. The Flowing Blessings was Muminah's favourite, whilst Naimah chose The Flowing Fragrance as her text.

It took me a while to get used to the idea of the open practice of polygamy, but since all the women seemed to accept it as the way things were ordered I decided not to question or discuss it. It was actually quite touching to see how the wives treated the young concubines as their daughters, saving them special treats, making sure of their comfort.

Once when I commented on this in my broken Malay, Carecontoe replied without hesitation:

'It comes as a relief to us older women when a husband takes a concubine. It gives us the opportunity to concentrate less on lust and pay proper attention to our homes and children. We don't have to go on bearing all the children of one man.'

She was looking at my belly and I suspect she felt sorry for me.

The condition of the 'rough and rarely travelled road' to Macassar soon changed and before long there was a remarkable improvement in the living quarters of the exiles. Volunteer workers appeared on Sundays, a day off for many slaves, to hammer and saw, build and cultivate. Donations from Free Blacks and the Malaysian islands poured in. No task seemed too great or impossible to enhance the comfort of the holy man and his companions.

I saw mature trees being transported on ox wagons in the middle of winter to be transplanted in the poor sandy soil of Zandvliet in the belief that they would flourish in the beatific presence. Reports of miracles performed by Shaykh Yusuf convinced his followers that he was not only a Sufi but also a saint.

The most prevalent account was of the incident on the journey to the Cape when, off the coast of Terra Natal, there was no fresh water left on the *Voetboog*. The holy man apparently had saved all from dying of thirst by putting his blessed toe in bucket upon bucket of sea water, turning it instantly fresh and potable. Olof told me later that he had no knowledge of such a miracle.

Since faith is the only quality required to confirm miracles and create an aura of saintliness around a man, it was easy to see how such a story could increase the popularity of the exiled Sufi. The passion that drove a growing number of people to flock to Macassar, meanwhile, was that of an oppressed people, some actually in bondage, all spiritually deprived, forbidden to practise their own religion.

It was not surprising that Macassar became the first place the Company soldiers looked for a runaway slave. To such as these the place was a haven of freedom, a place for spiritual comfort to ease the hardships of their lot. All were motivated by a new expectation that their Faith could be brought out of the dingy corners of suppression, be painted and polished and practised publicly with pride and dignity.

But Shaykh Yusuf was a war-weary old man and none of the exiled imams in his company ever expressed a desire to

stay to organise and lead the followers in a political move-
ment that would demand religious rights for the followers
of Islam. On the contrary, every exile believed that the
appeal for repatriation of the Shaykh by the king of Goa
himself would soon be granted.

This was very clear when I suggested in the spring of that
year that the indigo in the Gardens should be harvested
after blooming and the leaves processed into dye.

'Making indigo dye is a long process,' said Carepane.
'You need to build the tanks in which to ferment and crystallise the leaves. It takes weeks before you have even a
small amount of dye crystals. Why go to all that trouble
when we are not going to be here for very long? We have
enough dye available for a few more lengths of fabric.'

I did not want to discourage her by insisting, but I knew
how long appeals could take. I knew how long poor Dain
Mangale waited, how long I myself had been waiting. And,
indeed, they did have another ten years to wait until they
were repatriated, five years after the Shaykh himself had
passed away.

We did try to produce some indigo and madder to replace
their imported dyes but the amount of indigo was inadequate
and the tone of madder feeble compared to the rich brown of
the soga. By that time my husband had returned from Europe
and my contact with the people of Macassar had become
marginal. But my Malaysian costume I treasured and wore on
special occasions when fancy dress was required.

Macassar is still a place for pilgrimages where the disappointed followers of Shaykh Yusuf gather at his *kramat*,
praying for miracles and hoping that one day their communities will be adorned by mosques and madrassas where the
religion of Islam can flourish freely.

Chapter Twelve

The burden of bliss

OLOF'S RETURN WAS OVERWHELMING, to say the least. His large presence filled the house and the children and I, adoring him for so long in the abstract, scurried around, eager to show and tell him everything that had become important to us during his absence. The older children were soon quarrelling, each demanding Olof's attention; it became apparent that the revival of our family life would have to be organised.

Maria and Petrus, now thirteen and eleven, were early risers, and Olof bought them each a horse so that they could go riding with him in the morning. They were both healthy outdoor types and jumped at the opportunity to have their father all to themselves. This was a good plan, but I was also expected to be up and dressed to see them off.

Gone were the days of sleeping an extra two hours after little Dorie's five o' clock feed. Not wanting to appear lazy, I pretended it did not matter that the discipline and routine of the barracks were gradually being imposed on the household I had managed for eight years according to my own rhythms and inclinations.

Appolonia, now nine, hardly knowing her father, accepted the fact that she was too young to go riding early in the morning, but hung around him at every available opportunity, staring at him in amazement when she thought he was not looking. She became generally clumsy in his presence; she was so shy that she rubbed her eyes and stammered when she spoke to him. Olof kept his distance, giving her more time to get used to him.

Christina was a fully grown young woman, looking much like I did when Olof first met me. She spent every morning of the week as assistant to Pieter Davenraad, the town's most esteemed private tutor. She taught Latin at a primary level while Meester Davenraad concentrated on the more advanced pupils, all preparing to continue their education in Holland.

Employment gave Christina an air of independence and confidence that Olof found unsettling. It seemed as though he was uncertain whether praise would be considered flirting or flattery that would feed her vanity. Initially he almost ignored her in conversation, whilst frequently giving her gifts: a ring, a necklace a new dress or shoes.

Christina was a little taken aback, but not discouraged; she had a sharp intellect and a clever way with people. With Jan de Grevenbroeck's help, she found a copy of the accounts of Olof's two expeditions to Namaqualand, read the boring text and began to quiz him at the dinner table about the geography and the people of the hinterland.

She began to ask him endless questions, all with the air of a school marm, sure of a response.

'What is the best time of day for taking readings of latitude and longitude, Father? How was the surveyors' equipment transported? How did they communicate with the Amaquas? How long does it take to disasssemble and reassemble an ox wagon? Are there really so many elephants along the Olifantsrivier? Which were the most difficult mountains to cross in your opinion, Father?'

Christina always called Olof 'Father' instead of 'Pappa' as the other children did.

And it worked. Soon they were discussing the geography of Ceylon and poring over maps after dinner until Olof was convinced that his eldest daughter valued her active brain much more than her nubile body.

The largest problems of adjustment lay with me. I had enjoyed the status of a married woman all these years, but had the freedom of a single woman to organise my life according to my own taste and nature. It was lovely, to be sure, to have my husband in bed again; we always did enjoy each other's bodies. But after the initial flurry of love making had satisfied my starved appetite, I began to feel the insistent sexual demands to be an imposition.

Like Christina, the development of my intellectual and artistic personality had taken precedence over attention to my body in the years Olof had been away. Now, I had to concentrate on the duties of a wife: make love on demand, entertain on demand, and change my own plans on demand.

I did not want to appear ungrateful. The whole world regarded me as the luckiest woman in town: her husband returned with his inheritance in his pocket and his rank raised to the highest in the Garrison. Everyone knew he now received the third highest pay in the whole Colony.

How could the wife of the Honorable Captain Olof Bergh have anything to complain about? Ambitious Annie de Koning was poised to become one of the most prominent women in the Cape.

It puzzled Olof more than anyone else; he could not understand why I was not content to sit with the ladies, drink tea, and discuss fashions and gossip about the servants. This was what society women did. It was cultivated boredom, and I said so.

'I don't know what's happened to you, Annie,' he complained. 'You used to be so gregarious, so gracious in company when we were first married. Now I see you straining to get away from the women in order to talk to some man or other about plants or paints.'

'Plants and paints were my lifeline when you were away, Olof. How was I to survive otherwise? Those same women you now expect me to befriend shunned me when you were disgraced and our future was uncertain. Do you realise how difficult it is to sit in their inane company and forget about the things they said about me, knowing the venom is just below the surface?

'You may find it easy to pretend that all your former enemies are now your friends, but I will content myself with plants and paints a little longer. At least they have no malice in them.'

Olof seemed to have no quarrel with my musical activities and did not resent the time I spent practising or playing. Christina, Maria, Petrus and I made a fine quartet that produced some very pleasant sounds. Polla played simple recorder parts or percussion. We were happy to be able to include Olof, who had come back with a theobor. It pleased him that we were a musical family, and he often said that he wished there were a painter who could paint us at our music-making.

One day a parcel with music arrived from Holland. The sender's name was clearly marked on the outside. It was from Egbertus Wieland. Olof must have noticed my surprise and that little look on Christina's face.

'Who is Egbertus Wieland?' he asked.

'A doctor cum viol player who passed through some time ago. We all played together one weekend at Constantia.'

I was hoping this simple explanation would suffice, but Olof insisted on seeing what was in the parcel. I opened it. There was a letter, addressed to me, and a book of recorder music by Jacob van Eyck.

'Oh, look, Christina,' I exclaimed. 'The second volume from *Der Fluyten Lust-hof*! Remember, Doctor Wieland told us about this composer from Utrecht? The blind carilloneur?'

My nervous prattle, intended to divert, had the opposite effect on my husband.

'What does the letter say?' he asked abruptly.

I did not care for his tone of voice. It was cold and suspicious. I opened the letter with a pounding heart. I could not refuse to read the letter. Christina did not help, either. She exuded an excited curiosity as she stood there to hear its contents. The name 'Egbertus Wieland' seemed to trigger an animated reaction in her and her father did not miss the wicked twinkle in her eye.

I remembered how Egbertus's confident womanising had intrigued Christina, how his flattery mesmerised her along with everyone else, how her adolescent eyes watched me for any sign of indiscretion. I scanned the letter quickly, editing out the parts meant for my eyes only:

'*I am back in Utrecht,*' I read aloud, '*and have found this second hand copy of a volume much enjoyed by family and friends for many years. You may remember my mention of him? My mother knew him personally when he worked in the city as Inspector of Bells. I hope your little consort enjoys this music as much as many players here in Utrecht still do. You, yourself, should try the variations on Engels Nachtegaeltje, a very pretty, evocative piece.*'

I skipped over the invitation to listen to the nightingales in the woods outside Utrecht and went on to his description of his rotten time in Batavia.

'And that's all?' asked Olof when I finished.

'Yes,' I lied, folding the letter and putting it firmly into the envelope.

Later, when I was alone, I read the rest: how sorry he was not to have seen me before his departure, how he felt that any attempt to do this had been blocked on my instructions, how sad it was that a friendship with such an auspicious beginning did not blossom, but that it was not too late for me to get on a ship and come to Utrecht to listen to the nightingales in spring

I thought of those beautiful long fingers holding the quill that produced the fine hand conveying this outrageous suggestion. What a silly sentimentalist I had been. I burnt the letter to put an end to all thoughts of the predicament in which I could have landed myself had I been just slightly more irresponsible.

I realised also that my privacy was gone. As long as our incoming mail from abroad was delivered to Olof's desk, he would know about everything I received unless I made secret arrangements that, if discovered, would immediately cast aspersions on my integrity and motives. I had no need for concealment, but the mere possibility that it might arise made me feel that my personal liberty was being curtailed.

The turning point came shortly after Olof's first Christmas at home, when we were invited to visit Constantia.

Once again I managed to find an excuse not to visit that place that held for me such humiliating memories. This time Dorie had a cough and I thought it best to stay with her. Olof took Petrus, Maria and Polla with him. Christina, pleading her duty to her students as her reason, also stayed behind.

While Olof was gone, Jan Hartogh, the Master Gardner, called to say that he had heard reports that the first red disas of the season were blooming in the hidden crevices of the kloofs of Table Mountain. Johannes Starrenburg was in town visiting the Widow Oldenland and was keen to see the remarkable red lily in its natural habitat. Did I want to come?

It was an invitation I could not refuse. I had last seen the red disa when I went up the mountain with Heinrich and Marie. That was when I was still a novice at botanical painting. How well I remember what a mess I made of my first attempt to draw that rare and beautiful plant. Here was a chance to improve on the previous disaster. I left Johanna in Christina's care, bundled up the coughing Dorie and took her to my mother.

'Is Olof not expected today?' she asked with caution in her voice. She knew the form even if I was ignoring it: a wife is expected to be at home when her husband returns from a journey.

'It could be tomorrow. You know those Constantia parties have a life of their own; people come back when they run out of things to do,' I said, hoping that they would be there for a week. 'Anyway, Christina will be there to receive him even if we decide to spend the night on the mountainside.'

We set out at nine and climbed for three hours to reach the Platteklip Gorge. I was in my element, excited by the prospect of seeing the disas, but also made slightly lightheaded by the audacity with which I had escaped my domestic constraints. It was a feeling akin to that of a runaway slave.

I did not care much for the Widow Oldenland or Johannes Starrenburg, who were having a romance close on the demise of Master Gardener Bernhard Oldenland. I concentrated on the company of Jan Hartogh who was altogether more knowledgeable and caring about plants than his predecessor.

Bernhard Oldenland had come to the Cape after Heinrich Claudius was deported and, although he consulted me about his herbarium, our relationship had been a cautious one. He had no doubt been informed of my close friendship with the Heinrich and Marie and had been warned that I might be tainted with their lack of discretion.

Although Bernhard Oldenland had done a good job acclimatising trees from the East on their way to the botanical gardens of Europe, I disapproved of the manner of his collecting material for his own herbarium. Instead of personally finding specimens, selecting the best plants for drying and going back later to collect seeds or bulbs, he would send slaves into a location with instructions to pull up entire plants and bring anything they thought appropriate.

Apart from his own herbarium, he had assembled some smaller, and in my opinion inferior collections for sale, with the result that some species almost vanished from their natural habitat. Such irresponsible behaviour would have given Heinrich Claudius a heart attack. Heinrich may have been careless about enemies of the state, but he was always most respectful of plants and their habitat.

Whereas Claudius was a botanist purely for the love of plants, Oldenland's interest was entirely commercial. Starrenburg, for his part, professed a love of plants but, in reality, shared Oldenland's materialistic goals.

Margaretha van Otteren, Oldenland's widow, had inherited Oldenland's collection, but it was well known that she had no idea what to do with it. I suspected that Starrenburg's wooing of her might be his means to control of her legacy. During the time we took to rest on our way up the mountain, much of his conversation revolved around the best market for Oldenland's collection.

'His Excellency sent a detailed description to his cousin, Huydecoper, who will act as my agent in selling it to Witsen, the mayor of Amsterdam,' he said importantly, as though he already owned the collection.

'I am at present in correspondence with a James Petiver in London, who might want to buy it for Bishop Compton of London, but the price keeps changing. People don't seem to appreciate the value of the collection and the time and energy it has taken to gather and process all the specimens.'

Starrenburg liked to drop names. He seemed to forget that the collection of the specimens had been for him almost as effortless as it had been for Oldenland. His emphasis on material values made me furious.

'I should not count on Petiver if I were you,' I said curtly when he told us he was expecting the arrival of a certain James Cunningham with some sort of mandate from James Petiver to agree on a price.

'Oh, why is that? What do you know of the gentleman?'

'My friend Marie Claudius knew him in London. In fact, she met her husband at the Temple Coffee House Botany Club that both Petiver and the Bishop Compton frequented. Only once did she see the rooms at the back of his apothecary shop in Aldersgate Street. She said they were stacked from floor to ceiling with collections and exotic specimens from all over the world.

'The man is not a collector, he is a hoarder. It is not surprising he is looking for a bargain. I have done a little business with him and his pay is paltry.'

'Well, I don't think one can compare your little illustrations with a collection of such scope and value as Oldenland's,' he said, intending to silence me with his insulting manner.

'And Oldenland's it still is,' I fired back, rising abruptly to motion to the slaves that we were moving on.

It was late afternoon when we found the red disas hidden in a small cleft off the gorge. Twelve splendid blooms shyly arranged between the wet rocks, each with its two flat lower petals opened like wings, the upper petal cupped to hold the stamen. The combination of the simplicity of structure and intensity of colour took my breath away.

I found an observation point on the other side of the stream. It was as though the silent majesty of these magnificent flowers made me keep my distance.

'There,' I said, 'the pride of Table Mountain!'

'Yes, and twelve of them!' said Starrenburg. 'We could easily take half as specimens, right, Hartogh?'

'I should like to sketch all twelve of them, just as they are, in their natural habitat,' I said quickly.

'There's no time for sketching. We have to get back before dark,' he said impatiently.

But Jan Hartogh was on my side.

'I promised Mistress Bergh she could sketch the disas in their natural setting,' he said. 'That is why we came prepared to stay overnight. There is a woodcutter's hut not far from here for the women and we have a tent for us. The slaves will sleep in the open.'

'Overnight? You said nothing about overnight! I am expected back at my farm tomorrow. I can't waste time waiting for Mistress Annie Bergh to do her little pictures.'

'If you want any specimens at all, and I will allow you two at the most, you will have to wait until the morning,' said Jan Hartogh firmly.

Starrenburg accepted the Master Gardener's authority with some reluctance.

'Come, Grietje,' he said. 'Let's go and find that campsite. I hope you brought enough wine, Hartogh.'

The Widow Oldenland looked at me with a silent plea to rescue her.

'I'm going to stay here a little longer to make some preliminary sketches.' I said quickly. 'The light will be much better in the early morning with the sun on this side of the mountain. Why don't you men go and organise the camp and come back for Margaretha and me in an hour or so?'

'Thank you,' she said when they had gone. 'He was trying to get me alone again. Such eagerness in such an old fellow!' She gave a giggle that was mixture of boasting and embarrassment. I could see that she was eager to share confidences I had no desire to hear.

'When is the wedding?' I asked, trying to direct the conversation.

'Never, if I can help it. But he is so insistent, you see, it is as though he has a hold on me. He knows I cannot live without a protector. I am not strong like some women; I can't fend for myself. You know yourself that I married Oldenland soon after dear Blum passed away.' She began to cry.

Suddenly I saw the opportunity to undermine Starrenburg's plan to gain access to Oldenland's precious herbarium. The newly arrived Master Gardener came to mind.

'He is not the only eligible man in Cabo, Grietje. I'll help you find a less overbearing husband. Send him home to Stellenbosch tomorrow and tell him never to darken your door again. You don't have to put up with him.'

She dried her tears with a smile of relief, watched me sketch for a while and then wandered off along the stream.

Starrenburg had obviously started drinking as soon as they made camp. Soon after dark he needed his bed. The rest of us sat for a long time watching the stars while I told them about that splendid occasion when I got to see the satellites of Jupiter through a telescope. How I missed Heinrich and Marie. But Heinrich was dead and Marie remarried and living in Amsterdam.

The next morning, at first light, I found my way back to the disas and by the time the others arrived with breakfast, I had captured on paper these beauties nestled among the rocks. I would make a copy to send to Marie, but I would not tell her about the savage way in which Starrenburg had pulled up the two disas, fatally damaging three more in his attempt to dislodge his quota.

Watching this had upset me so that I started down the mountain ahead of everyone.

It was almost noon when we could see the detail of the town. There seemed to be a crowd gathered in the Heerengracht, particularly in front of my house. I looked to the stables at the back and saw the three horses in the yard.

My heart missed a beat. Olof was back and something was wrong. I knew the Assistant Forester kept a horse at his hut on the outskirts of the town. I descended carefully but quickly in that direction. He was there, his horse was there.

'I need your horse, please', I said, flushed and out of breath.

'I don't have a lady's saddle,' he protested feebly.

'I'll ride bareback. Please, this is an emergency!'

I thundered through the Gardens, scattering the strolling pedestrians, down the Heerengracht, up Bergh se Gang and into the yard. Wildly I rushed to the kitchen. Olof's bristling figure blocked the door to the voorhuis.

'*Fan*, Annie, where have you been?' he swore at me in Swedish. This told me how angry he was. Through the elbows on his hips I caught a glimpse of something on the dining table.

'What happened?' I asked in a panic. He turned sideways, grabbing my arm and pushing me into the room. It was Petrus, lying very still on the table; there was a wide gash in his forehead. My heart stopped; beds were for sick people, tables for the dead.

'He fell from his horse. Your only son, my son and heir is dead.' A terrible moan came from the depths of Olof's being as he clutched the sides of the table, bent over the lifeless young body. I stood staring, speechless and numb with shock and an overwhelming guilt.

And thus we remained for what seemed like hours, each separately encapsulated in grief. I remember Christina leading me to the bedroom, helping me with my bath and dressing in the only black frock I owned. The rest, the funeral, the floating weeks that followed, was like a bad dream that stays with one.

How sorrow makes every bone and muscle ache with regret. Olof and I spent night after dreary night next to each other, awake in the thick silence of detachment.

I was vaguely aware of the fluttering in my womb as the new baby innocently explored its domain inside me. How could I tell this stranger in my bed about this new life while he was still so much in the grip of grief? I believed superstitiously that I was a bearer of females; I did not dare hope that this child would be different

Even if it were a boy, how could it ever replace Petrus, his father's little Norseman?

During the day Olof spent as much time at the barracks as he could and often came home late at night. His manner was distant to all of us, but I was singled out for criticism: my running of the household, the children's table manners, the lack of formality in my clothing, my friendships and particularly my painting.

It was plain that nothing about me seemed to please him anymore. I felt my confidence dwindle, I felt constantly nervous, unable to perform simple tasks to my own satisfaction. And then the crying started. I would burst into tears for no apparent reason and began to spend a lot of time in my room staring at the floor.

It was Christina who finally called in my mother. They came together to my room, each carrying a chair and sat themselves down. I knew this was an interview rather than a visit.

'You have to pull yourself together, *shona*,' said Mai Angela in her gentle, caring voice, knowing that calling me her little golden one in Bengali always soothed me. 'We are here to help you make a plan. No, don't start weeping; there have been enough tears. Now you have to use your head.'

'But he blames me. I know he thinks if I were here it would not have happened, Petrus would still be here!' I moaned, trying to hold back another flood of tears.

'That is utter nonsense, Mamma,' said Christina, her strong voice filled with the confidence of youth. 'I was here when

163

they came back. Petrus was dead already. He fell from the horse near Bosheuvel. Maria told me exactly how it happened.

'If anyone was to blame it was Father for not taking Petrus to the nearest farmhouse. It was he who insisted on bringing him home. Petrus was in his care. It is his guilt that makes him blame you.'

A window opened on my dark spirits. Christina was on my side. Here was my younger self to console me!

'He doesn't speak to me, except to criticise. I don't know how to get through to him. If only I could get away!'

'Running away will solve nothing, *mamoni*. Does he know about the baby?'

'No, you know I don't show until the sixth month.'

'Then you must tell him. Perhaps that will end the stand-off between you. Whatever you do, you can't go on like this. Let's go for a long walk to my garden to clear the cob-webs from your head.'

Christina smiled; we all knew my mother was a wise old warrior beneath that mild exterior. I resolved to be brave, to pull myself out of this slump and have some results to show my loving mother and daughter.

That night the full moon shone into our bedroom. Once again we lay in bed side-by-side, awake, wordless. I put out my hand to touch his arm, but he pulled away, not turning his back, not a grand dismissal, just a small rejection; the kind that had kept me at bay since the death of Petrus. I got up and stood by the window looking down towards the Castle and the Bay.

'How long will we have to be so unhappy?' I asked the moon. 'Will we have to live like this for another twenty years? Or will Olof find another excuse to go away because he can't stand me anymore?'

'Olof is not going anywhere if Annie gives him enough reason to stay,' said the voice from the bed.

I turned my face towards his voice; his response gave me courage to go on.

'And Annie will be happier if Olof stops criticising her.'

'There is a lot I do not like in the Annie I found on my return.' I forced myself not to become defensive. He obviously had a list of grievances. Let him vent them. I would steel myself to listen.

'Such as?' I invited.

Pandora's box opened: He did not like my insistence on spending so much time painting, he did not like my friendship with Jan de Grevenbroeck, he did not like the way I let the children do as they pleased, he did not like the way I put myself above society and refused invitations from important people. Above all, he thought it unfair of me to blame him for Petrus' death. I gasped.

'So, that is really what has put us apart. You think I blame you and I think you blame me. All the other things can be changed or modified, but unless we agree to remove this thorn of blame we will never be happy again. We both know people who live like this, drifting apart because of unresolved unhappiness. Would we really end our days like that?'

I was talking to the moon again. Then I felt Olof's hands on my shoulders and when I turned towards him he buried his face in my hair.

'You have a way with words, Wife. We need each other.'

'And there's another little child that needs us too,' I said moving his hand to my belly. He held me for a long time in the moonlight by the window and much longer in the bed in lustless love. When we woke we were still in the same spoon position in which we had fallen asleep. Between us there was fresh hope, a new expectation that our future would draw on our joint energy.

Putting words into action takes time, careful planning and sacrifice. I was perhaps helped by the fact that this was my first difficult pregnancy and I was often reduced to staying in bed for days on end. This allowed Olof to organise the children in his own regimented way, but since they adored him they did not seem to mind. Christina temporarily took over the running of the house from me, and my paints stood in the studio gathering dust.

I persuaded Olof that Jan was not a threat and that, in fact, he could be an equally good friend to us both. In turn, he persuaded me to be gracious to the Governor and other high officials. All fences seemed mended when we gave a huge party to celebrate the baptism of Simon Petrus.

A new me had crawled out of her cocoon. As I spread my wings, it was soon forgotten that once upon a time I had been a wretched caterpillar.

CHAPTER THIRTEEN

Ostentation

I STILL FEEL A LITTLE dizzy when I think of the years Willem Adriaen van der Stel was Governor of the Cape. He arrived with his wife, Marie de Hase, determined to transform our little backwater to a Colony worthy of the splendours of the Dutch East India Company and, of course, to add to his own wealth.

Willem Adriaen and Marie swept into the Castle in their costly clothes and stylish wigs bringing with them furniture, paintings, china and books the likes of which had only been seen as collector's pieces. Those of us who had never sampled courtly life were convinced by the lavish entertainment and open opulence that we were at last participants in the style of the Sun King himself.

That, in fact, that was what Olof sometimes called Willem Adriaen in the privacy of our own four walls. 'Little King Ludwig with his face paint and his wigs.' This kind of irony was fine for Olof who had recently seen the wonders of Europe; I was less sophisticated and, therefore, completely taken in.

We were well placed to enjoy this spectacle of grandeur. Olof was now Captain of the Garrison and a member of the Council of Policy. The rules had changed and there was no limit on the property Company officials were allowed to own. Olof had already been given five morgen on the Moolenweg where we grazed our cattle and was expanding his farming to the Tijgerberg under the Rondebosjesberg where we could grow wheat and have a small vineyard. The rules also allowed Company officials to employ soldiers as farm hands to supervise the slaves. Everyone recognised that the Berghs had put misfortune behind them and were flying higher than ever.

Willem Adriaen had matured physically, but not in nature. His enthusiasms were still impulsive and passionate, but now he had the means to humour them. He was still an active musician and had brought with him a splendid harpsichord with a double keyboard. Marie was an accomplished player and an attempt was made to revive the Castle music club. One of the first things he said to me on arrival was:

'We'll make music again like we did in the olden days, Annie. I have become a very proficient viol player and I daresay you have put those recorders I left you on permanent loan to good use!'

This was a nostalgic notion that did not materialise until a few years later. Willem Adriaen was away so often, ostensibly on inspections, but also to find the ideal location for his manor farm. He found a site in Hottentots Holland, under the Schaapenberg, with a magnificent view of False Bay, a good six hours away from the Castle. He made no secret of the fact that he meant to install himself in greater splendour here at Vergelegen than his father ever achieved at Constantia.

Every available builder and craftsman was commandeered and soon the rumours were flying about the size of the house, the octagonal garden, the number of outbuildings and even the mirror on the ceiling of the bathroom. People said it was not a farm being built at Vergelegen, but a city!

While her 'palace' was being built, Marie van der Stel sought to make her mark on Cape society. She was ten years my junior, a pure blonde Dutch beauty with delicate features, clear blue eyes and hair a mixture of white and yellow gold. She had the figure of a young girl although she had already had four children including Simon, four years older than my Simon, both named after the same gentleman of Constantia.

Marie van der Stel was aware of every aspect of her physical appearance, which she sought to enhance with an endless display of new dresses, shoes and accessories. It seemed that her aim was to make everyone gasp every time she appeared. It was clear she wanted to impress on us that she came from the very top and meant to stay there. Many dismissed her as an incurable snob but the young, like my own Christina, were excited and aspired to emulate her style.

From the outset, Marie treated me with the intimacy of an old friend, based on my long acquaintance with the Van der Stel family. It did not occur to her for one moment that I might have reservations.

'I have heard so much about you, Mistress Bergh. My sister-in-law, Catelina, said I could count on you as a friend,' she said on our first meeting.

I was relieved. Catelina must have abandoned her grudge against me.

'She told me about your kindness to the family when poor Cornelia died. One of the first things I have to do is to lay some white lilies at the tomb of Cornelia on behalf of Catelina. Will you come with me?'

This was the first of many requests I could not refuse, mostly because they were all made with a curious blend of endearing sentimentality and imperious authority. I took her to Miss Cornelia's blue marble tomb the next day, after procuring with great difficulty an enormous bunch of white lilies from the Gardens.

Dressed in dark purple, she stood in pious reverence before the grave of someone she did not know, whilst the curious passed by, noting that the new Governor's wife was a devout woman. She sought to confirm the impression on Sunday after Sunday when she sat in her splendid new chair in the front row under the pulpit, singing hymns just slightly ahead of the congregation in her rich voice and refined Amsterdam accent

This, however, was all I saw of her piety. Our discussions revolved mostly around fashion and fabrics. She had brought with her not only an extensive wardrobe, but also bolt upon bolt of silks, muslins and chintzes, the likes of which I had never set eyes on. Her father had been Director of Persia and Bengal and she had access to weavers even the merchants of Batavia and Ceylon could not reach.

Marie was quick to observe my wonderment.

'Catelina said you were an excellent dress designer,' she remarked one day. 'You know I don't wear a dress more than once if I can help it. Soon I will need new clothes. Will you design them for me?'

'I haven't designed a dress in years, except for Christina's wedding dress. You know, my interest has shifted to botanical painting. Fashions have changed so much, have become so elaborate compared to what we are used to.'

'I have seen Christina's wedding dress and am convinced that your imagination and creative powers have not changed. I would have thought working in the new style would be more exciting, allow you more creative possibilities?'

'I don't know that I have the time. I still run my own house,' I protested weakly.

'But you're not painting so much anymore, Christina told me. And your husband would gladly hire a housekeeper for you. I know that. Come on, Annie, say yes! Think of what it would do for your reputation to be known as the exclusive designer to the Governor's wife. My gowns will be admired for their creator as much as for their model! Why hide your talent under a bushel?'

And so I was seduced back to my erstwhile profession. Vanity, and the love of those beautiful bolts of fabric before me, made me cave in even though I knew that I would now be at her beck and call like a doctor, a comforter, a glorified coiffeuse.

Surprisingly, Olof had no objection to the new plan. In fact, he encouraged it, suggesting we employ one of Shaykh Yussuf's daughters to be our housekeeper.

'How about Seity Labibah? You've always liked her. She looks to me the most sophisticated of the lot. She might enjoy living in town for a while since their repatriation might still take a long time. After you've trained her you can spend all your time on your social commitments and this designing project. I must confess, I like it better than botanical painting. It is much more like women's work, without all that climbing and scrambling.'

'I loved climbing and scrambling,' I objected, but with no serious regrets. Those silks were beckoning and I could not wait to get started. 'Anyway, Maria seems to following in my footsteps, after a fashion, though she is keener on small animals than plants. Have you seen her sketches of birds and lizards?'

'Maria is a wild thing. How are we ever going to find a husband for her?'

'She is also a very kind person and a capable cook. Don't worry; some widower will want a housekeeper sooner or later. My most immediate concern is to get permission for Labibah to come and work for us.'

This was not difficult, nor was it hard to persuade Labibah to come to the Cape. I found out later that she had a plan of her own. She had met the King of Tambora, the young rebel Sultan Abd al-Basi, soon after he arrived as an exile. He was detained in the Castle, but was allowed occasional visits to Zandvliet. Labibah and the Sultan fell secretly in love and began to set in motion the many formalities that had to be gone through before they could finally be married.

Being near the Castle and her beloved meant a great deal to Labibah. She took to the management of the house like a duck to water. She had for so long observed her mother and the other wives ordering subordinates about that she had no hesitation in being firm with my domestic staff. For most of her childhood she was a Dutch captive so she had a pretty good idea of our customs.

If she were officious with the slaves, Labibah was nothing but sweetness and light to our family. She especially deferred to Olof's authority, thinking it well to be on his right side; she knew his position on the Council of Policy could influence the decision in her marriage application. She treated me as a special benefactor because of the interest I had taken in her relatives despite their humble status as exiles. My keen participation in the *batik* production and my efforts in finding the supplies the small group of exiles needed had apparently been appreciated more than I had realised.

Labibah got along well with the older children, but she particularly loved the two babies, Simon and Martinus, though they were as different as chalk and cheese: Simon small, dark and intense, and Martinus fair and happy-go-lucky, much as his brother Petrus had been. The little boys provided her with a good excuse to walk to the Castle, where she might chance to meet with the Sultan. Taking the children for a walk was really Helena's work, but she was getting old and was only too happy to oblige Labibah.

I soon immersed myself in the role of exclusive fashion designer to the Governor's wife. I tackled the demands of the new styles with energy, counting. myself lucky to be working with such fabulous fabrics: soft silks and satins, gossamer voiles and organzas. I tried to complement the luxuriousness of each of these materials with custom-made lace as well as with original embroidery designs based on indigenous flowers.

My labours were a most rewarding extension of my work as botanical painter, which had given me an intimate knowledge of the shapes and colours of our own flora. I combined my experience of the overall patterns used in *batik* to fashion flowing designs of daisies and disas, pypies and ericas, thistles and geraniums blending reality and fantasy as I pleased.

Every able embroiderer in the Colony stood in line to be allowed to work with the new designs, not only because the flowers were familiar to them, but also because they were allowed to work with fabric and threads of such superior quality. It made us all happy to be thus involved in the dazzling lavishness that was championed by the young Van der Stels.

How curious it is that we are able to run our lives on parallel tracks, showing to the world a happiness and confidence we think it ought to see, but harbouring within ourselves a secret misery too awful to confess, all the while hoping to convince ourselves that the exterior pretence might overtake the inner despair. Perhaps that is what is meant by maturity, the bringing of the two together in a compromise, living without extremes.

From early on in my acquaintance with Marie van der Stel, I was privy to her inner struggle. It began after she broke into tears during a fashion consultation. I was shocked to see her lovely face transformed into such crinkled ugliness, her eyes red and lustreless.

I was tempted to leave her right then; she reminded me too much of myself ten years earlier. Her pitiful appeal made me stay, however, and tied me to her involuntarily as a counsellor.

'Oh, Annie, I am so unhappy!' she said, uttering the universal cry of a woman in trouble with her self. 'How am I going to manage in this godforsaken place?'

I could have given the standard Christian advice about how God was everywhere, how it was the challenge of every believer to discover His presence in the most unlikely places. Not being a lay preacher, I looked for a more down-to-earth reason.

'You're homesick, Marie. It is very common at first when you move so far from your own family and friends. Miss Cornelia was just getting over it when she so sadly died.'

'Lucky Miss Cornelia. How I wish for a fever to take me away!'

Don't even say such a thing!' I protested. 'You have to give it time. Everyone looks up to you. Your children, Willem Adriaen, the whole Colony, we all envy your position, your beauty, your possessions. You must be strong!'

Those were the days I thought that encouragement was all she needed. Her sobs unwisely made me go further.

'You can count on me as a friend,' I added, not knowing that she took my offer to mean that I would also be her sister, her mother, her confessor, while she continued to play the part of Governor's wife, showing off to Christina and her young set of Cruses, Van Brakels, Elzeviers and Linneses.

Meanwhile, I often had to deal with floods of tears and tales of her husband's demands, dissatisfactions and unkindness. I indulged her for my own selfish reasons, seeing her as an integral part of the new pomp and circumstance we were enjoying. She was essential in keeping the bubble from bursting. If she went to pieces the whole show would be over. No, I would prop her up as best I could. She could not be allowed to snap.

I did this with a mixture of discreet listening, common sensical advice, pious platitudes, homespun wisdom and diversions. This kind of attention kept her going for a number of years whilst her wealth increased and her spirit shrank.

When Vergelgen was complete, and not before, the whole world was invited to a *Sinterklaas* party that went on for a week. Some were accommodated in the house, some at nearby farms. Frans van der Stel lived not far away and took in as many as he could. The young set, full of bravado, camped in tents, tempting the appetites of nocturnal predators, still very active in that barely tamed wilderness.

Olof and Simon van der Stel set themselves apart from the comforts of the household. They offered to be in charge of the camp and so did not offend anyone, though I have no doubt Willem Adriaen made a mental note of their preference. He was already beginning to count those for and against him.

This house-warming party was, in many ways, an attempt on Willem Adrien's side to win people over. Little did he know that some of his adversaries were there with the specific purpose of gathering information, counting sheep and fruit trees, sketching vineyards and buildings, interviewing slaves and *knechte*.

These same people pretended to enjoy the events of the week, the visit of *Sinterklaas*, whom everyone, except the children, knew was the old Governor dressed up, followed by his blackest slave, Octavio, whom many children recognised. Then there was the tree planting ceremony, when Jan Hartogh supervised the planting of six camphor trees in front of the manor and everyone speculated how the fully grown trees would obscure the view.

There were hunting parties and shooting competitions, and escorted rides for the women and children to see the wild animals that ventured close to the cultivated farmlands. Shy Apollonia took her younger sisters and brothers on every one of these excursions and helped them keep a count of ostriches, antelope, boars and zebras. Once they even spotted a herd of elephants and some rhino.

The party was the epitome of high living. The octagonal garden was turned into an outdoor dining room with large marquees set up to accommodate the guests at tables laden with food and set with the finest silver, crystal and china. The eating and wine-tasting never seemed to stop. People came and went, some to walk, some to ride, some to hunt, some to do the unmentionable.

Every evening took on its own downward spiral into licentiousness. The musical entertainment was barely over when the chase began, ending in the most unlikely people finding themselves together in bed. Every night generated a whole new batch of gossip to be dissected and disseminated all over the Colony.

I used my new little baby girl, Engela, as an excuse to desist from taking part in the revelry; a nursing mother was at least given some respect. As I lay in my elegant bed in the north wing listening to the whoops and cries of lust and indulgence, I understood for the first time how often an affluent lifestyle dictates the abandonment of ethics.

175

'When money comes in the front door, morals go out the back,' my mother used to say.

I watched Marie as she skipped from day to day as the elegant hostess, the obliging wife, the caring mother. To see her thus, no one would guess that the following week she would collapse again in floods of tears, shaking her golden ringlets, moaning repeatedly, 'Will I never see the snow again?'

I had stayed behind after the party to 'help Marie get the house back to normal again' as Willem Adriaen put it. What he meant was 'to help Marie get her head back to normal again'.

I applied my usual prophylactic of hugging and comforting, promising snow on the mountains of Drakenstein next winter and seeking to divert her with a new design for a dress with a layered petticoat and a draped overskirt. But this time it was not enough. She wanted more from me.

'I found Labibah invaluable last week' she said. 'I don't know how I will run the house without her. Could you let me have her?'

'I employed Labibah so that I would have time to design your clothes,' I protested. But she was not going to permit opposition.

'You could easily find someone new in town. Your Appolonia is almost old enough, or your Maria?'

'You know very well Maria is at the point of getting married herself. She will have Albert Koopman's house and child to look after, and Polla is much too young.'

'What about your mother? She worked for you before, didn't she?' Her persistence was beginning to annoy me.

'That was different, and she didn't "work for me"; she lived with us while Olof was away. Now she is an old lady and deserves a rest. She has worked hard all her life. I'm not going to put her to work for me or anyone.'

My resistance prompted another display of dejection, no doubt to cover up the plan she had already made.

'Then what am I going to do? Here I am so isolated.

You're in town, you could pick from a dozen housekeepers!'

She added, almost as a threat, 'You talk to Labibah. You'll see she is most anxious to come and work for me.'

When I did, I discovered that Marie van der Stel had promised Labibah that she could arrange her marriage to Rajah Tambora if she came to work for her.

Soon after Labibah entered Marie's service she married the Sultan and both went to live at Vergelegen. Labibah ran the household and Raja Tambora, who was a *hafiz*, spent many months writing out the Koran for the Governor in his most exquisite Arabic calligraphy.

I did not get another housekeeper, and reduced my contact with the Governor's household as far as propriety would allow. The physical distance between Cape Town and Vergelegen made it easier to make excuses, but it was really the emotional effort that Marie's manipulations caused that made me anxious to avoid her.

Marie, however, did not seem to realise that anything had changed. On her regular visits to town, usually after ships had unloaded her orders from Patria, she would summon me and persuade me yet again to design new frocks to suit yet another crop of beautiful fabrics. Then she would fill my ears with tales of woe, each time telling me worse stories of her husband's temper.

Pity would take hold of me; I would capitulate once again and attempt to replenish her low spirits with new ideas to enhance her enormous wardrobe.

Marie van der Stel's personal misery finally turned to despair that grim January in 1706, when abnormal rainstorms caused irreparable damage to the crops and herds and we were all suffering from pink eye. I had come back from De Cuylen, where we were now living in a large manor built by Olof in keeping with our new affluence.

The townhouse on the Heerengracht had become known in the family as Annasrust because that is where I came for respite from the busy hospitality of De Cuylen, which had become a gentlemen's halfway house to Stellenbosch. An

KITES OF GOOD FORTUNE

endless stream of travellers came and went, expecting to be fed and housed. I gladly attended to all this hospitality, but sometimes I fled to town for a break.

This time it was to obtain celandine from the medicinal garden at the Company Gardens. The juice of this plant was the best remedy yet for sore eyes, especially when mixed with a little breast milk to reduce its stinging. Maria was still nursing my grandson, Albertus, and offered some of her plentiful supplies for my concoction.

It was early in the morning. My own little Albertus and I had just come back from Maria's house when there was an urgent banging on the front door. I opened it and found Labibah out of breath and terrified.

'She's going to do it, Miss Annie!' she wailed.

'Who's going to do what, Labibah? Calm down, for heavens sake! Come in and tell me.' In my heart I knew she was talking about Marie van der Stel.

'She has made herself a waistband with pockets for the stones she brought in a bag with her from the farm. She's filling them right now.' She ran to the window with a view on the Castle gate.

'Look, there she is. She's going straight to the millpond! You have to stop her, Miss Annie!'

Through my bleary, swollen red eyes I could see the familiar figure staggering up the path to the pond. Around her hips swayed bulging objects, dragging down her thin shoulders. Albertus, alarmed by Labibah's panic, clung crying to my skirts. I pulled him behind me as I rushed out the front door.

'I'll go. Labibah. You and Albertus sit here on the post office stone and wait.'

I ran down the street and then the track leading to my side of the pond. There were few people about, but enough to see that a drama was happening.

By the time I reached the pond Marie was already wading in on the other side. Never have I been so happy that I can swim. Giving no thought to propriety, I got rid of my petticoats and jumped in. She must have changed her mind as soon as her lungs began to fill with water for, by the time I reached her, she was struggling against the weight of the stones dragging her down, not thinking to undo the waist-band. Her head kept disappearing and re-appearing while she called out in hysterical frenzy.

As soon as I could, I undid the stone girdle to make her body buoyant and then proceeded to pull her to the bank. A small crowd had gathered, including the physician who helped her get rid of the water in her lungs. Someone had kindly collected my petticoats from the other side of the pond and handed them to me.

The Governor's wife was a pitiful sight.

'I wasn't brave enough to escape the excess,' she moaned repeatedly.

My one goal was to get her away from the crowd as soon as I could.

'Carry her to my house!' I commanded two gaping Hottentot youths.

Labibah and Albertus were still there, sitting on the post office stone, stunned by what they had just observed. Marie was in a compliant stupor. We changed her into the most humble garments she had ever worn and put her to bed. I noticed the bruises on her arms and breasts.

The crowd had now gathered in front of my house. I knew that those burghers of Stellenbosch who were trying to get rid of Willem Adriaen would have their spies out there and would make much of the incident. I went out on the porch looking only fairly respectable with my sore eyes swollen and my wet hair tucked hurriedly under a bonnet.

'The First Lady is going to be fine. You can go away now,' I said, ignoring the calls of 'Why did she do it?' and 'Tell us why she is so unhappy, you're her friend'.

I closed the door firmly and began gathering things together for a swift retreat to De Cuylen. Marie had to be removed from the Cape as soon as possible.

Labibah now told me about the argument the night before.

Willem Adriaen had apparently resorted to physical violence after Marie shouted that she 'wished the burghers every success with their deposition against the Governor because that would be the only way she would escape from this god forsaken country and the tyranny of such a husband'.

'He had been drinking a lot of wine. He was not reasonable. He is upset about all the dead sheep,' Labibah explained in an attempt to excuse him.

We escaped the crowd by mounting the coach in the yard and dashing out along Bergstraat and not Heerengracht as they had expected. Marie stayed at De Cuylen for a week, but it was difficult to secure any privacy, that place being such a public thoroughfare. Her father-in-law came over from Constantia and offered to take her back to Vergelegen, but she scoffed at his attempt to mediate.

'Such a hypocrite! Everyone in Amsterdam knows why his wife never came to the Cape with him. Like father, like son.'

She had no choice, however. Olof insisted her place was with her husband and I agreed that we could only offer her temporary asylum.

'In your position, appearances are all-important, Juffrouw van der Stel,' said Olof kindly, but firmly. 'It seems to me your choice is to leave the Cape immediately if you find your situation completely unbearable, or to stay with your husband and show the world a contented face. You can visit us any time, but your husband's subjects must know that you are a loyal wife.'

Terrified wife, dead wife, I thought. My husband was definitely a soldier, not a parson.

'If you want, I will go with your father-in-law to speak to him. I am sure will be able to persuade your husband of the importance of controlling his temper,' he continued.

And so the incident was resolved.

Marie van der Stel had to wait another four years before she could escape to Holland. During that time her husband was relieved from his post and refused permission to stay at the Cape. I know personally that this last decision was the direct result of a secret petition from some of Marie's influential family members in Patria.

There was never a person happier to sail away from the Cape. I thought Marie would leave Willem Adriaen as soon as they got to Amsterdam, but, curiously, she stayed with him. When I visited her at Uyter Meer in Lisse not so long ago, she told me that she could not face the deprivation of living less splendidly as a divorcee.

Life in Holland apparently was less of a strain on her husband's temper and by watching how much wine he consumed she avoided many arguments. I suppose she was not the first wife to run her life by such a strategy.

After the departure of the young Van der Stels, Cape society lost some of its gloss and we all settled into a new period of diminished display. To this day, however, you may see some splendid object or other in the houses of prominent citizens that dates back to the brief reign of 'little King Ludwig'.

CHAPTER FOURTEEN

Hot springs

IN NOVEMBER OF 1715, the *Vrijburgh* sailed into Table Bay. At that time we were living at De Cuylen, in a grand new house with marble floors and twin gables. At the beginning of that year, Olof had reluctantly retired as Captain of the Garrison on full pension. He was seventy years old and as spry as any man that age who had lived a life of sensible habits and vigorous activity. Now he was suddenly looking to me to abandon my own interests and devote time to him.

Olof's eyesight had weakened to the point where he found it difficult to read for a long period at a time. My job now was to read to him all those volumes for which he had had no time before. He had a collection of the accounts of many visitors to the Cape and of many protracted conflicts between the Company and various rulers in India and the Malaysian islands.

I learnt a lot reading these accounts aloud, not only from the information contained in them, but also from Olof's comments. He had known so many of the main players and details of the circumstances that I often thought to have him dictate a critique in response to our reading. But that would have been a completely new project for which I did not have sufficient enthusiasm. I was already spending less time on my embroidery designs and music, shifting my focus on the needs of my aging husband.

It was during this time that much of what happened to Olof in Ceylon came out obliquely. I gathered that his main task during those years was to befriend Shaykh Yusuf and to prepare him for his exile to the Cape. He told me in detail how the Shaykh was secretly put on the *Voetboog* and how he, Olof, was instrumental in passing misinformation about his whereabouts to the followers of the Imam.

Olof described to me in detail the beauty of Galle, where he went under cover to persuade two of the Shaykh's followers to follow him into exile. I could feel the atmosphere of Galle as Olof described the morning when he spotted the *Voetboog* from his window in the barracks and hurried down the street to the mosque to alert the Imams to their imminent departure. His obvious affection for Ceylon caused in me a new gratitude that he had come back to the Cape and me. It was a happy time and I did not resent his demands on me.

Still, I was only fifty-three. Lust had left Olof's body and I was expected to have none left myself. I found myself becoming more susceptible to the attentions and flattery of men. I warned myself that I was in danger of straying.

That November of 1715, Apollonia had her second miscarriage and needed me more than her father did. I left him in the good care of his two unmarried daughters: Johanna, already almost a spinster, and Engela, a month short of her fifteenth birthday, bright and amusing. I knew the one would see to her father's creature comforts and the other would make him laugh.

I myself did not expect to be at all diverted by Apollonia's low spirits; rather, I would be the one planning diversions to cheer her up.

Jan and Polla were now living next door to the grand double house built by Albert Koopman, where he and Maria still lived. When I arrived in town I was met with the news that Polla had a lodger, a sea captain who had arrived the night before.

'I think you will be interested to meet him, Mamma, you have the same name,' said Polla with a curious look on her face. She was not looking nearly as dejected as I had expected.

'He is Jan de Koning, captain of the *Vrijburgh*,' she continued. 'He says the ship is in need of repairs and he will be here for a while. Jan liked him immediately and offered him lodging for the duration of his stay. You will meet him tonight at dinner.'

'Has he spoken about his family? Could he be a relative?'

'You've always been quick on the uptake, Ma. I do believe he told Jan his father's name was David.'

I could feel my heart beating faster. In all these years there had been no contact between my father's family and my mother or myself. My annuity was paid by a lawyer from Enkhuyzen and stopped after my marriage.

I had never been bold enough to try to contact my half family and yet I often thought of them, so far across the sea. I imagined stepbrothers and sisters, glowing bright and Dutch, unaware of me, their shadow of a sister so many miles away. I imagined their puzzlement at the lawyers' insistence that a small sum be sent regularly to the Cape.

'We must send a chair for your grandmother, Polla, she must join us for supper tonight. We will tell her it's because I'm in town. We'll say nothing of Captain de Koning.'

'What if it really is your father's son? What if he looks like his father? Won't the shock be too much for Grandmother? You know how frail she is.'

'It's only her outer shell; her heart, mind and spirit are as robust as ever. No, she'll enjoy meeting this Captain even if he turns out to be only a distant relative,' I said with outward calm. But my heart was filled with excitement and I was wishing for a real brother.

We were sitting on the front porch under the vine pergola when they came up the street late that afternoon. Stocky Jan Alders and his tall, blond companion. My mother looked as though she had seen a ghost, her eyes wide, her wrinkled face animated. Her wizened body would not obey her wish to run up to the tall man. She held out her arms as though inviting an embrace.

'David!' crackled her once melodious voice.

The Captain went to her at once, stooping to take both her hands in his in an affectionate greeting.

'No, Madame, I am Jan, David's son,' he said simply, not letting go of her hands. I got up to give him the chair next to her.

Still holding both my mother's hands, he looked up at me, the ocean in his eyes.

'And you must be Annie? Mistress Bergh?'

'Yes, and are you who we think you might be? There was a Captain Leendert de Koning here a few years ago, but he showed no sign of knowing about any connection between us,' I said, hoping the sudden rush of blood to my cheek was invisible, the rapid beating of my heart inaudible.

He must have felt my trembling when he finally let go of my mother's hands and rose to kiss mine.

'That was my cousin, who was as ignorant as I was at the time.'

'This is such a surprise, you must forgive us if we show too much excitement.'

'I am equally excited, believe me, and so lucky to find you both alive and well. It was shortly before my departure from Holland that I learnt of your existence. The lawyer who managed my father's affairs told me of you on his deathbed.'

My newly-found brother and I talked until late in the evening, basking in each other's warmth. I took in his lively, enthusiastic face, his darting blue eyes, the way his mouth curled upwards when he smiled. He told us about his family, his wife and three children living in Amsterdam. The youngest was a daughter, Deborah.

Mai Angela quizzed Jan in detail about the relatives now living in the family home at Enckhuysen and all the changes that had taken place in the town since she left it almost sixty years before. Jan was amazed at her memory for detail and was eager to inform her.

'Do they still fly kites on the hill above the harbour wall?' she asked nostalgically.

'Sadly, we have to go further into the country these days, Madame, since the city has outgrown its walls and houses

have been built on the hill of which you speak. I was there
shortly before my departure to visit friends from my childhood. I myself live in Amsterdam now.'

During that whole evening David Koning was not once
mentioned by name. As she was leaving, however, Mai
Angela invited Jan to her house the next day.

'I have a book I would like you to see,' she said. 'I don't
read, but I have the engravings imprinted on my mind. It is an
account of the shipwreck of the *Aernhem* which, as you know,
was the only ship to survive that terrible storm that took
't Wapen van Holland. I should like to look at it with you.'

Without hesitation, he agreed to visit the next day if I would
be so gracious to show him to her house. This I consented
to do, knowing that there was little I could refuse him.

As we walked up the hill to my mother's house the next
morning, I told Jan of how my mother had risen steadily
throughout her life. The original two-roomed house she
built when she was first given the garden against the Lion's
Tail had been enlarged and improved many times. It was
still a modest abode by modern standards, but it had an
attic and a cellar and several outbuildings to accommodate
livestock and slaves.

My mother lived comfortably here next to our friend of
many years, Hester Weyers, the widow of Wouter Mostert.
Martha and Susanna, her devoted slave women, looked
after her with great care and three male slaves saw to the
animals and garden. She also had a small farm called
Hondswijk in the Tijgervallei where three slaves managed
her herd of cattle and sheep.

'It is on the way to our farm at De Cuylen,' I said to Jan.
'If you have time I could show you both farms. How long do
you have before you sail for Batavia?' The eagerness in my
voice must have told him that I was hoping he would stay
longer than it usually took to take in water and provisions. He
gave me a searching look before he replied.

'The *Vrijburgh* is in need of repair. The name De Koning
is remembered here because of the problems my cousin

Leendert caused when he sailed for Mauritius without having his ship properly checked and had to return. Were you aware of that?'

'Yes, my husband was one of those preventing him from getting into serious trouble and had him assigned as Captain of the *Beveland*.'

'Your husband is a powerful man, I am told, wealthy and influential even in his retirement?' I recognised the intimacy disguised as curiosity. In asking about my husband he was really asking about me.

'My husband has worked long and hard for the welfare of this Colony, contributing to it his talents in security, construction and administration. If, in the process, he has become rich and influential, it is because he is respected as a man of sound judgment, not only for his own benefit, but also for the benefit of the common wealth.'

'Well spoken Mistress Bergh,' he said with a touch of irony. 'You sound like a loyal and devoted wife, Sister.'

'I have no reason to be otherwise, Brother,' I answered quickly and, unable to stop myself, asked quite rashly: 'And you? Are you a loyal husband, a devoted father?'

'I am not easily tempted. But, then, neither was my father. The secret of his love for Angela of Bengal drowned with him; we were never to know about her or you, Sister Annie,' he said putting a brotherly arm around my shoulders.

Was he calling me 'Sister' for his own protection? If I called him 'Brother' we might both succeed in keeping each other at arm's length, which would be the proper thing to do in the circumstances.

Susanna saw us coming and came to meet us.

'The Mistress is very excited,' she said. 'Not one wink did she sleep last night. And up with the birds this morning telling Martha what to bake and making me dust and clean the *voorhuis* from top to bottom for the important visitor. I even had to take down and polish the frames of Master Willem's portrait and those pictures she has of Meester and Juffrouw van Riebeeck.'

She looked at Jan with special curiosity. Mai Angela must have told her who he was.

My mother was waiting for us at the front door and insisted on showing Jan the whole place, even hobbling along to the garden and the stables. Back in the *voorhuis*, she ordered tea and told me to get Andries Stokram's book on the shipwreck of the *Aernhem*. This ritual was familiar to me. As others visited the graves of their loved ones, we read the account of the storm that took my father.

For as long as I can remember, somewhere between the ninth and the eleventh of February every year, I was called upon to join Mai Angela in the ceremonial reading. We relived the battle against the wind and the waves as though we were on board *'t Wapen van Holland*. We imagined my father giving orders first to lower all sails, to drop the anchors and cut down the masts, all to no avail. The gale had continued mercilessly, and the decision had been made to abandon ship and the precious cargo with it.

After reading about the storm I would read one of the 'Prayers for Sailors Everywhere' from the *Groote Christelijke Zeevaart* prayer book. Then we would pore over the engravings in Stokram, especially the one showing an officer hacking off the hand of a black slave in an effort to lighten the load on the lifeboat.

'Your father would never have done such a cruel thing! It was probably his good heart that sent him to the same grave as that slave!' speculated Mai Angela in that voice reserved for tragedy. Jan and I kneeled on either side of her, stroking her hands and shoulders. He seemed to have a natural talent for comforting old ladies.

'How often have I wished I were there too!' she wailed.

'But you had me, Mai, and your other children to live for,' I said, trying to distract her. 'You did not abandon us to the storms of life. Your good heart saved us. And we survived! Look at you now, a rich old dowager! Aren't we fortunate to have lived to the day we could meet David Koning's own flesh and blood?'

188

She cheered up slightly, but lapsed into sadness again when Jan told us a curious thing we had not known in connection with the loss of *'t Wapen van Holland*. Six weeks after the departure of the fleet, Johan Maetsuycker, Governor General of East India, had had three successive dreams in which he heard Admiral Arnout de Flaming cry out and perish. The Admiral had travelled on my father's ship. Johan Maetsuycker had personally told this tale to the orphaned Koning children.

That evening Jan Alders proposed a trip to the hot springs in the Overberg. For years now people had benefited from the waters in the Zwartberg. Jan thought it would be an excellent cure for Polla.

I had long wished to visit the hot springs myself, but the amenities had only recently been improved. Olof and Izak Schrijver had camped there on their way to and from the wreck of the *Nossa Sehnora* and sat in the steaming waters. Since then, baths had been dug in the side of the *bronbult* and a site cleared and levelled for tents.

Before Ferdinand Appel bought the farm next to the springs, one had to take every necessary provision when camping at the site, depending on the Hottentot from Boontjeskraal for milk and honey. Appel did not provide board and lodging, but he did supply visitors with meat and vegetables at a goodly profit.

Jan de Koning had no hesitation in including himself in the party, confessing to bouts of gout for which the springs were a renowned cure. His ship had been examined and it was obvious that extensive repairs would have to be carried out. He trusted his deputy to oversee these. We encouraged Jan Alders to make the arrangements as soon as possible. In the meantime Jan de Koning would go to De Cuylen with me, and Polla and Jan would call for us on the way to the Overberg.

On our arrival at De Cuylen it was clear that Olof had received advance notice of who our visitor was and the amount of time we had spent in each other's company. He was polite to Jan, but not cordial. At the first opportunity he had to speak to me alone he said:

'So, this is the half brother who has swept you and your mother off your feet? Another De Koning with an ailing ship!' His hostility surprised and annoyed me, but I tried to be persuasive and conciliatory.

'Be generous, Olof, it is not every day that a son of David Koning visits. Can you blame us for being a little excited?'

'You seem more than a little excited, Wife, you seem infatuated. And he, well he looks as though he owns you.'

I patted his liver-spotted hand and kissed his bald head.

'You have no cause for jealousy, Husband.'

But I knew that delicate persuasion would be required if I were to join the expedition to the Overberg.

I encouraged Olof to take the initiative in showing Jan our estate and the adjoining farm at Saxenberg. His humour usually improved when he could impress a visitor from Patria. I stayed at home supervising the household and preparing for the trip.

Jan was quite dazzled by our vineyards and cornfields, our sheep and cattle and the number of slaves and *knechte* employed to run the enterprise.

'I hope I will have time to see the famous Constantia,' he said at the end of the first day. 'Everything Captain Bergh showed me today was compared unfavourably with that estate.'

'It is his ambition to buy the place when Simon van der Stel dies. The old man is very frail now. My husband is one of only a few visitors he entertains these days.'

'You don't sound enthusiastic,' he said, looking at me closely.

'I feel we have enough, but Olof's ambition lingers on,' I replied, trying to sound as neutral as I could.

190

The thought of Constantia brought back not only the memories of my humiliation, but also of the last time I went a little crazy because of a starved appetite. I told myself that I was older now, that I could resist the strong physical attraction I felt for this man who was my biological half brother but really a stranger who was paying me the kind of attention that could easily seduce me

I knew any physical enjoyment would no longer be threatened by fertility; my menses stopped soon after I was fifty. For the first time I would be able to be spontaneous. I caught myself wishing I were a widow and that shocking thought pulled me back from the brink, made me remember the realities of my life, my responsibilities to husband, children and grandchildren. I would not want to be remembered as the grandmother who went mad in her middle age. But I did not abandon my plan to make the trip.

Jan and Polla arrived soon after with wagons and tents and slaves. They had also brought a Hottentot with the knowledge to get us to our destination. Olof inspected the equipment and quizzed Jan Alders as to contingency plans in case of bad weather or attacks by wild animals. Rashly Jan said:

'Why don't you come, Father?'

'Too old,' sighed Olof. 'I can hardly make the journey to Constantia these days.'

'But you don't mind if Mother comes? Polla needs a female companion.'

There it was, out in the open; my plans for gentle persuasion gone in one swoop. Olof looked surprised.

'Annie?' he asked, 'I did not know you were planning to go? Why not take Johanna and Engela?'

'Engela is too young and Johanna has no taste for adventure. Besides, I am beginning to stiffen up. The exercise and hot baths will invigorate me. I need a cure.'

I noticed that Jan de Koning had gone into the house so as not to be part of the discussion. Olof looked doubtful, but when he saw Polla's pleading face, he gave in.

'Be sure to behave yourself,' he whispered as he kissed me goodbye.

Our expedition turned its back on Table Mountain and headed for a kloof in the Hottentots Holland mountains. We resisted the temptation to call at Vergelegen, which was still a magnificent estate, albeit subdivided.

The instructions to raze Willem Adriaen's house to the ground had been ignored and the hexagonal garden was still a place known for its roses. But we were in a hurry and Jan de Koning had to be satisfied with our elaborate descriptions of the place.

That day we saw many ostriches, zebras and antelope. After we crossed the Eersterivier, there was even a group of rhinoceros in the distance. Jan was like a creature on a new planet, bristling with curiosity and excitement. We camped at the foot of the kloof, ate a sumptuous supper and watched the stars for a long time amid the sounds of the wild. Jan Alders instructed the night guards to keep the campfire burning all night.

The next morning we set off on horseback up the kloof, following the wagons that had been disassembled for the crossing. It was hard going and near the top we had to lead the horses and climb the rest of the way. I began to think myself foolhardy for attempting such a difficult trek, but Jan de Koning stayed with me, cautioning, encouraging and lending a hand up rocks and over crevices. When, at last, we reached the top and could look back towards Table Mountain and the whole archipelago stretching along False Bay, I felt proud. Descending was hard work, but was done mostly on horseback.

We crossed the Steenbras River and proceeded to the valley of the Palmiet. We were lucky it was before the rainy season, which made the rivers easily fordable. It was said that in the rainy season one could wait for days until the floods subsided before crossing.

The second night we camped on the banks of the Bot River, at Boontjeskraal. No star-gazing for me. As soon as I could excuse myself, I sought my bed in the tent I shared with Polla. Stiff and sore the next morning, I pretended as best I could that I was fine, but when I was offered a ride on the wagon, I did not hesitate.

Jan accompanied the wagon on horseback, asking endless questions about the vegetation. I was pleased to supply him with informative answers and even more pleased that I had brought a sketchbook. There were species of *sewejaartjies*, ericas and marsh lilies here that I had not seen on the Peninsula or at Drakenstein.

We followed the wagon way a while longer until we came to the track that led across the river to the *bronbult*, the hill on the southern slope of the Zwartberg, where the source of the Yzer Bad was to be found. The high peak of the mountain loomed above and, despite my aching muscles, I felt a strong desire to climb to that peak.

'Wait until you've taken the waters,' cautioned Jan Alders 'Their effect, however, tends to differ from person to person.'

It was late in the afternoon and we decided to wait until the morning to take the waters. While camp was being set up and provisions from Ferdinand Appel's farm collected for our evening meal we took a stroll up to the source. Steaming water bubbled out of the rock running down to two cisterns that had been dug to serve as baths.

That night I could hardly sleep, partly in anticipation of the unique experience that lay ahead, but also because of the sounds of prowling beasts and the nervous reaction of the horses and oxen to these. I was glad to see the bright glow of the campfire and to hear the occasional conversation of the night guards.

Before breakfast the next day we took the waters.

This was the procedure: One sat in the hot bath until the skin turned a bluish red. Then, one made a rapid escape to the tent, where one wrapped oneself in blankets to sweat. When the body had cooled to a normal temperature you took a cold bath before dressing.

The men had discreetly absented themselves while Polla and I took our baths in our petticoats and bodices. They returned only after they were advised that the coast was clear and it was their turn.

Jan Alders was right. The bath affected Polla and me very differently. I felt exhilarated and ready to eat a horse and walk a hundred miles while Polla was so limp that she could hardly move from her bed. It was with great difficulty that I persuaded her to take some breakfast. Weak tea was all she wanted.

My plans to explore the cliffs in search of specimens remained unchanged and I was happy to see that the baths had had an invigorating effect on my brother as well. Together we set out with provisions and tools towards the Zwartberg. Jan took a small rifle in case we should come across an antelope for the pot, though he confessed that he was out of practice. Hunting was not something for which a seaman like himself had much opportunity.

It was a bright day, the temperature on the cool side and perfect for exercise. We found some specimens of *suurknol* and *tontel* as well as different kinds of thistles. Jan marvelled at them, but I could see he was a man of the water, more knowledgable about seaweed and plankton than plants that grew on land.

I made a special effort to keep our conversation light and informative, asking many questions about the plants of Europe, Batavia and Madagascar where I knew he had been. His enthusiasm for this island surprised me.

'There is much money to be made in the slave trade these days. And Madagscar affords many opportunities for someone like me,' he said.

'I have to tell you, Brother, even though I use slaves myself, the slave trade is a practice that makes me uneasy. My husband thinks this is a particularly feminine point of view, out of touch with reality.'

'And he is right. I agree there are bad slave traders who think of nothing but profit, but I would not be one of those. The trade is a fact of life and needs people like me to counterbalance the excesses of those greedy traders.'

'So, you are seriously considering becoming a slave trader? You could just as easily become a Free Burgher here and make your fortune from the land rather than by buying and selling people. Look at us, we flourish from the land.'

I did not mean it as an invitation, but my meaning was misinterpreted. Jan gave me a deep and serious look as he put his hand over mine.

'Would you like me to do that? Be close to you forever?'

My heart beat faster, my throat tightened. Just then I heard a growl above us. Instinctively I grabbed Jan, who put his arm around me instead of pointing his rifle towards the gryskat, now clearly visible on a ledge to our right. It looked ready to jump at any minute.

I disentangled myself from his arm and hid behind him. His trembling was contagious.

'Shoot!' I whispered. 'What are you waiting for?'

He fumbled with the rifle and as the cat jumped a shot rang out. But it was not from Jan's rifle; it came from behind us.

The cat fell to the ground and I spun round to see Olof standing a few feet away, his gun still in the air. I propelled myself into his arms.

'There, you see, I'm not too old to save you,' he said, hugging me tightly. To Jan he said: 'It's a little different from whale-hunting, isn't it, sailor?'

That night Olof told me that he had become irrepressibly jealous as soon as we left the farm. He set out in pursuit of us to prove to himself and the rest of the world that although he was retired, he was still a warrior. I kissed him with more feeling than I had shown in a while.

'You have no reason to be jealous. I am attached to the brother in him, not the man. This trip has proven that to me.'

'But has it proven that to him?'

The story of how Olof saved us underwent several mutations in the mouths of the scandalmongers, especially when Jan de Koning kept trying to delay his departure. He was even arrested and his ship sent off under a different command.

Jan's request to become a Free Burgher was denied and he was sent to Batavia on the first available ship. Olof made no secret of the fact that he had used his influence to achieve this.

I remained at De Cuylen and Jan stayed in town, spending many days in the company of my mother. The day before he left I went to her house to say goodbye, taking good care that Mai Angela was always in our company.

'I will be back,' he said. 'I have two very good reasons to return soon.'

CHAPTER FIFTEEN

Scandal

WHEN I THINK OF my children, I think of them in two batches. The first I raised by myself in difficult times, the second when Olof was at home and we began our steady rise to wealth and importance. Those surviving from the first batch were all girls: Christina, Maria, Apollonia, Johanna and Dorothea, though I think of Dorothea as a 'bridge' child since she was born shortly before Olof returned from Europe.

It seems fortune did not only favour us in terms of prosperity, but also provided for Olof the sons he so desired. Of the second batch, only one was a girl: Engela, my nightingale, born in 1700, a child of the new century. Simon and Martinus came before her, and two years after her came Albertus. Dorothea is, sadly, no longer with us. She joined Petrus and Carolus on the other side when she was taken from us in 1714 during the terrible small pox epidemic.

People say we are lucky we lost only one.

Of all these children only two caused us some public embarrassment and fed the troughs of the gossipmongers for a while. The first was Christina, who married Jacobus de Wet under a cloud of ill will from certain quarters, particularly Johanna Victor. One can hardly blame the poor woman for trying to shift her own disgrace onto others.

Jacobus de Wet had arrived while Olof was still away. He was an Assistant, working for the Company, and was immediately favoured by Governor Simon van der Stel who soon promoted him to Cellar Master, putting him in charge of the export of wines.

Christina was already assistant to Mr Davenraad and was friendly with Josina Pretorius, who worked in a kindergarten close by. I had nothing against the young woman; she was gentle and soft spoken, though not Christina's equal in education and accomplishments. I was worried about her home.

Her mother, Johanna Victor, was a vicious gossip. She made no secret of her dislike for me since I refused to discuss with her any of my private business. She made my life particularly unpleasant during Olof's absence by claiming that she had a correspondent in Ceylon who overheard a conversation between Olof and another Quarter Master. According to her informant, Olof insisted that he was never coming back to the Cape. She spread the rumour that I was a poor deluded soul and that Olof was never coming back.

Johanna Victor also made a point of always including the ethnic background of any subject of her current gossip. I knew she referred to me as 'that illegitimate *mestiza* with her musselman mother'. It was this same mother who helped me from the beginning to ignore the woman and live my life as though she did not exist. When Christina befriended her daughter, there was little I could do but warn her of Josina's mother's reputation.

This warning and my obvious disapproval of the friendship made Christina secretive though she confided somewhat in Maria, who kept me informed of the main events as they unfolded.

Jacobus de Wet soon became friends with the Cruse boys next door so it seemed quite natural that Christina would meet with them in the street and have conversations over the back fence. Josina now sought to become part of these encounters and I noticed as time went on how Jacobus would talk to Christina and flirt with Josina.

I would watch as Jacobus walked with them, one on each arm, nodding at Christina and leaning towards Josina. Josina spent more and more time at our house and when asked whether she was not missed at home, she laughed it off saying her mother knew that she was with her best friend.

I did not like to think of Christina as Josina's best friend, but since Christina did not contradict her, I left it at that. They began to take long walks in the late afternoon, often returning in the company of Jacobus de Wet, who would stay and stay in my parlour long past my bedtime. I insisted on staying up, as it was not proper to leave young people unsupervised especially when it was clear that two of them were in love and obviously hot blooded.

It was the death of our Petrus and my subsequent sadness that brought an end to Josina's frequent visits. This happened after Olof's return from Ceylon. Christina began to frequent the Pretorius household, often coming home after dark though she knew how I worried.

Olof strongly disapproved of the way she was taking liberties, but before he could confront her, she apparently quarrelled with Josina and their friendship dried up. She gave me a vague answer when I asked her about the sudden break with Jo and Jaap, as she called them, but to Maria she explained the whole thing.

'It's all the fault of Jo's mother,' said Maria, 'she told Christina to leave Jo and Jaap alone. Why was she always hanging around them when it was perfectly clear that they did not need a second fiddle? Could she not see they were in love? Or was she hoping to get a piece of the cake herself? Imagine the humiliation!'

Maria told me that Christina did not want me to know this. She knew how I despised Johanna Victor and the incident only showed how right I was. Maria thought that Christina was better off, as Jacobus was taking all kinds of liberties and if Josina were not careful she would find herself in the family way before long.

This in fact was what happened and Josina gave birth to a baby whose patrimony Jacobus de Wet duly acknowledged, even attending the christening of his little namesake. Still, he did not marry Josina. The reason for this unconventional behaviour was that he was now secretly courting my Christina. But in our small community secrets have a short lifespan.

Olof was the first to get wind of the romance after he saw the two of them together in Stellenbosch at the October *kermis* in honour of Simon van der Stel's birthday. That year I stayed at home, but the girls went with Olof to stay with the Huisings. Apparently Christina was never seen outside the company of Jaap de Wet, though Olof saw to it that they conducted themselves respectably. As soon as he noticed them seeking each other out, he appointed Maria and Polla as their sister's constant companions.

'We had so little fun,' complained Polla on her return. 'Who wants to be around the older crowd all the time? Still, the gossip was quite interesting.'

'What gossip, Polla?'

'Oh, what Jo's mother is now saying about us and the Governor.' She was teasing me, feeding me the vitriolic bait bit by bit.

'I can imagine she is calling Christina a slut, but what is she saying about His Excellency?'

'That Jaap is his natural child. I suppose if you look hard you can see some resemblance, but you do need a bit of imagination.'

'She should be careful. People were sent to Robben or Dassen Island for slander like that in the past,' I said. 'What does Jo say? Was she at the *kermis*?'

'She says Christina is welcome to Jaap. She'll soon find out what a miscreant he is. If a man can do it to one woman, why not to another?' This was also my worry.

But Olof did it the proper way. First, we interviewed Christina, who insisted that she had a deep and undying love for the man and had herself done nothing dishonourable or compromising. She admitted that he had behaved badly in the case of Josina, but that this was not uncommon. As a Christian she could find it in her heart to forgive him and give him a second chance. She begged us to do the same, placing a heavy burden on my self-professed tolerance.

I was particularly irked to see how my daughter twisted her father round her little finger. She had his agreement in no time. Jaap was summoned for a formal man-to-man talk to state his intentions. Halfway through this I was invited to join them to air my misgivings. He was an attractive fellow, dark and vivacious like Christina, but that evening he suppressed his high spirits and assumed a convincing gravity, assuring me that he meant to marry my daughter and look after her for the rest of his life.

Before the end of the century they married, after the dust had settled from a civil suit brought by Johanna Victor on behalf of Josina. Fortunately for Jaap, Josina was already pregnant with the child of a farmer from Drakenstein. It was not difficult to convince the court that she was promiscuous. We were all happy when she married the father of her second child and went to live in the farther reaches of the Colony, taking her mother with her.

Of Christina's marriage to Jaap I knew what I saw, and that was much in the beginning and little in the end. He kept her in the manner to which she was accustomed, made her drop her assistantship and involved her in a restless social life, especially during the years of the younger Van der Stels. Her tear-stained eyes, especially when she was pregnant, told me that Jaap was not a faithful husband and was greatly enjoying the fashionable liberties of the times.

Olof had more information than I, but it is amazing how men stick together under the pretence of protecting women.

I do not think Jaap was ever violent, though violently passionate he certainly was from the evidence of lovebites I saw on his wife. They had two children, Olof and Johannes, both still alive today and making their way in the public life of the Colony. But that, I always think, was due to the patient tutelage of their Swedish stepfather, Matthias Bergstedt, whom Christina married shortly after Jaap died of an unexplained fever. Her second marriage was as sedate as the first was tempestuous. Sensible, proper little Elsabe, born from that marriage, seems to personify this.

It pleased Olof a great deal to see his daughter married to a home-grown Swede who knew of his family, though he came from Stockholm on the other side of the country. He was also a member of the Lutheran band of brothers of whom Olof was the senior leader. Christina put the dubious beginnings of her adult life behind her and was restored to respectability.

Much later came Simon's rebellion.

From the moment of his birth, Olof appropriated Simon. After the demise of two male children, my husband rejoiced in the gift of another whom he could mould to his own desires and inclinations.

First, there was his name. On his return from Ceylon, Olof made peace with Simon van der Stel and to show the world that they had put the conflicts of the past behind them they became best friends. I, of course, had my own opinion of the Governor and could only reluctantly manage an arm's length position.

When I opposed the naming of the baby, Olof was puzzled. That was the only time I nearly divulged my dark secret. But I desisted, not wanting to ruin an alliance so essential to our future well being.

Despite the fact that the boy was baptised Simon, not Olof, he received all the extra care and attention due to a son and heir. From the beginning I knew that Simon was not made of the stuff of soldiers. He had an imaginative intelligence far beyond his years, and loved nothing better than to spend hours with my paint brushes. Olof countered this natural inclination by planning for him a rigorous programme of riding and shooting that gave him barely enough time for a proper education.

Nevertheless, Simon found time to do what he liked after dark. He used more candles secretly than his father would ever know of. What he did like about his father's work was construction, and it was said of the bridge at De Cuylen that it was designed by Simon and built by Olof. In this way Simon sought to please his father without giving up on his own nature.

The biggest quarrel between them arose as a result of Olof's portrait. This unfinished work had been sitting in our attic since the hasty departure of Heinrich Claudius. Heinrich had only managed to paint Olof's face and his coat of arms with the unicorn and areca palm. He had added a pistol on a table to indicate that Olof was a soldier.

The portrait also bore the inscription indicating Olof's age: *Aetatis Sui 41, Anno 1685*, which I added after Olof was sent to Robben Island.

Simon found the painting and decided to add a body to the face. It would be a surprise for Olof. He made careful enquiries as to the style of dress twenty years earlier and, when he was satisfied that he knew where to put all the buttons and how to detail the lace cravat, he set about his task. The only trouble was that he had had no lessons in portrait painting and wanted to include too much on the limited space on the canvas.

The result was that the body was hopelessly out of proportion to the face and, instead of creating an image of dignity, the whole portrait was turned into something rather farcical. It looked as if Olof's face had popped through a hole in the canvas above a ridiculously small body with hunched shoulders, a protruding belly and thin arms devoid of the well-developed soldier's muscles for which Olof was famous.

I urged the boy to hide the portrait even deeper than he had found it, but Albertus, with the indiscretion of the baby he was at the time, told Olof about the funny picture and Simon was forced to produce the caricature. It was clear that the unintended insult disturbed him greatly and no protestation from Simon or myself could persuade him otherwise.

Olof Bergh, courtesy of Cape Archives, Elliott Collection

'This artistic mutilation must convince both of you that this boy is no artist!' he said sarcastically. 'From now on you will concentrate on soldiering, Simon. I do not ever want to see a paint brush in your hand again. And this aiding and abetting by your mother will stop!'

I thought he was going to slash the canvas to pieces, but all he said was:

'Remove that thing from my sight, but let it be a reminder to us all that Simon Bergh cannot paint!'

The canvas remained intact for posterity, but Simon's pride was in tatters. I do not think he ever forgave Olof that remark. But Olof was a powerful force and capable of imposing his will on stronger characters than Simon, who joined the Garrison under his father's command as soon as he was sixteen. He only took up painting again in the years after Olof died.

A year before Olof passed away, Simon fell in love with Sophie Tauken, daughter of Johann Tauken who came to the Cape as a soldier and was for a short while employed by Olof as a *knecht*, an overseer, at our farm Saxenberg. Olof's opinion of Johann Tauken was that he was lazy and not entirely honest, and he was supposed to have fathered a number of slave children. When Johann became a Free Burgher, he had tried to cheat Olof in a cattle deal, taking a hundred sheep more than he paid for, thinking it would not be noticed.

After that, Olof had nothing good to say about Johann Tauken and almost rejoiced in reports that Tauken's farm, in the Land van Waaveren, was not thriving. He often expressed his opinion that the drunk and the lazy will make a mess wherever they are, even on prime land like that in the newest district of the Colony.

'Poverty is a state of mind', was Olof's final dismissal. He was very displeased that when Sophie Tauken decided to leave her father's home and better herself in town, Apollonia, who was now married to Jan Alders and was living in the big double house that once belonged to Albert Koopman, had offered her lodgings.

I liked Sophie; she was shy and modest, a dreamer and lover of music, an excellent seamstress. She reminded me a little of what I was like before I had the opportunity to develop my talents. Simon saw this potential, much as his father had seen mine so long ago.

I pointed this out to Olof when he first opposed the marriage, but he was not convinced.

'It is not the same at all, Annie. You came from a background of strong moral fibre. Your mother raised you properly despite her disadvantages in life; she set you a good example. This girl has none of that to offer. I would not be surprised if her father put her up to this. I can imagine him saying to her "Go and catch one of the Bergh boys. Martinus is already taken, but there is still Simon or Albertus. Marry one of them and bring a little of their money this way to help us out of the fix we're in".'

'I don't think he said anything of the kind,' I protested mildly, thankful that he seemed to have forgotten my mother's several illegitimate children.

'Don't contradict me, Annie,' he said in that particular dictatorial tone of his old age when his manners were no longer tempered by tender feelings. 'We must stand united in making it very clear to Simon that this marriage will not happen under any circumstances. I will have him sent on an expedition and if this does not cool his passion, I will have him demoted. Under no circumstances will any of my wealth go to the seed of that disreputable character Tauken. If Simon marries her I will disinherit him.'

I knew he was serious, and I was caught in the middle. I conveyed Olof's opinion to Simon, who responded with stubborn anger. 'We'll see,' he said, his mouth a thin, unhappy line that tore at my heart.

I went around to lobby all his brothers and sisters, but got little support from them. They thought Olof was as unreasonable as I did, but they did not have to live with him.

Olof brought his influence to bear and had Simon sent on a lengthy expedition to the Overberg. Sophie waited patiently in Appolonia's house, sewing, and singing, until he returned.

By this time we were living at Constantia, where Olof was to die the following year. Simon was summoned and arrived smartly dressed in his Ensign's uniform, with Sophie Tauken in tow. Fortunately I saw her getting out of the carriage and spirited her away before Olof could see her.

'What are you trying to do?' I said to Simon. 'Showing a red rag to a bull? You don't realise how serious this is, do you?' Sophie looked at me in consternation.

'We thought if the old Heer Bergh could meet me and have a proper conversation, he might realise that I am not as unsuitable as he thinks,' she ventured bravely.

'He's not against your person, child. He's against the idea of you, your background, your father's reputation. He must not see you; he wants to speak to Simon alone. You and I will go for a walk.'

I was annoyed. Looking after Sophie meant that I could not be a buffer between father and son. We walked for over an hour during which time I made sure that the reason for the marriage was not a pregnancy. We returned to a raging quarrel, raised voices audible all the way down the avenue.

'You can do nothing to deflect me from my purpose, Father. Disinherit me, demote me, see if I care!' shouted Simon audaciously.

'Oh, you will care when the time comes, my boy. You are so soft, so used to luxury and privilege. You'll soon care when you are deprived of those things. And so will the young woman when she hears that she is marrying nothing but a common soldier without any prospect of wealth!' threatened Olof.

Sophie heard this as clearly as I did and the rush of blood to her face did not escape me. Nor did the trembling in her voice when she said: 'It does not sound too hopeful, does it?'

'Not at all,' I agreed

Olof followed through on his threat and Simon was demoted to the rank of soldier. The whole family stood aghast at this wielding of power, but no one, including myself, did more than protest mildly in an effort to dissuade him. No wonder Simon felt alone in his struggle.

He went to pieces when it was rumoured that Sophie was now beginning to show an interest in the attentions of Sybrand Steen, a farmer from Stellenbosch. The fact that her resolve had weakened, that her love for him was not strong enough to wait a little longer until his father had passed away, convinced him that he had been completely abandoned. To Olof it only confirmed his suspicion that the girl was a gold digger who, finding nothing but fools' gold, upped tools to look somewhere else.

Polla made a special trip to Constantia to inform us that Simon was on a hunger strike. He had intermittent fevers, taking nothing but water and refused any medical attention or remedy. His father dismissed it as passing hysteria, undignified in a man, but I rushed to town with Polla to see for myself. He had been moved from his quarters in the Castle to the hospital.

My poor child looked terrible. He had not eaten for three weeks. He was dishevelled, passive and pale, but his dark eyes glowed in his head. The hospital reeked of the fumes from the sudatorum where sailors were being treated for the pox.

'Why are you doing this, Simon?' I asked weakly. He raised himself slightly.

'To show the world, Mother, to show you and my father and Sophie and the whole family that I have the will to protest this injustice until my last breath.'

It was a long sentence for a weak man and he fell back on the rough hospital pillow.

'Simon, please, stop this, for my sake! You are breaking my heart!'

'Mine is already broken, Mother. But no one will break my spirit,' he mumbled.

I wept, I begged, but to no avail. His parting message to me was:

'Tell that stubborn old man that I would rather die than give in. Let my death be on his conscience!'

This I repeated word for word to Olof. He was outraged.

'That boy has forgotten everything he has ever been taught, including God's command to respect and obey his parents!' he shouted, adding divine authority to his own. 'We will write a letter asking the Council to send him to one of the Indian colonies. Batavia or Ceylon or even Melakka; as long as he gets away from here!'

When he saw my hesitation he added: 'I will personally present this letter.'

I knew it was fruitless to argue; my resistance to his plan would be seen as treason. But I made a plan of my own. Olof had already had two attacks of apoplexy that left his right side weak. He walked with difficulty though he insisted on inspecting the farm on foot every day. He managed to do this on level ground, but even the gentle slopes of the Steenberg he found too difficult to negotiate.

When the time came to deliver the letter I persuaded Olof that he was too frail for the journey into town. I would present the letter to the Council.

Polla's husband, Jan Alders, was at this time a member of the Council. I saw to it that I arrived in good time on the Monday before the meeting on Tuesday, the 21st of September. This would give me time to have a serious word with Jan, who would have time to consult with Caje Slotsboom and Jan de la Fontaine and perhaps even Governor Maurits de Chavonnes himself.

It also gave me time to play with my latest little grandchild and first namesake, little Anna Rincina, who was just beginning to smile.

I presented the letter and, because of prior consultation, it did not take the Council long to decide not to send Simon to Batavia, but rather to order him to take a leave of absence, which was to be spent at the home of his parents. This was in many ways a signal from the Council to Olof to reconcile with his son. Everyone also knew that Sophie was to marry Sybrand Steen within the week and that the hospital was opposite the church.

I took Simon back to Constantia with me that very day. He seemed to accept the authority of the Council, his resolve much weakened by a lack of food and Sophie's change of heart.

So, for a while I had two 'patients' to contend with. Simon insisted on staying in the guesthouse, which forced me to overcome my disdain for the place. I, who had never allowed a wet nurse near any of my children, would feed this special son of mine the gruel and porridge that would give him the strength he needed to make his peace with his father before he died.

In nursing Simon I had the excellent help of Moeda van Slaaijer and his wife, Sien, who watched him for me night and day. I visited Simon often and took walks with him when I was not required to do the same with his father. Olof ignored his presence and maintained a heavy silence whenever there was a chance of Simon's name being mentioned.

Towards the end of November Simon began to take walks up the mountain, carrying a small rucksack. Soon Sien conveyed a request for paper and pencil that I gladly gave but did not dare mention to Olof. I rejoiced because I knew Simon was on his way to recovery.

That Christmas we had a family celebration at Constantia. All the children came and stayed until New Year. There was nothing more natural than for Simon to be in the presence of his father as one of the crowd and Olof accepted this oblique reconciliation.

For Olof those were the last golden days, surrounded by his children and grandchildren, getting over-excited, speaking with difficulty, but very unwilling to miss any of the fun.

We indulged him. He drank far too much wine than was good for him and stayed up far too late, though he did take many little catnaps in his chair during the day when he thought no one was looking. Simon told Martinus and Jan Alders that he would be going back to the Barracks when everyone went back to Cape Town.

A month later Olof had his final stroke. He was eighty years old, an age reached by few. We held a Lutheran service on the farm but he was buried with military honours in the churchyard in town.

I looked at my place next to him and wondered how long it would be before I would fill it. Little did I know that I still had ten years of widowhood ahead of me.

Chapter Sixteen

Bombyx mori

THE MAGIC OF METAMORPHOSIS touches me every time I watch silkworms. I never fail to be excited by the process year after year.

It all begins when the tiny, black silkworms hatch from minuscule eggs the size of pinheads. The minute they free themselves, after a year of maturation inside the pewter-coloured eggs, they wave their hungry heads in the air in search of the only food they eat – mulberry leaves. Like all caterpillars, they are voracious eaters and when they all munch together it sounds like softly falling rain.

During the six weeks of apparent non-stop feasting, they do take a break to molt. This happens four times in the life of a silkworm. The first instar, as the stages of molting are called, happens when the caterpillar is barely the length of the nail on my little finger. Miraculously prompted by nature, the tiny creature removes itself from food and friends to sit for twenty-four hours with its head raised, motionless as though in prayer.

When I saw this the first time I was alarmed, thinking the poor little creatures were sick, but the next morning I saw small shrivelled black tubes scattered all over the place. The worms had shed their skins and appeared bigger and whiter. I stopped worrying about their health when I saw how they were attacking their food with renewed appetite.

The moulting can easily be observed at the fourth instar when the worm is about the size of my little finger. The smooth grayish-white skin takes on a brownish hue and becomes like wrinkled parchment. The scab over the nose has changed from light to dark brown. The little black dots that mark the breathing holes become connected as black stripes appear on the sides of the insect. I am told this is when the new skin inside secretes a liquid as lubrication to separate the old skin from the new.

Soon the contractions begin and continue until the worm leaves the shrunken old skin behind. The last thing the worm does it to drop the old nose scab. Now the pale-skinned, pale-nosed creature is ready to eat again without stopping until impelled by nature to the next stage.

The worm stops eating and adopts a yellow translucence as it looks for a corner to anchor the first threads of the silk filament from which its cocoon is spun. Back and forth it goes, side to side, building the outer layers of its cocoon. Within a day it has trapped itself inside an oval-shaped silk fortress, leaving behind only a patch of liquid. The patient observer will wait for two weeks for signs of activity from that golden cocoon. Then a wet spot appears at one end of the cocoon, dissolving enough silk to make a small hole through which the moth crawls.

Those who are too curious may open the cocoon to find inside a pupa covered in a brown carapace. It is inert, the only sign of life a tiny wiggle when poked. The creature is best left untouched, but may be covered in kapok for artificial protection. By removing the cover from time to time the mutation of pupa can be observed, the shape of wings gradually becoming visible under the glossy outer shell

Finally the thrilling moment arrives: a furry white moth with feathery antennae and beady black eyes appears. From tiny black caterpillar to handsome white moth, the metamorphosis of *Bombyx mori* is complete.

Breeding begins almost immediately. The male, its body much thinner than that of the plump, egg-laden female, begins to flutter his wings frantically in search of a mate. It is said that the female emits an odour that attracts the male to her. With protruding procreative organs they hitch themselves together back to back and remain in happy copulation for at least a day.

Upon detachment, his usefulness at an end, the male is destined to die. The female now methodically deposits her fertile eggs side by side on the closest flat surface or on the nearest empty cocoon. For a day or so the eggs are yellow, but soon turn grey, a sign that they have been fertilised. And thus they remain until the next spring, developing a slight indentation in the centre as the maturing worm arranges itself around the outer walls of the egg.

There are two things to watch at the beginning of spring: the eggs and the new leaves on the mulberry tree. If there is the slightest sign of hatching before there are delicate new leaves on the tree, the coldest place for those eggs has to be found to delay the hatching.

The ant is the natural enemy of the silkworm at every stage of its life. I have seen ants attack caterpillars, moths and eggs with ferocity, leaving behind only nose scabs, antennae or yellow egg shells within a few hours. During one year, after we lost almost all our silkworms when the ants were really bad, Olof provided a military solution: surround the worms with water.

We put the baskets that held the worms into watertight containers inside a large vat filled with water, making sure that there was no way the ants could form a bridge to their prey. So you see, the successful silkworm breeder has to be constantly vigilant and ingenious, ready to apply the 'moat' as soon as the ants are spotted in the vicinity of worms, moths or eggs.

My passion for silkworms began during those years when Olof was away in Ceylon and Occum Chamnam called at the Cape on his third voyage to Europe. Apparently he had attempted to bring me some eggs on his second voyage, but the eggs hatched at sea and there were no mulberry leaves.

That time we were also not allowed to communicate because Occum Chamnam was in contact with Father Tachard who had just revealed to the world the 'strategic' information given to him by Heinrich Claudius. Simon van der Stel considered this an act of deceit, if not treason, and Heinrich was deported to Batavia. Those were times fraught with misadventure and dashed hopes and so the fact that the attempt to bring silkworms to the Cape was unsuccessful came as no surprise to me.

But when Occum Chamnam arrived at the Cape for a third time, the Governor's paranoia was a thing of the past and I was able to entertain him at my house in a manner befitting a nobleman. This time he was not an envoy, but was visiting Europe for his own pleasure. He had retired from public life and was occupying himself with his estates in general and his silk farming in particular.

He had brought the tiny eggs in a wooden box, but carried with him a bamboo basket in which the hatched silkworms were to be fed and a light wooden frame with small compartments in which they were to spin their cocoons. He advised me to move the moths to a bigger wooden container where the eggs could be laid.

'My previous experience gives me good hope that the eggs will hatch despite the fact that the seasons are reversed and they have only been in the eggs for six months. I have heard of a technique by which the eggs can be forced to hatch after six months to produce a second crop of cocoons, but on my farms we get so many cocoons every spring that the spinning and weaving takes the rest of the year. Besides, we are too far north to expect leaves on the mulberry trees all year round.'

We inspected the supply of mulberry leaves in town as well as at Rustenburg, where large mulberry trees flourished. Occum Chamnam inquired about the colour of the berries. As far as I could tell they were always dark purple when ripe.

'That is curious; our berries are white. I wonder if it will make a difference to the colour and quality of the silk?'

It was only after his departure that this question was partly answered. Our cocoons turned out yellow, some pale lemon, some gold, some a deep saffron. The quality would

KITES OF GOOD FORTUNE

not be determined for many years after the first serious attempt at producing silk for the market was made.

Those first eggs hatched soon after Occum Chamnam's departure and I began to keep silkworms as a pastime rather than a business. What kept me back was my reluctance to put the cocoons with the live pupa inside in to boiling water in order to obtain a continuous thread of silk from each cocoon.

I was told the pupae would be in great demand as a delicacy and eagerly sought after by the Chinese exiles from Java who were beginning to open eating houses specialising in their own exotic cuisine. But for many years I was like a person who enjoys fishing up to the point where the fish has to be taken off the hook. A sentimental reservation, I agree, and one that has prevented me from trying to establish a silk industry of my own.

It is only now, in the autumn of my life, that this has become a possibility. Francois Guillaumet, an expert in sericulture, travelled with me on the *Berbices* on my return from Holland. He is a Protestant from Languedoc and has been employed by the Company to produce silk on a commercial scale.

Guillaumet's presence was the result of years of lobbying by a younger, more enterprising generation of young men born at the Cape looking for agricultural diversification. They have been acquainted with my silkworms since boyhood and are not afraid to take the fish off the hook. Nicolaas Heijning and Captain Pierre de Chavonnes, spurred on by my Martinus and sons-in-law Johan Rhenius and Jan Alders, have been at the forefront of the petitions and requests to the Lords XVII.

Under my instruction, Nicolaas was placed in charge of breeding enough silkworms to justify a small industry. He even went so far as to dunk some cocoons in boiling water and have a nimble-fingered slave girl unwind the thread. Our ignorance about the process and equipment needed for spinning the yarn made it imperative, however, to find an expert to help us.

When I left for Holland the silkworms were moved to a room at the back of the house of Pierre de Chavonnes. Nicolaas Heijning promised me he would give them his personal attention and this he did faithfully.

When I went with Monsieur Guillaumet on his first inspection, the eggs had only just begun to hatch and numerous little black specks were wriggling on the leaves, munching holes through them. Many eggs remained unhatched, but the process is unstoppable once it starts.

'It seems I arrive right at the beginning of the season, Madame Bergh,' he said, pronouncing my name with a soft 'g'. 'The eggs and worms are in excellent condition.'

'Oh, we know how to cultivate the worms, Monsieur. It is for the winding and spinning that we need a silk master.'

'You know I will soon need a shed to accommodate the tanks for the cocoons,' he said. My heart shrank at the thought, but I resisted expressing a sentiment that I knew he would find ridiculous.

'We requested your house with that specific need in mind. You will have noticed that within the walls there is enough space for one large shed or perhaps two smaller ones. It is also conveniently situated close to the mulberry trees that grow along the stream in the Gardens.'

'That I have noticed, Madame, but you know those trees will not provide nearly enough leaves if we are to produce silk on a commercial scale.'

'Don't you worry, Monsieur. Tomorrow we will go out to Rustenburg to see the proper mulberry groves. And if you still don't think there are enough, we can plant some more. We have the space and the means as well as the backing of Governor de la Fontaine.'

My optimism reassured him. I wanted him to think of this as a real enterprise rather than an old woman's obsession, which it was. But I could sense my own decline and it worried me that commercial motivation might not be enough to sustain this undertaking. My love had kept these silkworms going for so long.

217

Monsieur Guillaumet did well.

The first year after his arrival we produced eight pounds of wound and spun silk. In my excitement about the product I managed to overcome my scruples about the sacrifice of pupae and watched with fascination as the threads were wound from several cocoons at once to form thin strands that were spun and rolled onto spools.

I caressed the first spool of soft yellow yarn as if to bless their journey. My dream was beginning to come true.

The silk was sent to Holland, four pounds to the Chamber of Amsterdam and four to the Chamber of Zeeland. Reports came back praising the quality of the silk. It seemed to make no difference whether the worms were fed on the leaves of white or of red mulberry trees. My bevy of silk enthusiasts was encouraged to proceed and another wooden shed was built in the yard of the silk master. The street on which he lived and worked was renamed Spinstraat.

Two years later the ants got to the eggs before the silk master. His plan to hatch a second batch failed. We sent out an appeal to all non-commercial silkworm growers to donate eggs and we managed a small crop the next year, keeping enough moths to bring us back to our original production the following year.

That was where I left that business and sought to complete this narrative. Every day I feel the creeping paralysis escalate, making the act of writing an effort. I raise my arms with difficulty and shuffle when I walk. I need help with bathing and to get in and out of bed.

The excellent eyeglasses I obtained in Holland four years ago afford me some vision, though I find myself peering, my nose close to the page, most of the time.

However, I still have a few things to tell you to make the story complete. I am fortunate to have my loving children and grandchildren around me and enough trustworthy hands to help in the house. I am happy to be living at Annasrust rather than Constantia, where I know Olof would have liked to see me.

This is my cocoon, to which I will retreat for my final phase, having partaken so voraciously of life's mulberry leaves. And when I appear in Heaven, I wonder if there will be angels with the wings of *Bombyx mori*?

Chapter Seventeen

Journey

ALL MY LIFE I HAVE felt divided, as though the ground on which my life was based, my melody and harmony, rhythm and tempo were African, but every ornamentation, every improvisation, every trill and grace note were European.

The thoughts, ideas and beliefs that nourished my heart and soul, the language in which I expressed myself, came from distant places, transported across thousands of miles of heaving oceans. Africa nourished my fertile body, provided the means for my considerable fortune, but European culture governed every way in which I conducted myself.

My mind possessed concepts my eyes had never seen, natural phenomena like snow and frozen ponds, animals like bears and beavers, trees like chestnuts and birch. These were all common in reading and conversation, represented in engravings and illustrations, described by friends and travellers. Fragments, pasted together in my mind's eye to create the place where I was supposed to belong, to make of me a European.

And yet, all along, I had the uneasy feeling that things did not quite fit, that, in order to fully comprehend this world, I needed to see with my own eyes and feel with my own skin the seasons and landscape of Europe. I often wondered how much of me was real, how much simply a European imitation. Was I merely a copy of a European flower, painted in African pigments? I had the strongest desire to measure my authenticity and in order to do that I would have to go to the source, and see for myself.

The letters of condolence that came after Olof's death were filled with invitations for me to visit Europe. Marie Claudius was one of the people with whom I had maintained a correspondence, partly in honour of our brief closeness, but also to assure myself of contact with the outside world, to keep me outward- rather than inward-looking. Marie was now living in Greenwich with her third husband, an elderly musician. It was her confidence that I could make the long journey that encouraged me to be brave enough to follow my lifelong ambition.

'I have so much to tell you, so much to show you, such a desire to see you and share your laughter,' she wrote. Who could resist such an invitation, such an opportunity to recapture the happy times of more than thirty years before?

Francina van Rheede was more mysterious: '*You must certainly visit me at Te Vliet although I spend more time in Utrecht in my humble townhouse than on the estate. Utrecht is full of music and cheerful people, a cure I need after the succession of sad losses of the past years. I have the pleasure of talking often with an erstwhile acquaintance of yours, but have been sworn to secrecy in naming him. Why don't you come and find out who it is?*'

She knew the child in me would find such an enigma irresistible. Annie Bergh was always up to the challenge of solving a mystery!

From Gothenburg came a warm invitation from Olof's sister, Christina Ruth, to come and stay for as long as I liked. It was as though they all realised that, freed from my wifely responsibilities, I had the energy, the means and the curiosity to undertake such an arduous and dangerous journey. The lure of promises to shower me with music and culture, expose me to all the new trends in style and fashion, and arrange meetings with the botanists to whom I had for so many years sent copies of Cape flowers convinced me that it was an opportunity I could not pass up.

The idea did not initially appeal to most of my children. My married daughters thought it my duty to be a devoted grandmother to their children and Johanna objected to being left alone to manage my affairs. Albertus and Marthinus seemed more concerned for my safety and well being, trying to discourage me with tales of danger and disease. I realised my children were spoilt by my ever available presence; it would do them good to depend on themselves for once.

Simon was the only one who thought well of the enterprise. I decided that he would be my travelling companion. A trip to Europe would be just the thing to broaden his horizons, relieve him of the discontent he felt in the narrowness of colonial life. He was artistic and curious, temperamental and imaginative, passionate and intense, all qualities discouraged by the limited opportunities of our small society.

After his rebellion in the matter of Sophie Tauken and out of respect for his ailing father, Simon had settled down to a pretense of acceptance of his life as a soldier, but I was not fooled. The long hours he spent in his room at De Cuylen drawing plans and building models was a constant reminder that his passion lay elsewhere. Convincing him that he should accompany me was not difficult. It was as though the proposition suddenly let sunlight into his life and brought forth an enthusiasm and sense of adventure that had been dormant during the difficult years of his early manhood. He threw himself into the details of all our arrangements and left me little to do, but pack and say goodbye.

Seeing that I was determined to go, Marthinus and his friends charged me with the final negotiations that would bring to the Cape the master sericulturalist, Francois Guillaumet. They were keen to turn an old lady's hobby into an enterprise and the detailed proposals for a future silk factory at the Cape were entrusted to me for hand delivery to the Lords XVII. No doubt, they counted on my personal appeal and the assurance I carried with my name to get the whole project off the ground. Having business to conduct gave validity to my journey, made it seem less capricious.

We awaited the arrival of the return fleet with anticipation and rejoiced that this year there were no major delays in continuing the voyage to Patria. Admiral Hans Bergman had no hesitation in offering us the best accommodation on board his flagship, the *Castricum*. I was to travel in style as behove a sea captain's daughter, albeit one who had never braved the outer ocean.

On the morning of our departure, the quay was crowded with children, grandchildren, friends, soldiers and slaves all come to see us transported to the *Castricum*. I knew that many of them feared they would never see me alive again. In my tearless, confident farewell I tried to convince them that I never doubted my return. I barely looked back at dear Table Mountain, the Castle and the flag on Signal Hill, so much did I focus my anticipation and desires on the adventure ahead.

We had what is known as a prosperous voyage, uneventful, save for one tempest off the Skeleton Coast to remind us of our mortality and the risk we were taking. Apart from that we weathered well, enjoying the seascapes and the company of Admiral Bergman. I was surprised to find how little the cramped quarters and reduced elegance bothered me.

The Admiral had a wide general knowledge and was an informed astronomer who took great pleasure in explaining the sky at night. Every night we would note the stars that had vanished from the sky. This was how we knew we were sailing toward the northern hemisphere, from spring into autumn. After three months at sea we reached Amsterdam, its impressive skyline imposed upon a background of an immense expanse of grey cloud. The absence of Table Mountain brought a wave of longing. I knew that however much I tried to push Africa into the background to make room for this new experience, this next year, in these foreign parts, would inevitably be an exercise in comparison.

And so it was: Amsterdam was bigger, busier, more developed in terms of paved streets and walled canals than I could ever have imagined. It set my head spinning to be in a place where the canal boat took several turns before it finally delivered us to our lodging on the Heerengracht. This canal was lined by so many splendid houses that I could understand why visitors to the Cape sought to hide their amusement at the name of our street which had, running along it, not a canal but a stream. How naively rural our city must have seemed to them. Here everything was on such a much grander scale, gradually acquired over centuries of habitation; it had the confidence and maturity that, by comparison, made the town in the Table Valley seem as though it was truly still in its infancy.

People of every description and station were everywhere, the wealthy in their chairs and carriages, those in trade and service thronging the streets, all well dressed and seemingly prosperous. But what was very noticeable was the absence of brown and black faces, particularly of those doing menial work. Simon, who knew perfectly well what to expect, could not keep himself from remarking,

'Look, a white fellow sweeping the street, Mother, and there are some white women doing laundry.'

'They're all white here, Simon,' I replied quietly. 'We with our sallow complexions are the ones out of place.' I wondered whether this would be for or against us. As it turned out, it was the way we were dressed and the company we kept that determined the respect with which we were treated.

Only occasionally did someone refer to our colour when the conversation turned to the number of Cape colonists who, like myself, came from mixed parentage. It was generally agreed that if Simon and I were examples of mixed marriages, there could be nothing against it. Privately I wondered if this would have been the case had we been less refined and poorer, but I was not here to court controversy nor to test the prejudices of those so elegantly hosting and toasting us.

We were lodged by Jan de Koning's sister, Barbara, who lived on the modest side of the *gracht*. Her house was already more than seventy years old and, although gabled in a less ostentatious period, the interior was elaborately decorated in Italian plaster work. Simon thought the proportions and subject excessive, but I adored sleeping below the cherubs and waking to the sound of bells coming from several nearby church carillons.

It took us a few days to recover our land legs, but somehow in Amsterdam I never recovered my equanimity. I felt as though I was being drawn into the vortex of Europe without the ability to control myself or my surroundings. I forced myself to get up every morning, eat three meals a day despite the messages my stomach sent, see the sights, meet whoever our busy social schedule expected us to meet and, above all, remained cheerful.

I managed to present my petition for the silk factory and was given permission to engage Monsieur Guillaumet who was already in Amsterdam awaiting instructions. It was agreed that he would go back to Languedoc, wind up his responsibilities in the silk factory there, gather the necessary equipment and join us on the voyage back to the Cape. In a way, this arrangement reassured me that I was going back and made the sense of rootlessness bearable.

Simon had no such problems. He took to the place like a duck to water and rushed around with his sketchbook drawing everything in sight. He wore himself out visiting buildings and studios, churches and guildhalls. He soon found himself adopted by a set of young artists and seemed grateful when Caspar Commelin, retired from his position as botanist of the medicinal and rare plant garden in Amsterdam, offered to take me to Utrecht.

'Leave the young to themselves,' said Commelin, 'I hardly understand what they are talking about these days. But your boy is obviously enjoying himself.'

'I suspect he is an amusing diversion for his sophisticated new friends, though I don't doubt their sincerity in befriending him. As for Simon, he finds everything here highly stimulating He tells me that it feels as though he is at the university he was never able to attend.'

I could see Caspar Commelin suppress a smile and wondered whether it was to hide his amusement at my old-fashioned Dutch or the keenness with which I pointed out our colonial disadvantages. He was a little younger than I and had been the most recent recipient of my copies of Cape flowers.

Caspar took me under his wing and introduced me to the botanical community in Amsterdam. Being one of those who insisted on calling the Cape 'the Promontory', he called me '*Flora promontoriensis*' and, as he paraded me round, proudly made it known that I was the only Cape woman he had ever known who could read Latin. I did not confess to the fact that my Latin was limited to the under-standing of Herbaria and kept a low profile when the learned professors of Leyden conversed in that language.

These august scholars treated me with the respect they reserved for exotic specimens. I felt like a rare bulb or root to be examined. They subjected me to an endless array of ques-tions, well aware that I could enhance their understanding with my local knowledge. We talked for hours on end about the Cape soil, the habitat of various plants and the climate. They were fascinated to hear about my expeditions with famous botanists whom they only knew from books.

I became sought after as a dinner guest. But the more I talked about the Cape, the more foreign Holland felt. I looked at those transplanted disas and *pypies*, struggling to survive in the conservatories of Amsterdam and I wondered if they too were homesick.

Francina van Rheede's's frequent inquiries as to when I would be coming to Utrecht began to weigh on me and I decided that the time was ripe for a visit to Francina's 'humble townhouse' on the Nieuwe Gracht. I left Simon in Amsterdam with a promise that he would join me again at Christmas at Te Vliet.

Caspar joined me. He knew Francina well. As a young man he was involved in the publication of the Baron van Rheede's opus magnum, the *Hortus Malabaricus*, and had published his own alphabetical index to all the volumes. In a way, both Caspar and Francina shared in the prestige of her father's work: she to raise her equity; he to add to his scholarship.

At first glance I knew there was nothing humble about Francina's townhouse. It was as grand as Constantia with far more ostentation in interior decor than Willem Adriaen van der Stel ever achieved at Vergelegen. The walls were laden with paintings and tapestries, the floors strewn with oriental silk carpets, the furniture as ornate as the ceilings in the fashionable Italian style. Rich brocade in gold and blue covered the dainty chairs and sofas, catching the light from large windows.

Francina herself, when she appeared, was like a metaphor for opulence. Her neck and fingers were heavy with jewels, her rotund figure clad in dark blue silk velvet and French lace. I felt dwarfed by her appearance and the shyness and hesitation of the country bumpkin took hold of me. But when she smiled, her wide mouth turning up, her dark round eyes narrowing, she was the friend of my youth again.

My anxiety fell away as we embraced.

'Annie, my dear, how well you have aged!' she exclaimed. 'Ten children and still the figure of a young woman! How do you manage it?'

'It's all the climbing in search of flowers and horseback riding that does it. And then there is the lack of confections of which you seem to have an abundance in Holland. I have already had to have my clothes altered once because of my indulgence. But you, Francina, your smile has remained exactly the same.'

We hugged each other again before Francina greeted Caspar and took us to our rooms up the sweeping central staircase.

'If this is a humble townhouse, Francina, how grand is the manor at Te Vliet?' I asked teasingly. A shadow passed over her face.

'This is the only place I can afford to keep properly. We've had to close off part of Te Vliet after Pankhuizen's death. It appeared he had debts I did not know of. And I, myself, am not exactly a genius at management. Still, there is plenty of room and provisions left for all of us to celebrate the holidays properly at Te Vliet. Did I tell you I have managed to persuade Marie and Willem Adriaen to join us? He is apparently quite frail but has agreed to risk the journey.'

'What a lovely reunion that will be!' I was truly thrilled. It would be good to see a happy Marie van der Stel; for her sake I could be tolerate her husband.

Francina began to list our engagements. I was delighted to hear how many dinners would be preceded or followed by musical performances. It seemed Locatelli was the name on everybody's lips and although the maestro lived in Amsterdam, he had a devoted following in Utrecht who performed his works and attempted, in vain according to Francina, to equal his virtuosity.

'But we also have some who still play the recorder and viol music I know you love so well. In fact my neighbour at the back is very involved in amateur consort playing.' There was a mischievous twinkle in her eye. 'You'll meet him tomorrow.'

The next morning I insisted on taking my recorder into the walled garden behind the house. Autumn had taken its toll on the vegetation, frost had already shrivelled the leaves on perennials and the wind had relieved the trees of their summer garb, revealing their inner shapes. It was a sight unimaginable in the temperate climate to which I was accustomed. For the first time in my life I was experiencing a menacing cold that made me cover my hands in gloves, not as a fashion accessory, but to keep warm.

Removing these gloves to play the recorder seemed foolish, but I thought to challenge the cold. Perhaps I could create my own warmth with my music. I played the tune of the *Engels Nachtegaeltje*. The notes rose through the thin crisp air. As I paused to play the first division, I heard the opening notes of the theme from the adjoining garden. The player paused at the first imitation of the nightingale's call and I immediately responded by playing the repeated notes of the counter call.

It was an amusing game. We played thus through all the divisions, answering each other. A door in the wall connected the two gardens, and at the end of the musical conversation, I saw this door open, revealing a stout gentleman in an old-fashioned coat and wig. The face, though broadened, was unmistakable.

'Egbertus Wieland,' I said and moved quickly to meet his embrace and wide smile. 'So, it is you who are the mysterious neighbour?'

'Annie, my dear,' was all he could say.

And suddenly I felt young again. All the ardour I felt for him so many years ago came flooding back. I forgot I was an old lady and he, probably, a married man, and stayed in his arms as long as he would hold me. His smell was still the same, his long hands still tender and possessive.

'This is such a shock, such a pleasant surprise,' I said when we finally disengaged, 'but it seems so appropriate that I should meet you here in your native Utrecht.'

'Indeed,' he said, 'and I hope you will allow me to show it to you. I am now fairly free of medical commitments. I have two sons to carry on the practice. I can do what I please with my time.'

'And your wife?' I asked.

'Gone, these last six years,' he answered with a hint of regret that pleased me.

And so destiny brought Egbertus Wieland across my path once more. Egbertus, the only man, apart from Olof, who ever set in motion a sequence of interest and desire that possessed my whole being. It seemed completely natural that he should be my guide and companion. I approved of the way he had aged. He had the comfortable appearance of a man who had made his mark in life, but he was devoid of pomposity, still brimming with the enthusiasm I knew in the young Egbertus so many years before.

It pleased me that Egbertus left fashion to his sons and their young wives. His apartment in their house was filled with books and memorabilia. The furniture was ample and solid, the drapes and upholstery in browns, ochre and dark green. There was a small harpsichord and his viol was the same one he had brought to the Cape. It was a place where I could relax, a place in which I was not bombarded by the new and unfamiliar.

Egebertus and his friends met around noon every day to play music that was familiar to me, in the style to which I was accustomed. I was invited to join in the music-making. La Folia became a tune to which we returned time and again. They called my own variations Dona Anna's Madness and introduced me to subsequent versions composed by Falconieri, Corelli and Marin Marais. They played for me the suites of Marin Marais, a repertoire neglected by the new generation of musicians who preferred sonate. It was refreshing to them to find someone to whom this was all 'new music', someone appreciative, but not entirely uncritical.

Day after day I immersed myself in the mellow sounds of Marais, now vigorous and energetic, now soothing and dreamlike. I allowed my imagination to be led by the titles the composer had given to each piece. Le Bijou, La Reveuse, Le Labyrinthe and Le Tourbillon were my favourites and the company of musicians indulged me by performing these over and over again. Sometimes during Le Tourbillon and La Reveuse, Egbertus would give me a special look as though he wished to read the thoughts that I was discreetly hoping to keep to myself.

There was much talk of the new music and performances were discussed in detail, but in playing the old airs and dances, divisions on grounds, ricecare and canzonas, the gigues, gavottes and galliardes, the voltas and pavans, Egebetrus and his friends saw themselves as guardians of a tradition in danger of being swept away by virtuosity and stylised invention. My unconditional approval and enjoyment of their musical taste made me into an ally, perhaps a little curious like themselves, but a person worthy of inclusion in their company without the slightest reserve. Even my out-dated Dutch was never commented upon.

Caspar Commelin, seeing that I was well installed, went back to Amsterdam, and my life gained a tempo of its own. Most mornings I walked with Egbertus, exploring the city, meeting his various learned friends.

I was like a sponge, soaking up the layers of history in which Utrecht was steeped. I took great delight in having actual Roman remains pointed out to me. To touch stones that were actually part of that ancient civilization gave me such a sense of immediacy that I felt as though the centuries were erased and I was part of the pageant of history.

Willem Wieland, Egbertus's cousin, was an antiquarian who was ingenious at conjuring up the city as it used to be. He often accompanied us on our walks choosing each time a theme for our exploration, be it antiquity, the Middle Ages or the Renaissance. Of more recent history, he had first hand accounts. His parents had experienced the French Occupation and the tornado that followed soon thereafter and wrecked the nave of the Dom. Fifty-one years later, debris from this disaster was still apparent, the tower of the church standing separate from its transept, vegetation occupying the space between.

'Yes, that was what a natural disaster did. But the man-made tornado that preceded it did the same to the lives of most people in this city,' Wieland remarked. 'I'm referring, of course, to the Occupation, brief though it was. I was a small boy, but even I can remember how the French ripped through the place, particularly the churches, imposing on us altars and images. They thought that if they changed our place of worship they would change our faith as though a new suit could change the heart of a Protestant. We Batavians have always been a proud and stubborn people.'

We were standing in front of the mausoleum of Admiral van Gendt, which had been placed on the site of the high altar after the Occupation. The organist was practicing a fugue by Bach. My mother's religious adaptations ran through my mind: not only Batavians are determined, I thought.

'But the local Catholics must have been pleased?' I asked provocatively.

'So they were,' he conceded. 'Unfortunately for them, their triumph was short-lived. Soon they had to take their popery underground again. However, the Occupation made them show their true colours. It also taught the rest of us how precious freedom and autonomy was. And it brought into the open those in this town who collaborated with the enemy so willingly.'

'Mind you,' he continued, 'fifty years later many of them are again walking around uncensored, but people like my father have never forgiven those whom they saw as traitors. It left part of his peace of mind ruined like this building.'

'How fortunate we were, then, at the Cape, to experience this threat only at a distance, never to be actually under enemy rule! I remember there was a great deal of vigilance and several additions to the fortifications and, of course, a ban on any Catholic religious practice, as though the host would somehow pave the way for a French take-over,' I said, with the flippancy of someone whose only knowledge of real civic peril was hearsay.

'I daresay such vigilance would have been justified,' countered Willem.

We were now experiencing the onset of winter with a cold that menaced my skin. Every day was noticeably shorter than the one before and the sun, when it appeared, seemed diluted and drained of its strength. I borrowed furs from Francina to go out for the St Nicholas parade, still feeling chilled to the bone.

Francina suggested that we invite Egbertus to spend Christmas at Te Vliet with us, but I hesitated, not knowing what Simon might think to see his mother so at ease with a widower. Fortunately, Egbertus himself made it clear that he wished to be with his children and grandchildren at

Christmas. On the day of our departure for the country he handed me a large box.

'This is for you, a belated St Nicholas gift,'

It was a long cloak made from the finest mink. There was a matching muff and bonnet.

'It's beautiful, but I cannot possibly accept this,' I gasped. 'Besides, I will have no use for it in the Cape.'

He looked at me gravely, 'I'm hoping that it will help you when you consider my offer.' He took my hand and drew me closer. 'Why go back, Annie? Stay here and marry me. Let us take up where we left off so abruptly years ago.'

The young girl in me wanted to cry 'Yes, yes', but the rational habits of a lifetime inhibited me, made me consider.

'It is a gracious proposal, Egbertus, but we both know I don't belong here,' I objected.

'You belong with me, you know we can be so happy together,' he insisted. I pressed his hand, but kept my distance.

'It is true,' I said gently, 'but many of the reasons for which I turned away from you when we were young still apply.'

He tried to draw me closer, 'It's different now. You are free!'

'Yes, free to marry, but not to live in this place so foreign to me. I am compelled to be where my children and grand-children are, my property and possessions, all my memories of my life with Olof, the grave of my mother. Those are the imperatives of my life, that's where I belong, Egbertus.'

He looked at me sadly.

'Would you be willing to sacrifice your whole life here for love?' I asked. 'If I asked you to marry me and come to the Cape, would you be willing to leave Holland, your home, your children?'

I read the answer in his eyes. Yet he persisted:

'I took "No" for an answer too easily when we were young. Consider it when you're at Te Vliet, discuss it with your son and your friends. In my heart I know it would be the right thing for you to do. You are my prize, Annie.

Accept the cloak and may it keep your body warm as I intend to keep your spirit warm for as long as I live.'

I took his hand in both of mine, unwilling to allow argument to sour our parting, promising to think about his proposal, but in my heart I already knew the answer.

Undeterred by my reluctance, Francina produced many good arguments as to why I should accept Egbertus's offer,. We would be neighbours, I needed a husband, everyone in their circle who had met me thought it was a perfect match, my children were grown up and did not need me anymore, wouldn't it be lovely to spend the last part of my life at the hub of European civilisation rather than in a colonial backwater?

But Francina did not know me. She did not realise that I was not some rare bulb wrested from its native habitat, forced to grow where it was transplanted. No, I was in charge of my own life and decisions, in touch with the way my needs related to my nature. Every insipid cold day convinced me of how instinctively African I was. Even the snow, which I found exciting and beautiful, was an alien phenomenon that belonged to them, not to me.

How does one possibly catch up on the gossip of seventeen years? This was what Marie van der Stel and I did with unrivalled intensity that Christmas at Te Vliet.

After the exchanging of biographies of all our children, their adventures in life and love, detailed descriptions of their spouses and children, their houses and chattel, we launched into a review of the fortunes of the people we knew: how Starrenburg had had to abandon his ambition to own the Oldenland herbarium and had married that battle-axe, Johanna Victor; how Johan de Grevenbroeck had become a recluse at the farm Welmoed, writing his Latin volume on the Cape and producing a Hottentot/Latin dictionary for which neither the Hottentot nor the average inhabitant at the Cape had any use, dying a fussy old bachelor obsessed with the amounts of money various people owed him.

Willem Adriaen, a sickly shadow of his former self, sat through all this talk, hardly participating and frequently nodding off. He only perked up when we spoke of a death or a funeral and demanded a detailed description of the ceremony and the gravestone. He did take a mild interest in the fact that, although divided, no one really had the heart to destroy any of the splendid buildings at Vergelegen, that the octagonal garden still harboured many splendid flowers and that his camphor trees, orchards and vineyards were flourishing.

Marie and Willem had reversed roles. She was the energetic one in charge of every decision, he the passive partner overwhelmed by ill health and the inevitability of his imminent end.

We stayed at Te Vliet much longer than expected, trapped by mountains of snow piled up by successive snow storms before and after Christmas. It was said to be the worst winter in living memory, but since it was my first I knew only how threatened I felt, how the confinement depressed me. The long nights seemed endless and the short frozen days offered no evidence of life outside. The countryside was a white wasteland, canals solid, all living creatures apparently trapped indoors.

While I was petrified and convinced that spring would never come, Simon went out of his way to enjoy the winter, apparently undeterred by the dangers and discomforts of the weather. With the young crowd he went skating and sleighing, returning red-cheeked and bright-eyed, full of praise for the beauty of the winter.

One dark and foggy day he persuaded me to go for a sleigh ride to the nearby village of Vianen to take tea with the clergyman, Jalabert, and his wife. I must admit that I was transported into a fairyland that day. The freezing fog turned every bare tree into white confection. A layer of frost highlighted the mouldings and plasterwork on every building and it looked as though the gargoyles on the ancient little country church had grown beards.

'You seem to like Holland so much, Simon,' I asked him

that evening, 'Do you think you could live here?'

His answer surprised me. 'I have had a letter from Sophie, Mother. Her husband had a riding accident shortly after we left. He is now bedridden and not expected to live very long. So, while I'm making the best of my time here, there is nothing that will dissuade me from going back. I know Sophie and I will be together as soon as it is possible.'

'You know your father was against such a thing, Simon, and I supported him,' I replied weakly.

'But that was out of loyalty, not because you felt it in your heart. You will not cross me this time, will you?' His voice begged me while his eyes gleamed with confidence. He knew he could wrap me round his little finger.

'Your determination overwhelms me, Son,' I said, 'and your unhappiness over that affair tore me apart. If fate brings you a second chance at happiness, so be it.'

He hugged me and asked: 'And what about your second chance at happiness, Mother? Aunt Francina told me about the gentleman in Utrecht, an old flame from your past. Are you going to marry him?'

'Only if he is willing to come to the Cape, and I think that highly unlikely. You will meet him when we go back to Utrecht. He is a fine person, but even though the time might be right, the place is not. I cannot imagine never seeing our home again, the Bay, the Mountain, the faces, fair and dark, of people I have known all my life. The sacrifice would be too great.'

We returned to Utrecht towards the end of January only to pack and make our way to England where I planned to visit Marie Claudius and from where Simon would make his way to Gothenburg. Egbertus had thought to accompany us to England, but decided instead to see us off at 's-Gravenhage. I was relieved because it would have been difficult to accommodate him at Marie's small house in Greenwich. Even Simon would have to lodge with a neighbour during our stay.

Egbertus and I parted at the dock in 's-Gravenhage in

silent agreement not to lament the impossibilities of the future but rather to savour the joys of our recent time together, a resignation that comes more easily to the old.

England was already rid of its snow when we arrived. Soon signs of spring were everywhere on the trees and hedgerows. Marie met us in London and took us down the river to Greenwich. The angel had aged, but she still looked as ethereal as when I first met her with her slight body and unruly hair, now grey instead of blonde, barely contained by her bonnet. Her brilliant smile still lit up the day and her ready laughter rang out as clearly as ever.

Simon watched with amusement as Marie and I forgot our age and immediately launched into intense conversation about music and botany. When we apologised for excluding him he responded with the indulgence of the young.

'It gives me a chance to see what my mother was like when she was my age!'

The two months I spent in England passed like one long happy dream. It was, perhaps, the rejuvenating effect Marie had on me or it could have been the onset of spring and the excitement of seeing Nature awake from its winter sleep. My energy and enthusiasm returned in abundance. We rushed around London visiting gardens and drinking coffee with London's most famous botanists, including Bishop Compton and Doctor Hans Sloane who paid me compliments on my drawings that had been amongst a collection he had bought from James Petiver.

Marie was now married to Christopher Simpson, a man ten years her junior, an unassuming though brilliant musician. He afforded for us many opportunities to attend private and public performances of oratorios and orchestral concerts on a scale I had not experienced even in Holland. It appeared Marie had abandoned her own music-making, content to listen rather than play. Her explanation was a little sad.

'With Heinrich it was so much fun; music was one of the games we played together. You can see for yourself that Christopher is very different from Heinrich. I prefer it this way. It's easier to keep the side of myself that belonged to Heinrich intact. I always find it amazing how one can love in many different ways.'

It was wisdom I understood. I had loved a soldier and a surgeon, each so different from the other. I loved all my children, each in a different way. It was because Marie and I shared these little insights into the workings of the world that I knew we would be friends forever though we might never see each other again. It was this thought that made my departure from England bearable.

We returned to Amsterdam in May to await the arrival of Monsieur Guillaumet. His family was already in town, but the silk master had gone back to France to bring his own supply of silkworm eggs just in case ours at the Cape failed. We had had no word about their condition, though I assumed that they would be as they had been year after year, safe in a cool place where the ants could not reach them. The silk master was anxious, however, knowing the many perils that could befall the eggs, the worms and the moths. He seemed a little dubious when I told him that the silk from our cocoons was yellow. White silk was of a superior quality.

I spent the last month before our departure furiously shopping for brocades and chintzes, velvets and lace, buttons and bows, gloves, wigs and boots, china and glassware, even knives and forks, the new fashion at tables all over Europe. I spent hours selecting music and books, paints and brushes, paper and pencils. Then I turned to toys, dolls and kites, stilts and hoops. I even bought a pair of skates just to show those children of mine in Africa what they would never be able to do!

At the end of July we boarded the *Berbices* with Francois Guillaumet and his family. For the Dutch it was the 'outward' journey; for us it was definitely homeward! The voyage was rougher than the year before, but I had no doubt that we would reach our destination safely.

When the weather was fair, Monsieur Guillaumet, Simon and I spent much time talking about the proposed silk factory, examining the plans for the sheds that needed to be built, the vats and racks and specialised threading equipment that would have to be made. Simon knew all the suppliers and craftsmen in Cape Town, Stellenbosch and Drakenstein. He gave the silk master an optimistic view of the viability of the enterprise.

And now the wheel has gone full circle and we are back to the beginning of this long account of my life. I have told it frankly in the hope that you will think as well of me as you would of one of my drawings executed with an honest attempt at true representation. But it is not uncommon, even for those of us who profess to portray realism, to slip sometimes and take artistic liberties to suit our palette.

I cannot tell when I will die, but I can feel myself fading. Apoplexy has already weakened my left half and I am writing this last part with great difficulty, propped up in bed. Soon I will surrender to my cocoon.

I can no more see the ships in Table Bay, though I know they must be there. I hear the South Easter and I imagine the flags on the Castle proudly waving

There are voices of those working in the house, of pedestrians and horses going up and down the Heerengracht and, when I peer into the darker corners of the room, I can conjure up the beckoning figures of my mother, of Olof.

And I am ready to follow.

GLOSSARY

Batavia	seventeenth century name for headquarters of the Dutch East India Company in the East, situated on the Indonesian island of Java, now Jakarta
beryani/biryani	rice dish found in Asian cuisine
Bombyx mori	scientific name for the silk worm
bronbult	hill containing the source of hot springs
carduus	thistle; early European botanists had no other word to describe the dried flowers brought from the Cape by travellers. Clusius was the first to give the name *carduus* to *Protea neriifolia*.
Free Burghers	settlers who were given land to cultivate produce to provision ships passing between Europe and the East
Free Blacks	manumitted slaves or their descendants
gracht	canal or moat
Heitsi Eibib	Khoi deity
Hottentot	recorded by early visitors to the Cape as the name given to the Khoi tribes by the Dutch; apparently derived from a ditty sung by 'Hottentots' when dancing: 'hottentotten, hottentoo, hottentotten, hottentoo'
kasturi	a mountain goat from which musk is obtained
kermis	fair, bazaar
knecht	paid Company servant
kolwadjib	uncooked sweet rice cake

kramat	tomb of a Muslim holy man
Lords XVII	governing body of the Dutch East India Company
madrassa	Muslim school for religious instruction
momm	wine
musk	fragrant substance used as a base for perfume
Occum/ Ok-khun	Siamese honorific i.e. The Honorable
opstal	farm house
Orixas	animist deities, still worshipped as such by slave descendants in Brazil, especially in Bahia, in candomblé ceremonies
Patria	name for Holland in the Colonies
pinang	betel/areca nut
placaat	official order, by-law
redoubt	small watch tower
samosa	triangular deep-fried snack found in Asian cuisine
stadholders	municipal officials
stuiver	VOC copper coin from Galle in Ceylon
tjanting	tool used in batik to draw wax designs on cloth
tromba	trumpet in Portuguese; sea bamboo can be blown like a trumpet when dry
VOC	Verenigde Oostindische Compagnie, i.e. the Dutch East India Company
voorhuis	parlour

TIMELINE

This timeline is the skeleton of dates and facts around
which the story was constructed.

Date	Angela & David	Olof & Annie	Bergh Children	Visitors, Friends & Exiles	Commanders & Governors
1643		Olof born in Gothenburg, Sweden			
1652	David Koning captain of the *Drommedaris*, lands at the Cape				Commander Jan van Riebeeck lands at the Cape
1655	Angela arrives at the Cape				
1662		Angela is sold to Gabbema David returns to the Cape; leaves for Batavia; drowns at sea			Jan van Riebeeck leaves the Cape
1665		Olof joins the VOC, serves in Ceylon			
1666		Angela is set free; given a plot of land			
1669	Angela marries Arnoldus Basson				
1672				Paul Hermann, botanist, visits the Cape	
1673				Willem ten Rhyne, botanist, visits the Cape	
1676		Olof comes to the Cape as Sergeant			

242

Date	Angela & David	Olof & Annie	Bergh Children	Visitors, Friends & Exiles	Commanders & Governors
1678					Governor Johan Bax dies Simon van der Stel arrives at the Cape as Commander
1679		Olof sent by Simon van der Stel to bring back three deserters	Christina is born		
1681		Olof promoted to rank of Ensign		Dain Mangale and Dain Manjampe arrive at the Cape	
1682			Olof sent to salvage the wreck of the *Joanna* Leads expedition to look for copper	Maria is born	Heinrich and Marie Claudius arrive at the Cape
1683		Olof leads another expedition to search for the Copper Mountain		Claudius accompanies Olof on his expedition	
1684			Petrus is born		
1685		Olof becomes a member of the Council of Policy		Father Guy Tachard visits the Cape Heinndrich Claudius accompanies Simon van der Stel on his expedition	Commissioner van Rheede visits the Cape Simon van der Stel leads expedition to the north-west
1686		Olof is promoted to Lieutenant *Nossa Sebnora dos Milagros* runs aground near Cape Agulhas	Appolonia is born	Occum Chamnam arrives at the Cape	

Date	Angela & David	Olof & Annie	Bergh Children	Visitors, Friends & Exiles	Commanders & Governors
1686		Olof is sent to salvage the wreck of the *Nossa Sebnora*			
1687		Olof is sent to supervise building of church and *raadsbuis* at Stellenbosch Olof is accused of theft; Bergh possessions confiscated			
1689			Carolus is born		
1690		Olof is exiled to Ceylon			
1691			Johanna is born		Simon van der Stel becomes Governor
1694		Olof leaves Ceylon for Holland		Shaykh Yusuf smuggled to Galle; arrives at the Cape on the *Voetboog*	
1695		Olof becomes Captain of the Garrison	Dorothea is born		
1696			Simon Petrus is born		
1697			Martinus is born		
1698			Christina marries Jacobus de Wet		
1699		Olof goes on trading expedition	Olof de Wet is born to Christina	Shaykh Yusuf dies	Governor Willem Adriaen van der Stel arrives at the Cape
1700			Engela is born		
1702			Albertus is born		

Timeline

Date	Angela & David	Olof & Annie	Bergh Children	Visitors, Friends & Exiles	Commanders & Governors
1706		Annie saves Marie van der Stel from drowning			
1707					Willem Adriaen van der Stel leaves the Cape
1710		Olof is charged with supervision of the hospital			
1711		Olof's post as Captain is confirmed	Christina marries Matthias Bergstedt of Stockholm		
1714			Apollonia marries Jan Alders		
1715		Olof retires		Jan de Koning arrives at the Cape	
1719			Martinus marries Catherina Ley		
1720	Angela dies				
1723		Olof and Annie ask the Council to send Simon Petrus to 'India'	Simon Petrus goes on hunger strike Albertus marries Elizabeth Bisseux		
1724		Olof dies			
1728			Johanna marries Daniel Karnspeck		
1734		Annie dies			

245

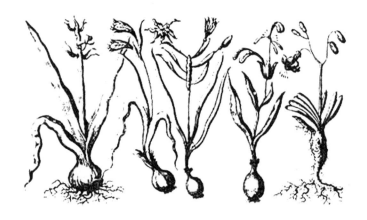

The Kirstenbosch identifications from left to right are: unidentifiable,
Gladolius sp., *Pancratium* sp., *Synnotea* or *Lupernusia* sp.,
Coryledon sp.

From *Voyages to Siam*, 1685, by Guy Tachard (1688).
Thought to be the work of Heinrich Claudius.